Acknowle

First, I would like to thank Mr. Steven Hammond ("Rise of the Penguins") for his support along with his ability to make himself available for brainstorming the self-publishing idea. Thank you, Steve.

Second, to Mr. Scott Saunders of design7studios for his hard work in getting my cover design done to my liking. It wasn't easy. Thank you, Scott.

Third, to Ella Medler and her "Shifty tenses" for her thorough editing talents, her criticisms, her pep talk, or I guess it's pep type, and especially the extremely kind review of the characters and story line. "You have a winner" is something every author wants to hear. Thank you, Ella.

This is a work of fiction. Any resemblance to historical events, locations or persons, living or dead is purely coincidental. Charmaine and Carpel are fictitious cities, as well as all characters within.

Grudge Count

ISBN: 978-1-7322763-0-7

Cover images: Shutterstock, inc.

Cover design by design7studio and an extremely patient Scott Saunders.

Editing by Ella Medler.

Author Website: Jonlathambooks.com

Grudge Count

A Willow and Birch novel

(Okay, enough of this prelim. Let's get to it.)

Prologue

He sat in the boat, leaning back, with his arms across the cabin roof and his legs extended, staring at Geri Ann. She was unmoving and just lay there on the deck. She wasn't dead. At least not yet. She was passed out from the additive he'd mixed in her drink.

He could do her and she wouldn't even know. He won't, though. He was saving that bit of action for number seven. Geri Ann had her purpose and it had nothing to do with sex. Her purpose was to die. Just as Chloe and Jennifer had before her.

He looked at her and wondered how many women out there actually wore bikinis under their clothes. Geri Ann hadn't needed to go home to change. She had just stripped right there on the boat, all the way down to her bikini.

He glanced out at the Pacific and still saw no signs of other vessels. Whale spouts aplenty, but no ships. They were alone. He took a swig of his beer and stared up at the sky, admiring the tiny puffs that passed themselves off for clouds, as his sailboat drifted aimlessly with the waves.

He guessed enough time had passed. He stood and made his way to his cabinets and pulled out his camera, then grabbed her arms and dragged her to the bow and leaned her against the rail, draping her arms over. Next, he crossed her right leg over her left, tilted her head as though she was looking at the sky, and straightened her hair. He backed up, focused and snapped the shot.

Then he repositioned her legs, with one bent slightly, tilted her head a little, and snapped another.

He put the camera away, went into the cabin and retrieved his equipment—his ice pick, his knife, a bottle of dish soap, his nail brush and file—and placed them on the cabinet top. He laid down the plastic sheeting and pulled Geri Ann onto it. She was really out of it. He wondered if he had given her too heavy of a dose. Would she even feel her death? Would she know she died?

What beautiful hair she had. It literally shined. Her brown curls fell just past her shoulders. She was a beautiful woman. To him, though, she was nothing more than a number. Number three, to be exact. Maybe in another time or another life, he and Geri Ann would have been an item. Not this time, though. Not this life. He was on a mission, and she was nothing more than a tool to achieve that mission.

He cleaned her hands, brushed her nails and then tied her wrists behind her back with the zip ties. Then he rolled her on her back, which did cause her to moan, and tilted her head to the left.

"Wakey! Wakey!" he said, but she didn't.

He picked up his ice pick and carefully inserted it into her right ear canal. When he thought he was close to the drum, he straddled her and slowly pushed it in. That woke her. At first, just a moan, but then her eyes flew wide and she screamed and began thrashing and kicking her legs. The screams became louder and he began to laugh.

"Whoop! Careful now, you're rocking the boat." He laughed out as he slammed the pick into her brain and began jerking it back and forth, up and down, around and around. The screaming stopped and the convulsing and jerking ceased, leaving nothing but the twitching. The pick broke off at the handle. He looked at the handle in his hand, then into her ear.

"Well shit, sweets. You broke my pick. Bitch. No worries. I have more." He stood up and quickly donned his mask before the purging started.

He stood over her, looking down at death. Not so beautiful anymore. He looked again into the oozing ear. "That matter really doesn't look all that grey. But what does it matter? It's kind of a grey area, anyway." He laughed again. He curled the plastic sheeting up so that none of the blood got on the boat.

He checked the body, careful of the areas he had touched. He wet a rag, squeezed some Dawn onto it and began cleaning the ear, face and anything else he had touched. He wouldn't need to be as intense with his cleaning on Geri Ann. She was going diving, anyway.

He folded the plastic over her hips and once again straddled the body. With his hunting knife, he lifted the bikini top off her breasts. He placed the tip on her left breast and pushed hard. He repeated the process on the right breast. Then he placed the knife point between the breasts and pushed again, stood and admired his work.

"Number three," he said. He used the knife to pull her top back over the breasts and then laid the knife next to the pick handle on the rag. The blood was starting to pool, so he stepped up the pace.

He placed the restraint over her ankle and secured it tightly. He padlocked the cable to the restraint, and took the other end to the railing, padlocking it to the anchor. He wrapped Geri Ann in the plastic and then taped it loosely, so no blood would fall out when he lifted her.

"Hooey. What the hell did you have for lunch?" he asked her as he threw her over the side. He watched her float a minute, as the water encompassed the body. She drifted out, with the cable beginning to drag her down. The anchor flew over the side, and he watched the body descend into the deep.

He used Dawn and the ocean water to clean the knife, throwing the pick handle over the side and stashing the knife back in his cubby along with the rest of his tools. He began cleaning everything she had touched with his bathroom cleaner, put everything away and started the engine, turning the sailboat back toward the coast.

"Oh, blow the man down, bullies, blow the man down..." he sang on the journey.

One year earlier

Sandman

Mike watched Blake stand at the steps watching the doors. Melissa would be coming out at any time. Blake's chest heaved as he took a deep breath to calm himself. This was absolutely the girl of Blake's dreams and he sure didn't want to come off as some college dork, but if Mike knew Blake, he certainly would. Blake looked back at the small group of friends providing support. Mike, Rick and Jada were all looking at him. Mike couldn't believe they had roped Blake into this.

Blake would have no excuse if she said no. He sure wouldn't be able to blame it on the weather. It was gorgeous out. Mike watched him look himself over and laughed. He probably thought he should have chosen a different shirt, and Mike agreed. He looked like a farmer. Mike chuckled.

The door opened and a few students filed out and then Mike saw her. Maybe Blake was over-dressed. She wore jeans and a Cardinal jersey and had her beautiful locks in a ponytail. She looked Blake's way and smiled. She actually noticed him. Mike could tell Blake's calm fled as he began rubbing his hands on his pants, but he got himself under control and walked toward her. Mike snuck behind a closer wall so that he could hear.

"Hey, Melissa. We're going over to Gravity after classes. Why don't you stop by?" Blake asked her.

"I might do that, Blake. Who's we?"

"Sandman. Jada. Estelle. Rick. A couple you haven't met said they might show. It'll be fun, if you make it. If not, maybe next time."

Don't ramble, Mike thought.

"Well, I hope you can come. See ya."

Blake left Melissa, rolling his eyes with self-disgust, and made his way back to his group that had sent him on the dare. This was one good-looking woman. One that Blake had been pining over for some time but never quite had the nerve to ask out. The guys knew his eyes were only on her, and they had been relentless in goading him on.

Blake reached the group and got querulous looks from all, but it was Sandman who approached him. Mike Sanders had gotten the nickname from Blake. They had been buds since grammar school. Blake had tagged him in the fourth grade and the name stuck.

In fact, Sandman was probably Blake's longest and most loyal friend. They grew up together, lived only blocks apart, went to all the same schools, hung out at each other's house and even went on each other's family outings. Their parents had become friends, as well. There were many times that even the parents shared interests.

Mike-the-Sandman-Sanders was a steadying influence on Blake. He was also the more daring of the two. Blake was not a risk taker. He didn't rock boats or push envelopes. He was laid back and took things in stride. Blake would back away from confrontations.

Mike, not so much. He would be right up in the face of the instigator.

Mike would push every envelope he could find and would not only rock boats, he would tip them over. He had been on Blake quite some time about asking Melissa out. Blake wanted to wait for the perfect time. There would only be one chance with Melissa. If she denied you, then you might as well move to Siberia. You wouldn't get a second opportunity.

If it were Mike after Melissa, instead of Blake, they would probably be married already, but it wasn't Mike, and it never would be. Mike wouldn't do that to Blake. It was Blake that had the eyes for Melissa. Now the man just needed to set the hook.

"How'd it go?" Mike asked.

"I guess we'll know when or if she shows up," Blake offered.

"I don't get you, man," Rick added, "You nearly drool every time you see her. Why don't you just ask her out? Even if she says no, at least you'll stop wondering and move on."

"You're such a pussy," Mike added, "I guess we know who'll wear the pants in your family."

"Spoken like a guy who already has a girl," Blake said to Rick, and then, looking at Mike, "I'm going to take this slow. Maybe if I play my cards right, she and I and our two kids will move into our dream house with our servants and never have to work a day in our lives."

Mike, Rick and Jada all busted out in laughter as they began to meander back toward the University steps, and class. Mike was now in a hurry to get through his last two classes for the day, to see how this turned out. Professor Wilson was pretty good and that class was usually quick, but his last class was with Professor Windbag, which sometimes went five to ten minutes long.

Today was the only day Blake's classes and Melissa's classes ended at the same time. On Monday he was out an hour earlier than her. She only had one class on Wednesday, and Tuesday and Thursday she was gone two hours before he was finished. This was it. She certainly wasn't going to hang around for him to finish.

Blake's major was engineering. Melissa's was Medicine. She would have four more years yet to go, but this was Blake's final year. At the end of this year, he would be a full-fledged engineer. He was close. With his diploma in hand, he told Mike, he would be heading right to Granger. She would be impressed.

The last two classes just went on and on. Mike was sure they would never end, but they finally did. He was in such a hurry to get to Gravity, he nearly forgot to wait for Rick and Jada. The two lovebirds eventually ended up in the back seat, and with Blake alongside he took off for the sports bar, breaking every speed limit along the way.

It took no time at all to find a parking space, despite it being Friday. Mike and his three friends entered the establishment and found the others of their group already there and seated. Blake took a chair with a clear look at the door. He received a couple of chuckles, but he didn't appear to care.

They decided on Mussels and Prawns for appetizers, and each ordered a wine that suited their current mood. Blake decided on a glass of the Portugal, which Mike had always wanted to try but never had. Blake threw a prawn on his plate and when the wine came, he nibbled and drank, and drank and nibbled, continuing to watch the door. Blake had to know his friends were laughing at him when he wouldn't answer their questions, but his attention was elsewhere.

After twenty minutes Melissa entered with one of her girlfriends. Blake must not have wanted to appear too eager, because he just stared at them entering. He waited for a few seconds too long to wave them over but he was saved from doing so as Jada had also seen them and did the waving. Rick jumped up and grabbed two chairs from an unoccupied table, scooted his over and put the two new arrivals between Blake and himself. His Cheshire grin was met with a scowl from Blake. The scowl disappeared right away as Melissa took the seat next to Blake.

Mike slid his chair a little closer to Blake so that he could eavesdrop properly. Blake was not the best there was with the female gender. He was too shy. Mike needed to hear what was said so that he could provide his friend advice later.

"What's good here?" Melissa asked as she looked over the menu.

"I like the ribs," Blake said, "but the others say the chicken is the best. Would you mind if I paid?"

"You invited me, Blake. If you don't pay, I'll make a note in my journal." Melissa's face was stoic for a moment, but then she smiled at him, causing him to smile back despite the flushing.

Blake was introduced to her friend 'Lucee-with-two-Es'. When he looked confused, Melissa explained that Lucee spelled her name with two Es instead of a Y. Blake then did the honors introducing Lucee to the rest of the group. Mike guessed Blake knew Melissa was already familiar with the group and didn't bother introducing her.

The server came to get the drink orders for the new arrivals. Both ladies decided what Blake was drinking looked good, so they ordered the Portugal. Once the server returned with the drinks, she took everyone's order, and about a half hour later, the four different conversations ebbed and everyone began eating. The exchanges prior to the food arriving had been light and jovial, as well as uninformative. Blake took the next step and spoke so softly Mike had to lean in to hear.

"How am I doing so far?"

Melissa afforded him a querulous glance, but then obviously understood the question. She put on the sexiest look Mike had ever seen. One that could not only melt butter, but the icecap too. He was feeling a little warm himself. She set her fork down and moved in close, licking her lips. Just as he thought she was about to kiss Blake, she said, "My wine glass is empty." She smiled and winked. When her glass was full again, she looked over at Blake.

"Why do you think you need to be judged, Blake?"

"To be honest, Melissa, I was hoping we could do this again, without so many chaperones. Maybe a quiet dinner and a movie, a walk in the park, a drive along the seashore." Finally, Mike thought, he said it. He actually got the words out. He asked Melissa out on an actual date.

She took a deep breath and looked over at Blake. "Was that so hard? What took you so long?"

"Sorry," Blake answered. "As long as I'm being honest, I'll admit being a little intimidated by your beauty. Is that a yes, then?"

"I'd love to," she said, but then hesitated a moment. "As long as you realize this may not end up as you hoped."

"You've already exceeded my expectations for tonight but lay it on me."

"You know that second base, third base, home plate thing? You're going to have to earn it. I don't sleep around, Blake. If you hope to take me to a movie, dinner and bed, it's not going to happen."

"How about if we make that your idea? I'm not sure, otherwise, how I would know I've earned it."

"Fair enough."

"Might I ask how you got here? Did you drive? Do you need a ride home?" Mike shook his head as Blake was spouting questions faster than any sane person could answer. Blake caught his disapproval from the corner of his eye and tried to slow himself down. He met Melissa's eyes, smiled and shrugged.

"Wowzers. You have a lot of questions. Lucee drove, and I'm a little old-fashioned, Blake. I will never leave the party except with whomever brought me. Relax. I was hoping you would get around to asking me out. I'm not going anywhere."

"Are you telling me I'm trying too hard?" Blake asked with a smile.

"Just a little," Melissa said, indicating by how much with her thumb and index finger.

"Okay. This is me being cool." Blake turned his chair slightly away and threw his arms behind his head. Melissa pinched the back of his arm, and the two laughed. She had a nice laugh.

"So, what does Melissa do when she's not dissecting frogs? What are your weekends like?"

Melissa laughed at the frog comment. "I spend them at home. It's not that much longer that we'll all be together. I have a brother and sister that are older than me and will be moving away soon. I love my family and I'm going to enjoy it while I can. How about you?"

"I'm from San José. My parents are divorced, but that was the only bad point in my childhood. I was ten at the time and an only child. It was pretty rough. Once I learned that I got two of everything, it got better. Where is home?"

"I tell everyone Carpel. That's the closest big community, but our house is north of there. I went to school there, though. Red Hawks, baby. All the way."

"School spirit. That's good," Blake said. "Cheerleader?"

"Our parents didn't allow us to get involved in anything non-educational. Bands, debate teams were okay. Sports were not. Tony wanted to play football really bad, but Mom and Dad wouldn't budge. It created a rift for a whole three days." Melissa laughed again.

"Parents were pretty strict, huh?"

"Just the opposite. We made our own decisions for the most part. We just weren't allowed to project ourselves as better than others. We had to get our school clothes at Target or Walmart. We had to ride the bus. We weren't allowed to join anything that would make other students feel inferior. It actually worked out well. We had more friends that way."

Mike could tell that Blake had a million more questions, but for the last five minutes Lucee had been listening in on the conversation, which usually meant boredom. Blake noticed it and nodded toward her, and Melissa looked over to her friend.

Melissa turned back to Blake and whispered so low Mike had a hard time eavesdropping, "Lucee is a little on the naïve side. She does well one-on-one, but crowds give her a problem. She becomes very introverted. She only came because she has her eyes on someone here." Melissa winked.

"Really? Who?"

"That, she hasn't told me yet," Melissa answered. Mike looked the table over, suddenly struck by the thought that he and Andre were the only ones unattached. He looked hard at Lucee. She was nice-looking but kind of paled compared to Melissa. Then again, almost anyone paled next to Melissa.

Melissa apologized and said it was time to go. She and Blake exchanged phone numbers. Blake told her he would call her tomorrow and get her schedule for the upcoming week. He stood when they did and then walked them to their car.

Sandman

Eight months ago

Blake had been dating Melissa for four months now. The last time he and Blake were together, Mike had asked, as carefully as he could, how the intimacy aspect of the relationship was going. Blake had said it was none of his business, but Mike could tell by the tone, Melissa was being a bitch. It was also obvious to others. Rick and Jada had said several times that Blake was not himself and was wound pretty tight. Four months? In four months, she couldn't spread those legs?

Blake was coming over after school, on the pretense Mike had set of helping with his car. Mike knew Blake had invited Melissa to his place that night for a quiet dinner. The two of them had spent every date out on the town and it was time for a calm evening. They had planned on dinner, wine and a movie. Mike intended on giving Blake some of his 'Spicer' mix when he came to the house. That should loosen her up a bit.

The lecture was over. Mike gathered his items and made his way out of the class, out of the school and to his car. He drove down to the liquor store, bought a six-pack and went straight home to wait for Blake. He arrived at his house, put everything away, and while he was waiting, laid out his car manual on the kitchen table. It wasn't much of a wait. Blake knocked on his door almost immediately after.

"Hey, Bud," Mike greeted him as he opened the door. "Come on in. Believe it or not, I actually found the problem myself. It's nothing but a fuse." Mike pulled out a couple of beers, walked Blake to his table and made a visible show of putting the manual away. "I had another reason for asking you over, anyway."

"What's that?" Blake asked.

"I want to talk to you about your sanity. We're worried about you."

"We?" Blake asked, looking out the window and showing disinterest.

"Me. Rick. Jada. A few others. You seem to be off your game. What's going on, man?"

Blake hesitated, took a drink of his beer, looking forlorn, and answered, "It's been a rough semester. Sorry for not being there. Everyone's okay, though. Right?"

"Everyone's fine, except you. Have your professors been dicks, or are you and Melissa having a spat?"

"Neither, and before you even think about it, I don't need the intervention. I appreciate the effort, though. School's going fine and Melissa is as charming as ever. She's still as beautiful to me as she was the first day I saw her. I'm just not sure she feels the same about me."

"Shit, man. Is she stepping out? You want me to keep an eye out?"

"No!" Blake spouted. "It's nothing like that, and you will keep your nose right where It Is. She kisses me, and they're passionate kisses, but every time I think it's okay for me to get handy, she pulls the hand away from that perfect ass or those scrumptious boobs, and… I can't believe I'm talking to you about this."

"Boobs?" Mike laughed. "We're not twelve anymore. A tit by any other name…"

Blake just shook his head, so Mike continued, "Look, man. Let me help you out." Mike walked to his desk and opened the top drawer, then pulled out a small lidded tub. "There's not much left, but it should be plenty." He handed Blake the tub.

"What is this?" Blake asked, looking the tub over.

"It'll help loosen her up a bit. It looks like powder, but it dissolves quickly and is tasteless. The rest will be up to you." Blake looked in the tub, and then stared at Mike. He closed the tub and threw it at Mike's face. Mike batted it, defensively, to the floor.

"Are you out of your fucking mind? You want me to date-rape my girlfriend?"

Mike picked the tub up off the floor and slid it back to Blake. "Use it or lose it, man. Your call. Save it for the future, then. I will say this: You are about as stressed as I've ever seen you. It will affect your GPA if you don't get someone to relieve that stress. Get a freshman to give you a blowjob. The shit will work with that, too."

The table became silent. Mike studied Blake. Blake studied the tub. Both men finished their beers and then Blake stood up, studied the tub some more, picked it up and shook it at Mike.

"I'll fix this just to keep you from using it on some unsuspecting junior classman. There's no fucking way I'm using it on anyone. Especially Melissa. You're sick, man."

With that, Blake took the tub, walked into the kitchen and dumped it down the sink, running water behind it. "What the fuck is wrong with you?" Blake screamed at him. "Are you using that shit on women? That's rape, dumbass."

"You're full of shit," Mike said. "Nobody's forcing them. It just relaxes them. It's not rape. You've never gotten a woman drunk? Gotten a little?"

"No. I haven't. For my part, they have to be willing, and the fact that you don't know that what you're doing is rape disturbs me. You know what? Stop talking. I don't want to hear another word. I will tell you this: If the police come to me and ask me about this? I'm going to tell them. So just stop talking."

With that Blake finished his beer, threw the bottle in the recycle tub and looked at Mike, shaking his head. "This makes you look pathetic, man. This is not the best friend I grew up with. Knock it off. Rape is rape."

"Quit saying that, damnit. It's not rape," Mike said angrily. Blake, however, didn't respond. He just glanced at Mike with a look of disgust, shook his head some more, walked to the door and left without another word.

Mike picked up his phone and dialed his supplier. It would be a nice weekend for a drive anyway. He would have to go to Charmaine. He'd learned long ago not to use anyone near the U. The Local police were always in the know here. He wasn't sure how, but he suspected one of the students was an informant. That wasn't a problem for Mike. He only provided to people he knew well and never took on new clients. The drive to Charmaine kept him away from local users, as well.

He was also clever enough never to use the same meeting place twice. Charmaine was a big enough city to make that easy. His supplier would use some of his people to stage a big enough disruption to draw the police away from the meeting place, but not so big as to cause an arrest. An argument inside a store usually did the trick. The police would show up and chase the loud and obnoxious combatants, and in the meantime the deal would be done quickly.

Mike was pretty sure his supplier had a lab of some sort, although he was not allowed in the actual rooms. He had been to the office—a travel agency, of all things—but he'd never been invited into the back. But Mike didn't complain. He could get anything he wanted, and it would be provided in any form he wanted. Capsules, powder, vials. You name it, he could get it. The only thing he couldn't get was marijuana. He didn't know anyone that wanted it anymore, anyway.

The ironic thing about Mike's hobby was almost laughable. He could pass any drug test known to man. He wasn't a user. Well, he was. Just not on himself. One thing he was not lacking was sex. College girls loved to party. Status was everything to them. If you didn't party, you weren't part of the 'in' crowd.

Getting girls to the party was easy. Once he had them there, a few well-mixed drinks got them into his bed. He had a few failures, but not many. That Lucee girl that Melissa had brought with her months ago was a tough nut to crack. He couldn't even get her to a party. She hung out with Melissa too much. What a looker, though, and seeming to be very nice, talking to Mike all the time. She seemed interested, but as soon as he mentioned a party, Lucee begged off for one reason or another.

There was one thing about Melissa that Mike was all in on. She was a brunette. Mike had a passion for brunettes. Lucee was a brunette, too. Melissa, however, was even better looking than Lucee, but she was already taken. If Blake ever got fed up with her, though, friend or not, Mike was going after her, and he wasn't the least bit shy about loosening her up. Date rape was bullshit. Women wanted to get laid just as much as men. They just needed a little push.

Mike made his appointment and decided to call it a day. He took out his calendar, sat on his couch and looked it over to decide on the best day for his next party. He pulled out his phone once again and began making invites. He wasn't going to invite Blake and Melissa this time, though. Blake and his passive attitude were beginning to wear Mike down. His first call was to Rick. He and Jada always got things going strong.

Logan

Chulo sat his car, waiting for Sanders. The man was usually prompt, but today he was a little behind schedule. Chulo decided he didn't need to wait in the parking lot, so he went to his trunk and pulled out his golf clubs, sat them on the pavement and opened his ball pouch. While leaning into the trunk, he looked both directions and glanced behind him. Satisfied it was clear, he quickly slipped the powder pack into the ball pouch and zipped it shut.

He closed his trunk, shouldered the golf bag and made his way to check-in. He sat his bag down beside a bench and waited there for Sanders. Sanders didn't know it yet, but he would be paying for today's round.

He didn't have to wait long. Sanders drove up and parked next to Chulo's Beemer. The two exchanged waves, but Chulo continued to wait where he was, sending a message to Sanders that he had the product with him. Within a few minutes, Sanders sat beside him on the bench and began to change shoes, so Chulo did, as well.

"You're buying," Chulo announced.

"No sweat," Sanders responded. "I was planning on it. This is what I call a beautiful day for golf. There's no wind and it's nice and sunny, so you will have to come up with a different excuse for that trademark slice of yours."

Chulo laughed as Sanders went inside to pay for a round. It was an executive course, and they would wait until the fourth hole to exchange their packets, white for green. This was the course they always used because the fourth tee was surrounded by trees and bushes and they had to walk all the way around them to tee off.

"How's business?" Sanders asked as they were walking off the first tee toward the fairway.

"Really good, Mike. How about yours?"

"Fantastic. I get to go to Minnesota next week to help put in a bid on an outlet mall. This intern stuff is pretty cool."

"Get to? Doesn't it snow there?"

"Yeah, it does. You do know they have heaters in corporate offices, right?" Mike asked, laughing.

"Hey, I don't get out much. I've been away from California all of once in the last six years."

The conversation, laughs and ribbing continued through the match and they did, indeed, exchange packages on the fourth tee. Chulo won the match by one stroke, so Sanders had to fork over a buck, which he did once they reached the cars.

"How's the love life?" Chulo asked.

"The love life is just fine, Chu. I don't need one of your girls, but thanks, anyway."

The two put their bags back in their trunks and Chulo pulled out an ice pick, a pocket calendar and a deck of cards and handed them to Sanders. Sanders threw the items in his trunk with a roll of the eyes. Chulo knew he was pushing the stuff on Sanders, but the more he gave away, the less time he had to spend at conventions.

Chulo worked for Mitchell Ice as an assistant manager. The pay stank, but that wasn't why he had the job. If it were, he could do better. He made enough money in his main business to put some away for an early retirement, if he chose to do so.

He not only was the local supplier for "Special K", he also had a nice selection of women that he used to make good money from some of the rather wealthy local businessmen, as well as those who would come to conventions, and there were quite a few. He needed the convention goers, because he was at a point now where he had as many girls as local customers.

∞∞∞∞

The two departed the course in different directions. Chulo headed back to the office to pick up the receipts. The thought was that he would be depositing them into the bank, but he never did. A man in his line of business couldn't really trust that his assets wouldn't be frozen at some time, so his bank was located in several locations, including his house, his car, the train station, the airport and so on.

If Chulo ever had trouble with the law, he would scoot his ass out of town and nobody had a clue where he had stashed the money, not even his wife. Chulo was not the type to get caught, he just wasn't loyal enough to anyone to trust them with everything.

He also knew if anyone thought him worthy of investigating, he would find out about it. Chulo had connections in law enforcement. He had also been very careful with those he had to dispose of. He had a crew that handled any cleanup. What he really needed was one of those guys who had the ability to make entire bodies disappear down the drain, bones and all.

Alas, his business was not prosperous enough yet to afford that kind of cleaning. He was stuck with having his people clean away all evidence and bury those who wronged him. Horace caused him a little concern, though. Chulo had made the mistake of giving him an ice pick, once, and now the man swore by them. Between Horace and Sanders, his sample collection wasn't all that overstocked.

Chulo's office was a travel agency. His girls made a percentage for every customer they booked, made good money when he sent them out on their "dates" and always made good tips, because they were good. Very good. The customer had his desires and they satisfied them, without questions and happily. Because that's where the tips came from.

He was a little concerned about Brittany. She always seemed happy with her work, but her tips being small were constantly a complaint on her part. Chulo wondered if she was putting on a façade when she was talking to him and becoming a different person with her date. She was getting up there in age, so it might be she had just lost her appeal, but he wasn't totally convinced. He would have to give it a little more time.

Sandman

Present day

A lot of time had passed since Mike had last seen Chulo. There hadn't been a need. With graduation looming, Mike had been focusing on his studies. He hadn't wanted anything to mess up his graduation, so he had been party-less-and-study-more for nearly a year.

Now here he was, degree in hand, no longer an intern and hired into the best architecture company in central California. He even had his own office, with his own secretary. Life was good, now that he was settled, and not only settled but settled in Charmaine. He had less than five miles to drive to restock. He would need to do that soon. His plan was to begin his party life now.

All of his friends had graduated. Well, all but one. Dumbass got caught. How do you not know where the mirrors are in your own damn apartment?

Some of his friends had moved off to continue their life elsewhere, and he would miss them, especially Rick and Jada, partygoers extraordinaire. They had gotten married and moved east of Carpel, but they promised to stay in touch.

Tonight, though... Tonight was about Mike. Tonight, he was clubbing. Getting back into the dating scene. He had made friends fast since being in Charmaine, and they had invited him to tag along. He would do it just this once and then he would strike out on his own and pick up a date. If he needed to. Being an alumnus, he still had get-togethers with college students, but nothing big enough to call a party.

Maybe he wouldn't need to. For the last ten minutes he had moved to the bar and struck up a conversation with a couple of lookers. Maybe they were lookers. Maybe Mike had one too many and they just looked that way, or maybe it was too dark to get a good look. Who cared? He just wanted to get laid.

Bruce was with him. He had taken the stool on the other side of the two and was working on the blonde. If he found a way to lure her out of here, great. If not, Mike would have to separate the two.

The other girl looked to be the same age as Mike, was a brunette, and had a very nice set that he was doing his best not to look at. It was difficult, with her sitting, to get a clear picture, but once again, who cared? He had already divulged everything he could think of about himself, all of which was a pack of lies, and tried to mask his intentions when asking about her.

"How do you feel about parties?" he asked.

"I love parties. Do you know where there is one?"

"I do," he said. "You interested?"

"I am. How many people are there? Do you know?"

"Including us?" he asked, tilting his head and raising his brows in a questioning way.

"Sure," she smiled at him.

"Two."

She laughed, shaking her head, and just stared at him. Then she looked at her friend. "Angie, I'll catch you later, okay?"

Angie looked at her, at Mike, back at her, and said, "Hey, don't call me for a ride. I'm going to be busy." The two shared a hug and then Mike let her lead the way out of the club, eyeing her figure before him. Holy shit! Jackpot!

They arrived at Mike's apartment and Mike took her sweater and draped it over the couch. He thought it might be a little early for a warm-up, but he gave it a shot, gently moving her hair behind her ear.

"Take it easy, hotshot," she said with a smile. "How about a glass of wine and a little conversation, first?"

"As you command, Milady," he said with a bow. "White or red?"

"Red, please," she said, looking around. "This is a nice place. A little surprising for a bachelor. You're not married, are you?"

"No. You're not going to get me drunk and fly me to Vegas, are you?"

She laughed again, and it was a nice laugh. "Maybe. We'll have to see how the night goes."

He brought out the two glasses of wine, one with a little extra boost in it, and the two sat on opposite ends of the couch. He began telling his life story with the most monotonous voice he could muster. With her already having had a few, no food, and the "Special K", it took less than fifteen minutes before she was out.

Sturgeon

Willow Sturgeon finished her interview at the burglary and made her way to the squad. She put away her items and climbed in and entered her destination into the computer as the station.

This was the third residence in her district in the last month that had suffered a burglary. She needed to get these dirt bags. It was the same group. Each house had been stripped of its flat screen, stereo and jewelry. Other things were taken, but those three were consistent. It was the same group or person. She felt it was a group.

They were careful on each occasion to hit a house without cameras, so she was pretty sure at least one of the perps was working in security equipment and knew what to look for. She needed to re-interview the previous victims. She had asked this victim if he had been contacted about security, or any other solicitation, and he had said he had, giving her the company's name. She didn't recognize it.

At the intersection of Parker and Tray, she stopped at the stoplight and noticed the woman beside her was talking on her phone. The driver had her window down, so Willow thumbed hers down and tried to get the woman's attention. The woman held up a finger and pointed at her phone, returning to her conversation. When the light turned green, the woman accelerated and Willow pulled in behind, flipping on her strobes.

She entered the plate on her computer and approached the vehicle with the woman still talking on her phone. Willow waited at the door, and the woman, after nearly a minute, told her fellow conversationalist that she had been stopped and to hang on.

"What is it?" the woman asked.

"Ma'am, I stopped you because it is illegal to be holding a cell phone while you're driving. May I see your license, registration and proof of insurance, please?"

"That law is only for teenagers," the woman said. "Do I look like a teenager to you?"

The temptation was there to say 'hardly', but Willow stayed professional. "We don't discriminate due to age, ma'am." Willow accepted the documents and entered the driver's info and violation into her EID. She showed the woman where to sign and then printed out a copy for her, handing it to the woman. After a couple of extra, and free of charge, angry comments from the sweet lady, Willow was back on her way to the station.

Willow arrived at the station and parked the squad in its designated spot, punched in the mileage on her trip-tick tab of the computer, picked up her gear and made a quick scan to make sure the unit was as clean as it was when she'd started her shift. Haniger had the swing today, and he was a pig, so she wasn't sure why she cared, but she did.

She walked into the locker room, put her gear in her locker, grabbed her clothes and began changing, still thinking about the burglaries. Her shift tomorrow was the swing shift. She would start at one PM and head right away to the Compton residence and ask them about solicitors.

"Captain wants to see you," Sarah said from the doorway.

"Okay, thank you."

Sarah was the captain's secretary, so Willow didn't find it necessary to ask if she meant the sergeant. She tied her shoes, attached her nine to her hip, locked her locker and made her way upstairs.

Willow began running her week through her head, trying to decide if she was about to be disciplined for something. It was not unheard of for the captain to call in a patrolman, but it was highly unusual. If she had screwed up somewhere along the line, she already would have been on the sergeant's carpet.

She arrived at the captain's office and her heart began to sink. The sergeant was in there with him, and the door was closed. This couldn't be good. She just stood there, looking moronic, she was sure. Sarah smiled at her and made a twisting gesture with her hand, so Willow flushed and twisted the knob, and entered the office.

"Sturgeon, have a seat," the captain said. "What's happening in your district, right now?"

"Three burglaries that I believe are connected, Captain, a few vandalisms, some stolen property, and the usual domestic disputes."

"Why do you think the burglaries are connected?" the sergeant asked.

Willow turned to him and explained about the missing items being similar, but he just nodded and looked deep in thought.

"Sturgeon," the captain said, stealing back her attention, "We have an opening in homicide and I'm appointing you to the position. I'm going to ask you to come in early tomorrow and put everything you have on the computer, including all your hand-written notes, and email them to officer..." He looked unsure and glanced at the sergeant.

"Crocket" the sergeant offered.

"Crocket," the captain repeated. "He's Baker's recruit, and Baker said he's ready, so they will be doubling over into your district tomorrow, and then Crocket will take over next week."

"Sir," Willow said, "I appreciate this offer, but I've only been a patrolman for four years. Won't this create friction on the team?"

"Let's talk about two words in that question, Sturgeon. One, the very fact that you used the word team tells me you're ready for this. Two, I don't remember using the word offer. I'm pretty sure I said I was appointing you.

"Yes, it is going to cause friction," he continued. "Some of the officers will say you only got the position because you're a woman. That accusation will be somewhat true. We have no female detectives, so you're it. Deal with it. The sergeant has spoken highly of your ability to handle the dissension. Is he blowing smoke up my ass?"

"No, sir. I'm just not sure how I feel about being a number."

"Tough shit! You have another option, and I'll certainly understand. You can think about it tomorrow while you're working on the email."

"I'm not resigning, if that's what all this is seeking. I'm not understanding why you find it necessary to be such an asshole about it, sir. Captain, sir. Feel free to demote me back to patrol for my insubordination."

"I love your grit. You'll need it. Miller is moving on to partner with Mercer. You'll be with Birch. That will be all. Be here Monday morning at nine sharp. My office."

"Birch?" Willow nearly screeched out.

"That will be all, Sturgeon."

After what seemed like minutes staring at the captain, Willow stood and walked out of the office as loudly as she could. Not only was she going to have to deal with the harassment, but she would be partnered with the department drunk.

Willow paused at the patrol floor contemplating whether she should get the email done now, but she knew she had company coming and had to get dinner started, so she continued out the door. The thought went through her head that this might not have anything to do with her being a female. It was no secret that her father was a recovering alcoholic. Partnering her with Birch might be intentional.

Her father's condition had left her sour about alcohol abuse. Regardless of whether this arrangement was intentional, she knew she and Birch were in store for a volatile relationship.

∞∞∞

"Pretty hard on her, don't you think, Cap?" the sergeant asked after Sturgeon left.

"I hope so. I can only trust your judgement on this. If she can't fix it, then I'm going to have to officially intervene, and that means I.A."

"I've known her since she was five," the sergeant responded. "She's never quit anything in her life, so I don't think that's going to be a problem."

∞∞∞∞

Willow would have stayed and continued to make a big deal of the sexist promotion, but it was too late to back out of dinner. Besides, she had already transferred the pork chops from the freezer to the fridge that morning.

When she was growing up, she had spent a lot of time with her mother and father as they took turns cooking. Never re-freeze was one of the many rules of the Sturgeon kitchen. If you had thawed something, cook it. Even if you didn't eat it that day, you could always make a sandwich the next.

Willow had had a good childhood for the most part. At least early in life. Every Saturday was a hike and a picnic. Then, when she turned twelve, her dad became very stressed at work. Neither she nor her mom knew why. Willow's mom developed hard feelings for her dad's boss, even though her dad never gave a reason for the stress. Mom was sure it was because of his boss.

It got worse as time went by and eventually dad would fix himself a drink as soon as he walked in the door. No hugs. No kisses. Just the drink. That led to two. Then three. After about three months of the drinking increasing, Willow found herself living with her Aunt Vic. She knew her mom and dad were in verbal skirmishes over it.

She stayed with Aunt Vic and Uncle Billy for nearly three months before Aunt Vic loaded her in the car one day to take her home. Willow hadn't wanted to go. She didn't like what her dad had become and she didn't want to see her parents arguing. When they arrived at the house, both mom and dad were waiting for her on the steps.

Aunt Vic left and her dad sat her down at the kitchen table with her mom on one end and him the other. That was when her dad told her he was an alcoholic and began to explain what an alcoholic was. He said he was getting treatment and wouldn't be joining them for dinner on Tuesdays or Thursdays.

The conversation had gone on for an hour, and her mom had encouraged her to ask any question she needed to. She and Dad had said several times during the family meeting that they were all in this together and each of them needed to know how the other felt. Willow had asked several questions. One, she asked twice. She asked her dad and then she asked her mom if either had hit the other. Dad hadn't hit mom, but mom admitted crying hard and hitting his chest with both hands. Several times.

The childhood was good because that was the only hiccup. Willow had many friends. She wasn't sure why, but she'd had more than most. Almost all of them had horror stories regarding their families. Willow knew she had it good, and she felt genuine concern for her friends. She had, on several occasions, been witness to some of the horror, when she was on sleepovers. Despite thinking about it all the time, she couldn't understand how parents could treat their kids so horribly. She still couldn't now. When she had kids, she would follow the great example set by her own parents.

Willow was twenty-eight now and had been thinking for a couple of years that she needed to become a Mrs. Someone. Every Friday and Saturday night she dedicated to herself. No friends over. She would get out and about with her female friends, and they would change their destinations daily. She had gotten many dates from the excursions. Some she had seen often. One man in particular lasted nearly four months. The sex was good, but she knew he would make a horrible father. Most, she wouldn't even award a second date. She had no intention of settling. Biological clock or not, the man she married would be a good husband and a good father.

When she walked in her door, she found one of the lamps on the floor next to the couch. "You guys are driving me CRAAAAZY!" she said. Pepper, her dog, was smart enough to recognize the tone and made a mad dash through the doggie door out to the back yard, but Salt couldn't care less, as she continued to sit atop her cat tree, licking her paws.

Pepper was a black and white Papillion and was acting like the typical three-year-old, but Salt was seven and should know better. Of course, cats always thought they knew better. Willow cleaned up the mess and went downstairs to begin her workout regimen. Pepper edged his way in about ten minutes later, so Willow stopped the workout and hugged Pepper to her, letting her buddy know she wasn't angry.

Birch

Travis Birch hated Mondays. Not so much because he had to work, but more because he had to work without the relief he got by the occasional drink he would consume. He needed the booze to drown out the drubbing his brain suffered when he had to deal with the losers he would come across nearly every day. That and the fact that it helped him forget Kris and the kids for a time.

His head was killing him. He needed a drink. He was somewhat fortunate that he had the entire weekend off for a change. Both of the previous days he had gotten rid of the headache by downing a morning scotch. Today he wouldn't be so fortunate. He had already shown up for work once after a drink and Miller had had a cow.

After he was shaven, had brushed his teeth and showered, he got dressed and headed to the garage and his Chevy beater. He only needed twenty-seven more miles to reach the magical 200K in the tan cruiser. Before Kris took the kids and left, it had been his baby. He had pampered it and been proud of its mint condition. Now, not so much. He started the ignition and she started up right away and purred like the kitten she was. She took better care of him lately than he did her.

With good traffic today, he would probably be in to the station ten to fifteen minutes early. That was a good thing, because having had the weekend off, he could only imagine what his inbox looked like. He might even beat Miller in for a change.

35

Travis was a big man. Dark skinned, with a receding hairline, large hands and feet. Both of which were lefts. It wasn't that he was all that tall—a mere five-eleven—but he did like to eat. He was a good two-eighty, easy. He was forty-two now. His mother had been a single mom, raising two boys, and she had done an amazing job. She worked two jobs and did some housekeeping on the side. They'd lived in an eight-story apartment building, and there was no shortage of people living there who needed their places cleaned, clothes ironed or pets watched. All of which his mom could do with him and Charles tagging along.

Neither of her boys had been involved in gangs, despite the neighborhood they grew up in. Neither had even been stopped by the police, much less arrested. On occasion, the neighborhood firehouse boys would come down to their block and join the basketball game. The firemen got their butts kicked every time, but they continued to show up anyway.

The downside was that Mom had worked herself into an early grave. Both he and Charles were grown and working when she died. It had been a horrible time in his life, but it did make an already strong relationship between him and Charles even stronger. Travis had been twenty-five at the time, and Charles two years his junior.

As horrible as it was to lose his mother, it got worse nearly two years ago. Charles died. It had effectively been the straw that broke the camel's back. Travis found he could no longer handle the tragedies of life without a little assistance. That assistance came in the form of a bottle.

Travis would pop a cork, so to speak, as soon as he walked in the door. It hadn't been that big a deal at first, but as time went by he found he enjoyed the taste and the comfort more each day. The kids didn't seem to care as long as he played with them, but

Kris became more and more belligerent about it with each passing day. Eventually, he came home one day just to find out he was the only occupant of the house.

His drive to the station was even more boring at this early hour than it normally was. There was less traffic, so he was making good time. The downside was there being little in the way of honking horns and flipping fingers from the hothead commuters. At least that was good entertainment, watching people try to get one car ahead of where they had been. The things people found to get angry about were mind boggling. He didn't find any humor in that joke about putting perfectly sane, calm people behind the wheel of a car, which turned them into mindless trolls. Jokes like that aren't funny when they're true.

Other than the normal stoplights, he only had to slow his drive once when granny was having trouble deciding which lane she needed to be in. Travis took a great deal of pride watching the newer vehicles dodging and darting away from his beater. Their insurance companies certainly weren't going to get rich off him.

When he arrived at the station he was more than surprised at what ten minutes did for the parking lot. Not even Miller's huge Hummer was here. He parked closer than he usually did and climbed the stairs to the bureau, turned on his computer and logged on. His part of the V-shaped desk looked like it always did, but Miller's side was unusually clean. He guessed the man must have had a boring weekend and had come in and cleaned his workspace.

With the screen on, he clicked 'E-Mail' and saw he was right. Three deaths. One an apparent self-inflicted gunshot, one the coroner had ruled an accidental fall from a roof, and one where a woman had been stabbed six times. Probably not self-inflicted, so they would start there. They were pretty much finished with the

Drake murder and had gift-wrapped the leader of the Perte gang for the ADA.

There was also an email from the captain telling him to come to his office first thing, so he went to the coffee maker, poured himself a cup of whatever the hell it was and went to the captain's office.

"Hey, Cap," he said as he walked in.

"Have a seat, Detective. Let me finish this email and I'll be right with you."

While the captain was finishing, Travis sipped the hot water that passed itself off as coffee and glanced out at the desks. He saw Miller planting himself at the Davis and Martin V. Martin had retired, leaving Davis on desk duty for the last week. Travis had an uneasy feeling he was about to become a desk jockey. Unlikely, since he'd had the death emails, which meant yet another new partner. He was starting to get a little paranoid. Better not be some gung-ho recruit. Damn, his head hurt.

When he looked back at the captain, the man was leaning back in his chair with his hands interlocked behind his head, staring at Travis. Travis was nothing if not kind, so he returned the blank stare.

"I've partnered Davis with Miller," the captain offered. "Your new partner should be here by now, so we'll wait. Any questions?"

"Why do I get stuck with a new man? Why not Davis? Miller and I are at 100% conviction."

"Yup! Two cases, two convictions. Not exactly high numbers to be judged by. When you have a say in staffing, I'll ask your permission before I assign, and I don't believe I said anything about it being a man."

"Oh, no. No. No. You did not partner me with a chick."

"Chick?" the woman asked from the doorway. He assumed this to be his new partner, and right away he was sorry. She looked to have a daily membership at some fitness club and quite literally looked like a Barbie doll, blond hair and flawless pale complexion and all. Probably going to rag on him about his eating habits.

"So, I'm going to be partnered with some short, fat, junior high-schooler? You look older than your vocabulary. I haven't been called a chick since I was twelve."

"Sit down, Sturgeon. You're late," the captain interjected.

"Well, if I'm going to be labeled, I may as well act the part. It takes us female detectives time to put on our makeup and decide what shoes to wear and shit." She took a chair next to Travis and copied his earlier stare-down with the captain. Hers lasted longer.

"Are we wearing jeans now, Cap?" Travis asked. "We went from formal to casual?"

Barbie bristled and snarled at him, "I'm wearing jeans, fat boy, because if we have to give chase, it's going to be just me doing the chasing." She stared at him and he stared back. He was ready with his retort but the captain ended the insults by slamming his fist down on his desk.

"Detective Travis Birch, this is Detective Willow Sturgeon. It's obvious you two are off to a rocky start, so I'm going to add my two cents. If either of you, directly or indirectly, cause through your actions or inactions harm to come to the other, I will bring you up on negligence charges. Am I clear?"

"Understood," Barbie said. Travis just nodded, but when the captain's stare returned, he echoed Barbie.

"We had a heavy weekend," the captain said. "Davis and Miller will handle what's left of the Drake murder and the attempted retaliation on Saturday. You two are to handle the rest. Three, to be exact. One is for sure a murder, but I want all three investigated. The stabbing victim's boyfriend is in lockup. Get to work."

Travis stood and his head pounded its objection. He made his way to the V with Barbie at his heels. Once there, he pointed at her chair.

"I'll email IT and have them come up and set you up. For now, pull your chair around and I'll show you what we have. There were three deaths over the weekend, but only one looks to be a murder." She complied, and he sent a quick email off to IT and loaded the files.

He tapped his finger twice on his desk, wording things in his head. "Look. I'm sorry for the chick comment. I was upset at losing my partner."

She reached for his mouse and opened the stabbing file. While reading the details, she replied, "I'll accept your apology for the chick thing, but you'll need to apologize for each future occurrence separately."

"I'm not like that. There won't be more occurrences."

"I have no doubt there will, Birch," she said. "I grew up with an alcoholic father. I'm very familiar with the mannerisms."

"God damn it! I'm sick of people telling me I'm an alcoholic. Yes, I drink, but I can stop when I want to. They can't. And you can call me Travis."

"There's probably only two people in this entire precinct who don't know you're an alcoholic, Birch. One is you and the other is the captain, or you would already be on A.L. You're the talk of the town. I'll call you Travis when you earn it. Admit you have a problem and get some help. Then I will call you Travis. Then you will have the disease. Until then, you are just a drunk to me. Someone whose reaction time I can't trust."

"Don't hold your breath... Sturgeon."

"Fair enough. I have to run downstairs and talk to someone about a few burglaries. Then I'll be back. I'm assuming we're starting with the stabbing?"

"Hey, Travis," came the shout from one of the other desks. "If you want to take a day off soon, I'll take the recruit for you."

Barbie flipped a middle finger in the direction of the comment, but her eyes were still waiting for an answer.

"Meet me in the coroner's office," he said. She nodded and made for the stairs.

Travis watched Sturgeon walk away, wondering what kind of a bitch he would have to put up with. She had on tight-fitting jeans and a floral blouse that fell below the waste, obviously hiding her service weapon. He would start with her attire and pick up other things he could use against her as time went by. Two could play that game.

He turned back to his computer after she disappeared into the staircase, only to see Kramer at his desk, looking back at him.

"Gee, Birch. What were you looking at?" Kramer smirked.

"You can have her," Travis replied. "I'll gladly trade you."

Travis transferred the three files to his cell phone and opened up three folders on his desktop. He read over the patrol report of the gunshot victim and the fall. He would do his due diligence, but he was certain he would find nothing foul with either. The stabbing victim, however, was another matter. He dragged the patrol reports, one at a time, into each folder, pulled out his notebook from his drawer and made his way to the coroner's office.

Fenowicz

Jacob Fenowicz had had a horrible weekend. Every time he settled in to do a little reading the phone would ring and he was right back in the van. Being the coroner was certainly not boring, and it paid well, but there were times when relaxing with a book and a glass of wine seemed to be more of a challenge than the actual job.

He pulled the first cadaver, the stabbing victim, out of the cooler, and he and Jack loaded it onto the scissor lift and moved it to table one. They repeated the process with the second cadaver, the gunshot victim, moving it to table two. The third cadaver had already been picked up by the funeral home. The officers had three witnesses who saw the man fall, so an autopsy was waved by the family.

Jacob attached his head lamp and microphone and turned on the overhead lamp. Then he unzipped the bag, and with Jack on one side and him on the other, they began pulling the bag off the body on table one. They then repeated the process on table two. Jack took photographs of both and moved the ultraviolet light next to table one. Jack started noting external findings on the one on table two while Jacob was starting on table one. Though Jacob had a recorder, Jack would need to list findings on a report, so it would take him longer.

"You forgot to remove the needle, Jack," Jacob said as he observed the arm the blood sample had been taken from on arrival.

"Sorry, Doc."

A knock came at the door, so he covered the body while Jack went to the door. It was Birch. Birch tapped Jack on the arm with a smile and walked toward the tables.

"Hey, Doc," he said, "What can you tell me?"

Jacob looked at the comb in his hand and then at the body. "Your victim has brown hair. She looks like a Caucasian to me. She is five feet seven and weighs 118 pounds. She has a butterfly tattoo on her right ankle."

"That's all you know, so far?" Birch asked.

"Did you know the coffee in this place sucks?" Jacob asked.

"Yup."

"Did you know the parking lot is too small for the number of people working in this building?"

Birch crossed his arms, provided a smirk and then answered, "Yes. That, I know."

"Did you know the coroner doesn't perform autopsies on the weekend?"

"No. That, I didn't know."

"Well, there you go. That's what I can tell you."

"Okay. Sorry, Doc. How about her personal items?"

Jacob unlocked the cabinet and handed Birch the woman's bag and the evidence report. Birch took a seat and began going through the items, so Jacob uncovered the woman's head. He could at least comb out and inspect the hair and head while Birch was nosing around.

Birch was one of the best detectives the department had at their disposal in quite some time, but Jacob also knew the man wasn't long for the job. Birch had a severe alcohol problem and had for a long time. The captain had been very patient, but the rumblings were going around now that the patience was at an end. It was a shame. The man was intense with his investigations, and almost never left them cold.

As he was under the microscope with the residue of the woman's hair, another rap came at the door. Jack was elsewhere, so he went to the door and found a young woman that he thought he recognized as an officer, but she was wearing jeans and a floral blouse.

"Yes?" he said.

"Willow Sturgeon, Doc. I'm looking for Detective Birch."

Jacob opened the door and pointed at the still-digging detective. Birch looked up long enough to introduce her as Detective Willow Sturgeon. Jacob pulled out his notepad and asked the new detective for her phone number and email.

As he was heading back to the hair residue, he found it necessary to wave a hand in front of the face of the returned Jack who seemed to have come down with a case of wide-eyed stares directed at the new detective.

After an hour or so, the detectives had finished with the victim's personal belongings and put everything back in the bag. Jacob locked it back up and escorted the two to the door.

"There was no cell phone found at the scene, Doc?" Detective Sturgeon asked.

"Not that I found. It doesn't mean the first responders didn't find one. You might want to check with them."

"There was nothing in the report except a bottle of dish soap, a brush and a fingernail file, but we'll check with them. Thanks, Doc."

With the detectives gone, Jacob left the residue in the event there was another disturbance and returned to the body. He uncovered her and did another count. Six puncture wounds. He adjusted his mic, grabbed his measure and began measuring the depth of each, reporting his findings, after each, into the mouthpiece.

He attached his loupes and began the intense and time-consuming job of searching every inch of the body for needle marks or pinpricks. Skipping certain techniques on some deaths was expected, but murder was not one of them. Especially not with Birch.

Sturgeon

"What are you thinking?" Birch asked as they made their way upstairs.

"There's no way a twenty-two-year-old woman would be anywhere without a cell phone, so either the killer has it or it's still at the scene. It wasn't in the report, and there's no way any officer would have omitted it. We need to call the next of kin and get the number."

"Once we have that, I'll shoot an email off to research and see if we can get the phone book," Birch said. "We'll probably need a warrant."

When they arrived at the V he sat and began his email. I.T. was occupying her chair so she stood behind him, watching. Birch was a big man, but not in height. In girth. He looked in his fifties, but she wasn't positive that wasn't due to the alcohol. She guessed that also contributed to his bulk. His eyes betrayed him as an alcoholic, as well. She needed to get this man some help and find a way to get him in her workout room.

Willow opened the paper file on his desk, and while he was typing she dialed the victim's NOK. The phone was answered on the second ring.

"Mrs. Simmons?" she asked after the hello.

"Yes."

"This is Detective Sturgeon, working on your daughter's case. I'm so very sorry for your loss. Is this a good time to ask some questions regarding your daughter?"

"Is that prick in jail?"

"He is. We're about to get set up for the interview, but we're missing your daughter's cell phone. I'm wondering if it was unusual for her to be without it."

"There's no way she went anywhere without it. She was a texting fool. She even got stopped and cited for distracted driving. That asshole probably has it. She dumped him and he killed my daughter."

The mother broke down, and Willow waited patiently for her to regain herself. When the sobbing reduced to sniffling, Willow continued.

"Mrs. Simmons. We want to do this right, so we need to gather every bit of evidence we can on her ex. The officers that contacted him found paraphernalia on him, and he became violent, so we have a little time before he makes bail. We'd like to work quickly and see if we can get the judge to deny bail. I see that you are the co-signer on her apartment. Would you grant us access so that we can gather evidence, if there is any?"

"Absolutely. You just say when."

"We have to make a run to the scene and see if we can find the phone, so maybe early afternoon?"

"I'm ready. I'll do what I need to do to make that asshole pay for this. You call me and I'll meet you there. I have a key."

"Thank you, Mrs. Simmons. Do you know, by chance, how she broke it off with him? Was it by phone?"

"I don't know. That's not the way we raised her, but it doesn't mean she didn't."

"Just one more thing, if I may. Can you provide your daughter's phone number and provider?"

While the mother was looking up the daughter's phone number on her husband's phone, Willow saw that Birch was now emailing the ADA for warrants on the residence of their person of interest and the victim's phone book. He was waiting patiently for a number and service provider to attach. As the mother provided the information, Willow repeated it for confirmation and Birch attached the info to the warrant request.

I.T. gave her a temporary password. Willow called the jail and asked them to have their guest transported to interview room one. She and Birch descended the stairs again and waited in the observation room for the subject to arrive.

Once the man was in and cuffed to the table, the officers left, leaving him alone. Willow started for the door, but Birch tapped her arm and held up a hand, so she waited with him and watched.

The man fidgeted a few minutes and then looked at the two-way with a questioning look and gestured with his hands. Birch looked at her with a smile and said, "Not his first rodeo."

She and Birch entered the interview room and Birch spoke, "Good morning Mr. Walker. I'm Detective Birch and this is Detective Sturgeon. Do you know why you're here? Did the officers explain your rights?"

"Hey, baby," the man responded, looking at her. Willow gave her best look of repulsion and bent over like she was about to barf.

The man took the hint and looked back at Birch. "Yeah, I know why I'm here. Those pigs stopped me, pulled me out of my car, threw me on the ground and threw a pipe in my car."

"You do know the officers have body cams, right?" Birch asked.

The man just shrugged, so Birch continued.

"Heather Simmons."

"Fuck that bitch. She called the cops on me?"

"No. She didn't call us. Good to know you're not denying you know her, though. Nice manicure. You have that done professionally or are you self-taught?" Birch asked.

"What are you talking about, man? So, I trim my nails. So, what?"

"Well, it kind of looks like you missed one," Birch observed, causing Walker to cover one hand with the other. Birch continued. "Oh, that's right. That's your emergency snifter, right?" Walker just looked around at everything except the detectives.

"Let's talk about the knife," Birch continued.

"What knife?"

"The one you used to stab her with," Birch said.

"I didn't stab that bitch. She's lying."

"Pretty hard to lie when you're dead. She didn't survive, Mr. Walker. You're now looking at murder one. We can talk to the D.A. about a reduced sentence if you care to tell us why you did it. Did you two have a fight?"

"Whoa! What? No way. I want a lawyer, right fucking now."

"No problem," Birch said. "Do yourself a favor, though. When your attorney gets here, tell him you were infuriated that she dumped you. That way he can argue it wasn't pre-meditated."

"She didn't dump me, man. I dumped her. She was always trying to fix me. Telling me she didn't need to spend her life chained to my dependency. Fuck her. I don't have a dependency."

Willow noticed a stunned expression on Birch's face, but he got it under control. "Then you might be interested in helping us find out who did," Birch continued. "You two spent some time together. Anyone else we should be looking at? People she didn't get along with? Maybe giving your supplier shit for keeping you in the stuff?"

"I don't know what you're talking about. Keeping me in what stuff?"

"Let's not play games, dumbass. The best way for you to get out of here is to give us a reason to release you. Right now, you're all we've got. You're a user, and you have motive. If you want to fuck with us, we'll just charge you with murder and watch you scramble to get some other dumbass to post your bail. Then we'll talk to that person. How many of your family and friends do you want us to fuck with?"

"Talk to her friends, man. They're the ones who were telling her I was trash."

"Why would they kill her for that? Think hard, shithead. Who wanted her dead? Was she killed by one of your enemies to get back at you? We don't mind talking to two or three hundred people. It's what we do."

"I don't have enemies, Dicktective. My friends like me. Her friends didn't. That Amy chick was always on her about me. Fucking bitch. Her parents were assholes to me, too. Maybe it was jealousy.

Maybe the Amy bitch wanted me for herself and offed Heather. I didn't kill her."

"Amy who? What's her last name?"

Walker just shrugged. Then he looked at Willow and winked. Willow pointed and laughed.

"I'll tell you what, Mr. Walker," Birch continued. "Even if you do get out of here, I'm going to be all over your ass. It might benefit you to think about what I said. Nothing takes the pressure off like having more than one suspect. Like I said, right now? You're it! Enjoy the pressure. Good luck getting supplied with us watching your every move. We'll be talking again, Mr. Walker. Tell your attorney you want to take a polygraph and you want your residence searched while you're still incarcerated."

"Fuck you, Dicktective. I know my rights. You need a warrant."

"We'll get that warrant, Mr. Walker. Have a nice day. We'll get you a public defender." Willow and Birch left, asking the officer to take the man back to his cell and let the ADA know he needs a public defender.

"We probably should have asked for a warrant on his car, too," Willow said. "The knife or phone could be in there."

"I'll try," Birch said, showing her the email, "but I've already got a denial on his apartment without more evidence. The ADA is going for the phone book, though."

Willow was ready to go, but Birch was still standing outside the interview room, checking his nails, scratching his chin and straightening his shirt. Then he opened the interview room door and was at Walker, again.

"Sorry it took me so long to get back," he said to the man. "My partner was distracting me."

"You just left, Dicktective."

"See," Birch said, "I told you I was going to be all over your ass. Sin paz, sin piedad. What is in the list of items you had on you when you were booked? Were you the one with the butt plug?"

"Fuck you. Go find out."

"Okay, I sure will." Birch left the room and closed the door. He checked his nails again and straightened his shirt, yawned and tapped his feet on the floor. He opened the door again.

"Do you hunt, Mr. Walkman?" he asked.

"It's Walker, Dicktective, and what's it to you?"

"Oh, nothing. Still looking for that knife, you know." Birch walked out and closed the door but resumed his previous actions. He opened the door again, but before he could get a word out, Walker screamed.

"HELP! Will someone take me back to my cell?"

Birch slammed both palms down hard and loud on the table and glared at Walker. A smile slowly materialized. "You ain't seen nothing yet, buddy." Birch's smile turned to a snarl. He stood and closed the door behind him. This time he made his way to the stairs. Willow followed.

"I'd like to make a run over to the scene, Birch, and see if I can find anything."

"You're seriously going to call me Birch for the rest of our career?"

"As it stands," she said.

"Okay, let's take a look. Then we probably should run over to her apartment." They went back to the V for the cruiser keys, which she snatched off the desk.

"I'm driving," Birch said.

"When I see you've stopped drinking," she said quietly. "You can wait here if you like." She turned without waiting for a response and left the building. Birch followed, fuming.

During the ride, she took note that Birch was using the ride time to call the witnesses of the fall death. There were three, and each call was short as Birch let them tell the story without asking too many questions. The questions he did ask were different for each of them. Good tactic. Hard to recite set stories that way. Each witness was believable, apparently. Birch made a few paper notes and then stuck the file at the bottom of the others.

When they arrived at the park scene, Willow checked the paper file to get the exact location the body was found. She held up the photo and turned in a circle to locate the defining tree with the police tape wrapped around it and walked toward it. She found the heavily treaded area right away amidst all the trees and began looking for the phone. Birch searched the opposite side.

The area was not very level, and looked to be that way by design, so there were a lot of ups and downs, but Willow made the best inspection she could. When she was about fifty feet from the scene, she saw what looked like fresh dirt. She began slowly brushing the area.

"Oh, shit!" she said quietly. She backed away, careful to tread in her same steps, and pulled out her cell, dialing Fenowicz.

"Coroner. This is Jack."

"Jack, this is Detective Sturgeon. Is the Doc handy?"

"Fenowicz," came the doc's voice after less than a minute.

"Doc, this is Detective Sturgeon. Care to make another trip to the crime scene of the stabbing victim?"

"Why?"

"I've just uncovered a shoe, and there's a foot in it. I'll wait here for you."

"Okay. Give us a few minutes to get the cadavers back in the cooler and we'll be on our way. Your self-inflicted is definitely self-inflicted, by the way."

Willow thanked him for letting her know. Two down, one to go. She hung up the phone, looking about trying to determine where Birch might be. She took her best guess and climbed the minor incline, spotting him.

"Hey, Birch," she screamed in his direction. "We have a whole new set of problems over here."

Birch came lumbering over the hill asking her what she had.

"I think Walker may have been telling the truth. It looks like our victim may have stumbled on another murder and was killed for it. There's another body here." Once she pointed out the area, she continued, "I've called the coroner. Do we want to snoop around a bit more before calling in the crime scene unit? Because they'll chase us."

"Nope, we do it by the book. I'll call them. There's nothing here that tells me he's not our guy. He could have killed the other one just as easily as Simmons."

"Doc said the suicide is confirmed," she told him.

"Okay, we'll turn that over to social services," he said as he dialed the crime scene unit.

While Birch was on the phone, Willow went to the cruiser and popped the trunk, then pulled out the yellow tape roll and flags. She began taping off the area. When she finished that, she carefully went back to the area of the second body and stuck a flag in the ground. She made a widening circle around the body, looking for other pertinent objects or loose soil. Birch was right. Walker could have done both. She wasn't sure why she'd spouted off like that. Now she felt like a rookie.

Her phone rang, and it was officer Crocket checking in on the burglaries. Willow continued to keep her focus on the crime scene investigation and answer his questions at the same time. He mainly wanted to know which pawn shops she had checked for the stolen goods. She gave him the name of the two she had visited and then hung up. Having checked as much of the area as she could, she walked back to Birch and waited for him to finish with CSU.

Once Birch finished his call, she said, "She might have heard something or saw something, and when she found this person being buried, she started recording it on her cell instead of calling the police. That's why she didn't have her phone. The killer took the evidence with him. I'm just offering up another possibility."

"He would have to be completely stupid to throw it, so I'm guessing you're right about him taking it, but it's also a possibility there was something on the phone he didn't want us to see. Like his face," Birch offered, holding up Walker's mug shot. Willow dug in her notes and found the cell phone number and dialed it. She wasn't sure why. Heather Simmons must have had a lot of friends, and one of them surely would have called it. If it was answered they would have called the police. To her surprise, the call was answered, although silently. Willow wasn't sure what to say, so she went with the first thing she thought of.

"I'm going to find you." There was nothing but silence on the other end. No clicking sounds, such as you would hear on a hang-up, or breathing, or anything. After a short time, a man started laughing. It was a low laugh, at first, but then it got louder and heartier. Then it stopped, and the man spoke softly.

"If only you could, sweets."

Sandman

Mike finished the call, closed up his desk, logged off the computer and walked out of his office, telling his secretary, Michelle, that he was going to lunch. He wasn't, of course, but she couldn't know where he was going. He was totally out of product, and he had made arrangements to meet Chulo at the grocery store. That was where they exchanged goods for cash, on occasion. They each had a shopping basket with identical shoulder bags and would exchange carts in the middle of an aisle.

No fuss. No muss. No questions. He and Chulo would always need something that would require a cart. With Mike it was always beer or wine. Neither of which were things he would need to worry about expiring. They were both things he used, regularly. So Chulo would put beer and wine in his cart. Mike would put 24 packs of water and beer in his. Chulo was not a wine man.

They would get into a conversation about nothing in particular and keep moving about and eventually leave with the opposite cart, pay for the items and continue their conversation on the way out the door. Once outside, however, the conversation would switch, as well as the volume, and they would begin talking about the transaction, future transactions, pricing, and general topics they both had in common.

It was by no means the only place they would meet. Sometimes the business transaction would also be pleasure. Such as a round of golf, which Mike never seemed to get the upper hand at. They would also get together at the cabin. Mike was trying to put that in the background, however. The last time they were there, Chulo had noticed the churned earth. Mike had said he was going to plant vegetables, in the event he became a hermit. However, Mike hadn't planted vegetables and never would. So, it wouldn't be a good thing for Chulo to see nothing had been planted.

It would also not be a good thing for Chulo to get curious about it and decide to drive out there alone one day and dig around in the churned soil. Mike didn't think so, though. Chulo was a pretty easy-going guy and not the curious sort. Mike knew Chulo had his own demons. He didn't need to shoulder someone else's.

Mike also knew Chulo was a pimp of sorts. Chulo had offered him a discount one day that Mike, at first, hadn't understood. It didn't take him long to realize what Chulo was offering. Then, after he had figured it out, Chulo brought out a photo album. A large one. There was no way that many girls had nothing better to do with their time. It wasn't even the only album. Chulo said he had three. Mike didn't want to know what the other two were for.

The temptation was great. The majority of the girls were extremely attractive and young-looking brunettes, but Mike also knew the photos had been photoshopped. Still, he wasn't at the point where he was that desperate. He made good use of the goods he bought from Chulo and didn't need help.

The only problem Mike had with Chulo, and it was selfish of him to call it a problem, was Chulo's obsession with giving out promotional junk. Chulo worked for Mitchell Ice Company and was constantly shoving pens, pencils, ice picks, plastic tumblers and everything else he carried at Mike. At first it was cool, but now Mike threw most of the stuff out.

Chulo made enough money off Mike and others like Mike to support a family of six, but when Mike asked him why he worked at all, Chulo had a totally sensible answer. Anyone who could support an entire family and never went to work became an immediate target of the various law enforcement departments. His work was just a cover.

Mike arrived at the grocery, found Chulo's car and parked a few stalls down, so as not to be too conspicuous. He found an unused cart, threw his shoulder bag in and pushed it toward the entrance, side-glancing here and there for occupied vehicles.

When he passed through the entrance he received the usual greetings from the nearby staff, and once he got past them, he began side-glancing again, while at the same time looking down each aisle for Chulo and finding him in the canned goods section.

"Hey, bud!" Chulo greeted him.

"Chulo. How goes it?"

"Good. Ready for another game of golf. Are you recovered yet from the financial drubbing you took last time?"

Mike laughed. "Oh, I don't think you got me for that much. You only won by one stroke. At a dollar a stroke, I hardly felt it. I think we ought to set something up for next month." Mike pulled up his schedule on his phone. "How does the seventeenth look for ya?"

Chulo copied Mike, checking his phone, and began typing in it. "I got you, Mike. I'll set up an early tee time and give you a text."

"Sounds good. How's it going, otherwise?" Mike responded as he entered the data himself.

"Can't complain. Business is good. Had a problem over the weekend, but it was easily taken care of. How about you?"

60

"The same, without the problem part. Business is up. Clients are happy."

"How's the love life? Still have that discount waiting whenever you're ready."

"No. I'm good in that area. Might have myself a keeper, actually."

"No kidding!" Chulo exclaimed. Mike could tell, though, that the false happiness was really a concern about losing some business. "Why don't you stop by the car on your way out? I might have some goodies in the trunk."

"Come on, Chulo. I have more ice picks, tumblers, stir sticks and calendars than I know what to do with."

"Really?" Chulo looked at Mike and smiled. "How about an ice bucket that just arrived? I know you don't have one of those. They just came in."

"I'll admit, I could use a new ice bucket. Is it a good one, or one of those cheapies?"

"First, it's free. Second, it's good enough that I don't think it should be."

"Well, let's take a look," Mike said as he grabbed Chulo's cart and checked to see that the product was hidden. He adjusted the bag as he made his way to the checkout. Chulo was behind him doing the same with Mike's cart.

They each went to a different clerk, paid for the goods, and exited, meeting up again at the back of Chulo's car. Mike looked over the ice bucket, decided Chulo was right and accepted the gift. He thanked Chulo, loaded his car and left the lot.

Logan

Chulo loaded his car and left the lot out of an opposite exit from Mike. He was troubled about this supposed 'keeper' of Mike's. He was going to have to do some research. Chulo didn't stay in business by being content with customers finding a keeper.

Chulo's livelihood was predicated on desire and addiction. He knew Sanders wasn't a user. He couldn't be and keep his job. The company he worked for conducted random drug screens, and there was no forewarning. Human Resources stopped in your office and handed you a cup. If you made mention that you didn't have to pee at present, they would remain in the office with you until the company medical nurse arrived to draw blood.

Sanders had told him all this during one of their meetings. Chulo had said it was a violation of human rights, but Sanders explained that the procedure was covered extensively during the hiring process, and Human Resources made it clear that agreement was necessary for the person to be hired. They also made it clear that changing your mind afterwards would result in immediate termination. A signed form and audio recording was a part of the employee's permanent file.

Having gained this information, Chulo knew he would never have Sanders for that form of client. Addiction was out of the question. That left desire. There didn't seem to be a problem in that area with Sanders. His need for the 'Special K' was a good business for Chulo.

Chulo could get more money out of the tightwad if he would just buy into Chulo's girls. So far, that side of his business wasn't interesting Sanders. It seemed he much preferred taking chances with variety. At least in the girl. Like Chulo, Sanders preferred darker hair, but Chulo had several brunettes on his list. Sanders just wouldn't bite. He wondered if Sanders' interest would change if he knew that his boss was one of Chulo's customers.

Chulo arrived home and found one of his men outside, lounging on the porch with a beer. Chulo didn't conduct business at home so he immediately became incensed. He pulled into the driveway, looked at the cars up and down the street, and got out, discretely checking windows in neighboring houses. Satisfied, he walked to the porch.

"Why are you at my house, Horace?"

"It's pretty urgent, Chu. You're not answering your phone."

Damn it. Chulo had forgotten he had turned his ringer off in the grocery store. He adjusted the phone as he asked the next question. "What's the problem?"

"Sam brought in another girl. A fourteen-year-old blonde, who should be profitable and easily trained, but he roughed her up pretty good. From looking at her, I'd guess it could be a month or more before we can even begin."

Chulo tried to hide the look of anger but could tell by the expression Horace was providing that he wasn't very successful. "That makes seven now, and only five clients," Chulo said through clenched teeth. "Brittany is no longer bringing in the business. She's twenty-eight, and our clients are looking for younger. Retire her."

Horace nodded and stood to leave, but Chulo grabbed his arm to stop him. "While you're at it, Sam needs to be retired, too.

We will be okay until I find another recruiter. Make sure you get his keys. Check his place and his car, and as usual, bring me his phone. Bring it to the office. Never come here again. I don't care how important you think it is."

"Understood," Horace said. He walked to his car and left.

Chulo took a long breath and let it out slowly, walking to the door. He walked in and was met by his wife and son with a hug.

"Who was that man, honey?" His wife asked.

"A friend from work, sweetheart. Just checking to see if tomorrow's deliveries were scheduled. How are you, guys?" Chulo asked, mussing his son's locks and changing the subject.

"I had a good day," his wife said. "I can't say as much for your son here. Apparently, he was a little unprepared for today's test."

"How unprepared?" Chulo asked, looking at his son and getting a look of shame in return. His son knew his dad was expecting an answer and also knew his mom wasn't going to provide it so he hesitantly told his dad the results of his test.

"No X-Box," Chulo said.

"But papa..."

"No buts, either. Go wash up for dinner."

With his wife returning to the kitchen and his son pouting off to wash his hands, Chulo picked up the mail and walked to his recliner, still thinking about the news from Horace. He had to balance that news with his plans for Sanders. Maybe if he found out who the keeper was, he could do something to dissuade her from hanging with Mike. Sanders had money, and Chulo wanted it.

Chulo felt the vibration in his pocket and told his wife he needed to get something out of the car. He walked out and answered the phone.

Birch

"I don't think we should waste time on Walker anymore," Barbie said.

"That was stupid," Travis spouted angrily, and with a look of disgust. "That was the epitome of stupid! Now he has your phone number."

"Good. Maybe he'll give me a buzz and we can go out for a couple of drinks."

"You don't get it, do you, Sturgeon? If he has the equipment and know-how, he'll be able to track your movement and know when we're closing in on him."

"I think you're giving him too much credit. This is a city park. If he's as smart as you suggest, he would have picked a less conspicuous place to dump a body. I'm going to look around for more loose soil."

Barbie headed off one direction, and he walked the opposite direction. Before she got too far away, he decided to antagonize her.

"Besides, if you just want to stop off for drinks, I could show you around."

"I have no doubt," she spouted back.

He obviously wasn't going to find the phone, so he concentrated his efforts on looking for the knife, or signs of more burials, and he deliberately stayed out of sight of the walking path. The killer would have tried to stay away from the path. Even though he may have failed once. Maybe even twice. If Barbie was right. If Heather Simmons had strayed onto a crime as well as the witness who'd found Heather, then that would be a problem without a lead. He just wasn't sure, but he had a nagging feeling the woman had been targeted.

If that was the case, it was possible she was killed elsewhere and brought here for disposal. Barbie had a point, though. This was not exactly a prime spot for disposing of bodies. Getting them here without being seen would have been near impossible. The killer could have dumped them in a dumpster, but that wouldn't have worked, either. Too many cameras.

Still, there were other places outside of populated areas that would have been less conspicuous. Unless, that is, he wanted the bodies found. Why hadn't he buried the Simmons woman? It could be he thought he had been seen and just left her. Maybe the man who'd found Heather scared him off.

Travis needed to stop overthinking this. Barbie might have been right. Perhaps Heather Simmons had just made an error in judgement. She should have called the police.

Travis guessed he had gone far enough away from the scene and turned back that direction. When he got back, Barbie was talking to one of the CSU officers, while three others were digging, brushing and sifting around the second body. Travis walked as close as he could but got an evil glance from one of the officers, so he stopped. He was able to ascertain the second victim was also a woman.

"Any sign of a phone or wallet?" he asked.

"We'll tell you what we have as we get it, Detective," the man standing with Barbie said. Travis assumed it was time to shut up, now. He called the evidence room. Hopefully Max was working today, otherwise he was going to have trouble getting his answer. Max answered.

"Hey, Max. It's Travis. Can you check Walker's basket? See if he was booked with more than one phone."

"No phone, at all. Probably draining in the impound lot."

"Perfect. Thanks, Max."

He saw Barbie walking toward the walking path and turned to see the coroner's van pulling up, so he followed her.

"I hate to act too eager, Doc, and I don't mean to push," Travis said as he reached the van, "but do you have anything for us yet on the Simmons woman?"

"I have a few things so far. She was not sexually assaulted, but we do have DNA. She put up a fight, and not just a little one. There are literally chunks of skin and blood under her nails, and a knuckle on her right hand is broken. My guess is this man or woman's face looks like a jigsaw puzzle.

"The knife you're looking for is a hunter's knife. Double edged. One edge is honed sharply, the other is serrated. I'm still looking for a cause of death. There wasn't enough blood residue around the knife wounds, and they appear to be carefully placed. Six wounds. Three above the breasts and three along the breasts. The blade measures six inches at the deepest. Considering the fingernails, I don't see how she would have survived long enough to obtain that much skin. The fight was obviously intense and must have occurred prior to whatever caused her first injury."

Travis dug out his phone, but Barbie was already dialing. They walked with Jack and the doc as they pulled the gurney from the back of the van and made their way through the trees.

"This is Detective Sturgeon," Barbie said into her phone. "Could you check weekend calls from hospitals and urgent cares and see if there were any about suspicious injuries? I appreciate it. Thank you. Either myself or Detective Birch. Yes. No, not child abuse. Specifically, facial scratches, cuts or abrasions. Okay, thanks."

"Was there enough under the nails to get a DNA match?" Travis asked.

"Oh, yeah," Jacob confirmed. "She got him good. I checked the mouth and teeth. It looks like he wasn't close enough for her to bite, and there's no sign, so far, of any scratches on her other than the stabbing. I have to check the stomach contents and medical records yet."

"Okay. Thanks, Doc. Let us know what you find."

"There's not much we can do here," Travis said to Barbie when she hung up, "that won't annoy CSU or the doc, so let's check out the Simmons apartment. At least now we know the reason for the soap, file and brush. He wanted to clean out those nails. Remove the evidence. When that guy stumbled on the body, the killer was right here, watching him. We're going to need to talk to him, too. The guy who found the body," Travis clarified.

"I don't like where this is heading. Why didn't he just kill the guy and bury them both?" Travis stuck his hand out. "I'm driving."

"You're not driving. In case you haven't noticed, you've been shaking for two hours now. Are you sure you can make the whole shift without bending that elbow?"

"You know, this was kind of funny for a while. Now I'm starting to lose patience with your shit. Knock it off and mind your own business, and while I'm thinking about it, you need to dress a little more professionally. I need interviews focusing on my questions, not your ass."

"Nope on knocking it off and be careful about your comments about my ass. I might file sexual harassment charges on you. I was promoted because I'm a woman, so I'll flaunt what I've got."

After Sturgeon called the mother, the entire drive to the Simmons apartment was made in silence. When they arrived, the mother was already standing by the front door of the building. Pleasantries were exchanged then Travis asked the mother if Heather kept a diary or journal.

"If she did, it was on her phone. Everything she did was on that phone. Did he have the phone?"

"Mrs. Simmons," Travis answered, "although we are still interested in Mr. Walker, it's beginning to look less like he's our killer, and he definitely doesn't have the phone."

"How do you know? Who killed my baby?" Mrs. Simmons broke down again, and Travis explained that Sturgeon had called the phone and a man who wasn't Walker had answered, as Walker was still in lockup. He went on to explain that Heather hadn't been raped, and had put up a valiant fight, but he couldn't comment beyond that as it was still an active investigation. He waited a bit for her to calm down and then continued.

"Mrs. Simmons, I can't even imagine what you must be going through right now, but for us to find the man who did this, it is imperative that you do nothing to hinder this investigation. You absolutely can't call the phone. Detective Sturgeon is baiting the man, and if it rings too often, he may turn it off. We need the phone to stay on. Did you have a GPS locator on her phone?"

"When she was a teenager we did, but she's changed phones twice since then, so we disconnected it, not wanting to invade her private life."

"That's okay. We'll try different means," Travis said, and they all climbed the steps to Heather's apartment. Sturgeon went right to the bedroom, so Travis sat Mrs. Simmons in the living room, and began the interview.

"Did Heather have any favorite hangouts that she mentioned? Favorite places to dine, sports clubs, clothing stores?"

"She liked Red Lobster. She ate there a lot. As far as I know, she never bought clothes anywhere except J Crew or Macy's. She had their credit cards and didn't like carrying cash or using her Visa except at restaurants or gas stations. As far as sports clubs, it would only have been with Amy or the asshole. She didn't drink herself. She and Amy walked all the time or went to Planet Fitness."

"Amy's last name? Phone number?"

"Gaudier. I never had her number. I'm not sure why. I guess I never saw a need."

"Do you know where Amy lived?"

"On Riverside somewhere. I'm sorry." Travis had to wait for Mrs. Simmons to calm again, but he remained patient.

"Where did Heather work?"

"She worked for Southwest Airlines in ticketing. Oh, dear. I suppose I'd better call them. That's where she met Amy."

"That's not necessary. We'll stop out. We'll have questions for them, as well. Amy works in ticketing, too?"

71

"I don't know. Heather never said."

"Any other associates you can think of? Anything at all that would have sent a mother's hackles up?"

"Not that I can think of. We were so happy at the job we had done raising her. Her life was so calm. Well, except for that dumbass."

"How did Heather get along with her dad? Would she maybe have confided something in him that she would have been afraid to talk to you about?"

"I highly doubt it. They worked opposite hours. She worked afternoons at Southwest, and he works days. He's in bed before she even gets off. Do you want me to ask him?"

"That's not necessary. If it becomes important, we'll call him. Can you think of anybody Heather may have mentioned that might want to hurt her? Co-worker? Associate?"

"No. I think she was pretty popular amongst her friends."

"Do you know the passwords to any of her social media accounts?"

"No. Sorry."

"We would like to understand her being found in the park. Do you have any idea why Heather would be walking alone in the park?"

"No clue. I never heard her mention even once that she had walked alone."

"Who is this man, Mrs. Simmons?" Barbie asked, walking in from the bedroom and showing a picture of Heather and a man standing in front of a sailboat.

"I... I don't know who that is. I've never seen him before."

Sturgeon

Willow left Birch to his interview and walked back into the bedroom. Mrs. Simmons had given the okay for her to make a copy of the photo, but she wanted it back. She went back to the secret compartment she found in the armoire and took a photo of the jewelry and coins and closed the drawer.

She opened the bedside stand, rummaged through the personal items and then pulled the drawer out. She ran her hand under and behind the drawer, looked inside the drawer slide and repeated the process on both drawers of both stands.

She lifted the lamps and looked under the bases. She pulled the bed away from the wall and checked the backside of the frame. She lifted the mattress and then the box springs, checking underneath. She went to the base of the bed frame and checked those drawers as she had the stands. Nothing but bedding. Nothing underneath the bed, either.

All the pictures were attached to the wall with Velcro strips. She pulled her pocket knife and carefully pried the Velcro apart, pulling the frame from the wall. Nothing behind any of the pictures or in the frames themselves. She placed them back on the wall.

"I told Mrs. Simmons we would lock up behind us," Birch said from the doorway. "She was struggling so I sent her home. Have you done the bathroom yet?"

"Not yet. Have fun, but if there's any whiskey in the toilet tank, leave it."

"Fuck you, Sturgeon."

"Not on your life."

Willow moved on to the dresser, pulling it slightly from the wall to look behind. She then started with the drawers, and there were a lot of them. Nine, to be exact. This woman loved her clothes. She found nothing there and made her way to the walk-in closet. She found the laundry basket right away and began looking through the dirty clothes. The only thing she found in the basket was a bedsheet with a spot on it that may have been spermatozoa. She folded the sheet in on itself and placed it on the bed.

It took nearly a half hour to rifle the closet with all the shoes she had to look inside and pockets she had to search, but she found nothing other than the sheet. As she was walking out, she realized the door to this closet would seldom be closed from the inside. She closed the door. There was a piece of paper held to the door with a thumbtack. She removed it and, on closer inspection, saw a lot of gibberish.

217fbHeSim

HS006Taw5

There were six different sets of numbers. Willow folded the paper and placed it on top of the bedsheet. She went into the living room, grabbed the notes on the desk, Heather's tablet and laptop, and walked them into the bedroom and put them on the bed.

Birch walked out of the bathroom, tying off the trash can bag, throwing it on the bed. "Give me a hand with the shower curtain," he said. The two of them began unhooking the curtain. "Find anything?" he asked.

"There was a bedsheet in the hamper with what might be sperm on it," she answered. "And her passwords. You?"

"Standard stuff. Nothing unusual. Ibuprofen, antacids, bandages and a shit load of rubbers, so that's probably not sperm. No guy was going to be able to say he forgot to bring one, for sure."

"Well, if Walker was my boyfriend, I'd probably make him double up."

Willow took the kitchen and Birch the living area, and after two more hours of cupboards, drawers and end tables, they were finally convinced they had covered everything they could. Birch went to the cruiser to get bags for the evidence, and they locked up and went back to the cruiser, throwing everything in the trunk.

It was one o'clock, and after several minutes of arguing healthy food vs. hamburgers, they stopped at Chipotle. Willow ordered a chicken salad and watched as Birch had them build a five million-calorie burrito. When they had their food, they made their way to a corner table.

"I'm going to talk to the captain when we get back," Birch said, not bothering to finish chewing first, "to see if he can find you a partner you can get along with."

"Sounds good," Willow answered quickly. "I don't think there's any hurry, though. The way you drink and eat, you'll be dead in a week and the problem will fix itself."

Birch just shook his head disgustedly. "You're a piece of work. You know that?"

"Careful with that piece word. I might file sexual harassment charges on you."

"Who the hell made you such a cynical bitch?"

"Who the hell turned you into a drunk? Once we get back, you can go see the captain and then call it a day. I'm sure you have a date with a bottle. I'm going to go out to the marina and see if anyone knows the dude in the picture or recognizes the sailboat. Then I'm going to re-interview the guy who stumbled onto the scene."

"You're not going anywhere without backup. You know that. I'll apologize ahead of time if it happens to be me. If you're going to the marina, we'll stop by your house so you can change into something not painted on."

"I'll accept your apology if it does happen to be you, but I'll hope it's someone I can count on."

"I'll tell you what I'll do," Birch offered. "I'll drink nothing tonight, to show you I can, if you can go the whole shift tomorrow without an insult."

"Deal," she said, trying unsuccessfully to hide the smile.

"What's funny?"

"You, Birch. You're funny. You know as well as I do you're going to crack that bottle as soon as you walk in the door. You also know I'm experienced with drunks. I'll know as soon as you walk in if you even smelled a cork."

"Well, there's nothing I like more than a challenge, so you're on."

They finished the rest of the meal and made the fifteen-minute drive back to the station. Willow opened the trunk and began pulling the bags out and Birch reached in to help.

"I have this," she said. "You go see the captain and cry on his shoulder. I'll take this to the lab and then wait for you at the desk."

Birch fixed her with an angry stare and then walked away. Willow took the items that needed to go to the lab, and the passwords, laptop and tablet to research, and then climbed to the desk and checked her emails.

There was nothing mind-numbing in her emails, so she took the picture and walked downstairs to social. Fred wasn't involved in anything critical and gave her his attention. She handed him the photo.

"What's involved in getting this out there?" she asked.

"I can crop it. Are we looking for the man and the woman both?"

"No. Just the man and the boat."

"Then I'll have to blur the woman's face. What's the message?"

"He is a person of interest in multiple murders. I want to make sure no one confronts him. He should be considered armed and dangerous. He also might be considerably disfigured, with scratches and maybe bruises. Then provide the usual crime-stopper info."

"One of the victims kicked his ass. Got it. It will take me about a half hour, and it will be posted."

"That's great. Thanks, Fred."

Next, Willow went to the patrol division and began showing the picture around, asking if anyone knew the man. There weren't a lot of officers in-house, and the attempt proved futile. She made a mental note of which officers she had asked so she could catch the others as she saw them.

Willow went back upstairs to see how many detectives were in. She would make copies and have them check with their CIs, something she would need to make a priority. She knew from listening in on conversations detectives had that confidential informants were pretty critical.

Birch

Travis walked to the captain's office. Finding him unoccupied, he knocked and walked in.

"Detective Birch. What's on your mind?"

"Cap, I'm not sure this is going to work out," Travis said. "The woman is obstinate, insulting and just plain antagonistic towards me. I think the department would be better served if she had a partner who didn't annoy her."

"Why?" the captain asked, daring Birch to admit he had a problem.

"Why what?"

"Why is she obstinate, insulting and antagonistic, and why do you annoy her? I did my homework, Birch, before I promoted her. She is very well thought of among the patrol team, and the sergeant had nothing but praise for her. What is it about you that's set her off?"

"She thinks I'm out of shape," Travis said, not about to mention the alcohol accusation.

"You are out of shape, Birch. Look in the mirror before you come to work and ask yourself if you could run down a fleeing suspect. If you want her to stop, ask her if you can join her after work. She has an entire gym in her house. Did you know that? Do you know anything about her? Did you try to get to know her?"

"I know she's bitchy."

"There is an average of two patrolmen a day that join her after work, Birch. They all say she is relentless in pushing them to their full potential. Her sergeant was even there a time or two. He said she is friendly and kind. She offers bottled water and even cooks for those who stay after the workout. I have not heard the words obstinate, insulting, antagonistic, or annoying even once from anyone but you."

Travis knew he was getting nowhere. The captain was running out of people to partner him with. He kept moving them to other partners. If the captain would have left Miller alone, everything would be fine. He and Miller were buds.

"She's your partner, Birch. It's not going to kill you to lay off the burgers and exercise a bit. Get back to work. Get these deaths solved."

Travis left the captain's office stewing. Not because he'd failed. More because Barbie knew he would. She was indifferent to it. She didn't really care who her partner was anyway. As long as her partner didn't relax with a stiff drink, that is.

As he was approaching the V, he saw her in her chair, probably reviewing her email. One patrolman and two detectives were looking at the picture of the man and the sailboat and shaking their heads.

He took his chair and began reading his own email but kept his ears open to what was being said. The patrolman was clueless as to who the man was, but he did strengthen the captain's words.

"What time are you getting off, Will?" he asked. "I was going to pop over after work, if that's okay."

"I don't know, Adam. I'll text you when I'm on my way home. I have a roast in the slow cooker, too."

"I'm all in with that. I'll wait for your text. Jessie said she might come, too. When she finds out about the roast, I won't be able to keep her at home, anyway." He laughed.

"Did she get that job?" Barbie asked the man.

"She did, and she's stoked."

"Okay. Well, thanks for looking at the photo, Adam, but I have to get back to work."

"Sturgeon, did you show this photo to the captain?" Kramer asked. Kramer was a property detective, and it was he and his partner looking over the photo.

"Willow is fine, Detective. No, I didn't. Why?"

"I'm Matt, and this is Rich. I don't know the guy, but this woman looks awfully familiar. She looks like Amy's friend."

"She does have a friend named Amy," Travis interjected. "Amy who?"

"Amy Gaudier," Kramer answered.

"Who's Amy Gaudier?" Barbie asked.

"Trevor Gaudier's daughter."

"The Trevor Gaudier?" Barbie asked incredulously. "The captain actually knows him?"

"Oh, yeah. Navy buddies from the old days."

Barbie snatched up the picture and headed off to the captain's office, while the two detectives made their way back to their area without so much as a 'See ya'. Travis was beginning to think Barbie was right. Maybe the captain was the only one who didn't know he drank.

He really didn't want to see the captain again, so he finished his emails and began entering his interview notes into the opened case file. He labeled the file 'Heather Simmons' and created a new folder and labeled it 'Second victim'. He would change it later, when he had a name. He scratched out 'at the coroner' on a post-it note and slapped it on Barbie's desk. One of the emails was from the doc. The captain's response had evidently bothered him more than he thought. His hands were shaking. He needed a drink.

When he got to the coroner's office, Jack let him in and he greeted them both. The coroner was finishing up the second victim, so he waited at the desk. It was a short wait.

"Detective," Jacob said in greeting.

"Doc," Travis nodded. "You wanted to see me?"

"Yes, although I think Jack would rather see your partner," he said loudly, looking at Jack, who was peering through the window at the steps. Jack got the hint and went back to what he was doing.

"I believe we both have a problem," Jacob continued. "My problem is the second victim is a Jane Doe. No ID of any kind. If I don't find anything in the clothing, I'm going to have to go back through missing persons. Your problem is a little more disturbing."

"Let's have it," Travis prodded.

"Jane Doe was stabbed, as well."

"Understandable," Travis said.

"Five times."

Travis dropped his jaw. He knew what the coroner was suggesting. There were four more bodies out there somewhere.

"It could be just a coincidence, Doc," Travis stammered out.

"Absolutely, it could, except for one thing. Heather Simmons and Jane Doe both were stabbed post-mortem. The actual cause of death was an ice pick through the brain. It has been shoved through the ear canal, and the killer did a very good job of cleaning the blood from the ear."

"Were you able to get anything from the fingernail DNA?"

"Like what? This isn't television, Birch. Get me the suspect's DNA and I'll send both to the lab. You know I'm going to have to call them, right?"

"Bullshit! You can't do that to us. They'll just muddle things up."

Barbie was let in by Jack and briefed by Travis. "Doc here is going to call in the feds."

"No biggie," Barbie said, causing Travis to flail his arms.

"It's our case," he screeched.

"It's murder, Birch," Barbie said calmly. "We need to stop him, and we're going to need all the help we can get. They have resources we don't. This isn't about collars. This is about stopping it at six."

Travis needed a drink. Everyone was against him, and his head was pounding.

"I'm going to the marina," Barbie continued. "Are you coming?"

"Let's do it," he said.

"Was there any sexual assault on Jane Doe?" he asked Jacob on the way out.

"Nothing violent. I'll need more time to determine if there was consensual sex, and there's close to three days' difference in the deaths."

"Will you help us out here, doc?" Travis continued. "Try to reconstruct her as best you can, take a picture and get it to research. I'll call them and have them check to see if she shows up in any of Heather Simmons' social networks."

"Good idea. Might save me some time. Jack, get on that."

"I wonder why he didn't bury the Simmons woman," Travis said as they were walking to the cruiser.

"Could be the person who called it in frightened him off," Barbie offered.

"Is Simmons a friend of the Gaudier daughter?"

"He thinks so. He's going to call and see if Amy has talked to her lately and try to get us an interview for tomorrow. He appears to think a lot of the family and didn't look all that thrilled at being the bearer of bad news."

"Two victims, so far. There must be a connection between the two. We just have to find it."

"Why do you think that?" Barbie asked.

"This guy has a plan. Twisted, but a plan. There are four more victims out there. This doesn't smell of random killings. There is something that connects all six. Even if they are all Caucasian brunettes, there is something else that makes them his target. Maybe they were all call girls. Servers. Executives. Something. Maybe they all knew each other."

"We're going to have to get to the airport," Barbie said. "Hopefully, there will be enough time today. Maybe they were all employed there. Maybe our killer works there."

Sturgeon

Willow still had the keys, so there was no argument about who was driving. When she called it a day, she would pretend to throw the keys in the desk drawer but had already decided to take them home with her. She knew the two of them had nothing to talk about and the thirty-minute drive to the marina would give her some time to think.

She needed to find a way to get Birch to realize he needed help. She could get him that help. Her dad was now seventeen years sober. It would be easy to get Birch help, but first he had to know he needed it. Otherwise he was just going to shrug everything off.

"The captain says I'm stuck with you, by the way," Birch announced out of the blue.

"Bummer, huh?"

She wondered if Birch was noticing any symptoms. He would think they were being caused by something else, of course, but maybe if she kept pointing them out, he would take them more seriously and go to a clinic and listen to the doctor tell him he drinks too much.

"Are you frightened?" she asked. "I can drop you off and do this myself."

"Why the hell would you think I'm frightened, Sturgeon?" he spat out.

"You're shaking. I'll drop you off at home. You need the bottle. Which way?"

"Knock it off. You're not my mother. Just drive and shut up."

"Nope. You're not sleeping well, either. You have pretty severe dark rings around your eyes, and they're bloodshot. How long has it been since you bent that elbow? Ten... twelve hours?"

"Kiss my ass."

"Not on your life."

Her cell rang and she pushed the wheel sync. "Sturgeon."

"Are you going to be much longer, sweets? I'm running out of things to do." Willow glanced at the displayed number.

"Hey, pigeon shit. How are ya?"

"Bored."

"Do I get to be number seven?"

"Maybe."

"I've never had a serial killer before. Are you fun?"

"Depends on what you call fun."

"Well, I'm getting all..." she let out a heavy breath and moaned, "...wet. What's fun for you?"

"Is that an offer?"

"Absolutely. If you think you can make it exciting enough. How long has it been since you had a blow job?"

"It's been a while. Is that another offer?"

"Absolutely. I swallow, too. Maybe we could meet up and go sailing so no one's around."

A second's hesitation. "Well, I've kept you long enough, sweets. I have to call my girlfriend now."

"You found a woman who likes you? How about that! Well, don't get all worn out. You don't want to go all soft on me. Maybe you can answer a question for me. What is it about these women that makes them better than me? You haven't asked me out."

"Not to worry. I might be doing that sooner than you think." She heard the click and disconnected.

"Hear anything in the background?" Willow asked, looking at Birch. She saw him looking back with big eyes.

"There is something seriously wrong with you, you know that?" he stated.

"Elevator dings and the sound of circular doors," she said. "Our perp is staying in one of the downtown hotels." She pushed the sync button again, and when the voice prompted, she said, "Research."

"Research, this is Mary."

"Mary, this is Detective Sturgeon. Can you call the front desk of every hotel with circular doors and ask if they have any heavily scratched-up guests?"

"Okay. It might take a bit while I dig up floor plans."

"No problem. Did the coroner bring in a picture yet? Who's working our case?"

"That would be Tara. I'll check with her."

"Thank you, Mary," Sturgeon finished.

After hanging up, she saw Birch writing down the time of the phone call. She knew he had the same thought. They would be checking video footage of the assorted lobbies. The guy may have just sealed his fate with his cockiness. She just wished she was more confident of it.

"You're sweating, too."

"Shut up about it, Sturgeon. I've had enough."

"Nope."

They arrived at the marina. Willow took the original and Birch the photocopy, and they headed off down separate docks showing the picture of the man and the sailboat.

It was an unmitigated disaster. Not even so much as a, 'Hmm'. The photo was a close-up, and both were standing on the sailboat, so there was no name and no numbers to associate with the vessel. No one remembered seeing the man or the woman, and Willow began to wonder if the picture had even been taken at the marina. There was nothing in the background except water.

When she got back to the cruiser, Birch was already there talking with research and asking them to have the desks hold the lobby footage of 3.15PM.

It was after five by the time they got back to the station. Birch shut down his desk and walked out without a word. Willow entered her notes in the case folder, shut everything down and went to her car, calling Adam on the way.

When she got home, Adam and Jessica were already sitting on the steps. Adam was fiddling with his phone, and Jessie had her head resting on his shoulder. She pulled into the garage with Adam and Jessie following her in. Hugs were exchanged, and all three entered the house.

"Yum. That smells good," Jessie said as the two went right to the equipment. Willow walked to and unlocked the front door, switched the cooker to warm and went to her room to change into her sweats.

When she got to her exercise room, she found Jessie on the lat pull, Adam on the bench press, so she went to the treadmill, elevated it to fifteen degrees and began walking, thinking of the case, Birch, and her day in general. She heard the front door open and close.

"Oh, my God! It smells good in here."

"We're in here, Mitch," she said.

"Like I didn't know that," he said as he walked in, greeting Adam and Jessie. Mitch went to the leg press and she went back to her thoughts, changing the setting for running. After fifteen minutes, Jessie abandoned her post and went to the shower. Willow ran to the machine, laughing at Mitch who'd had the same thought but was a little slower. Mitch and Adam switched machines.

Willow worked on the pull another fifteen minutes. She heard the shower shut off, and in a few more minutes, the cupboards opening and closing in the kitchen as Jessie was obviously setting the table, so she went to the shower, leaving the exercise room to the guys.

Showered and dressed, she opened her bedroom door to Adam standing and waiting for her shower. She guessed Mitch had beat him to the hall one. She made her way to the kitchen and found Jessie had everything nearly set and was chopping salad. She picked up a knife and began slicing cucumbers. Pepper wasn't allowed in the kitchen, but it didn't stop him from supervising from the edge.

"I heard you got the job. Are you excited?"

"You know it. It feels good to have a job that falls more into line with my education. I'm kind of low on the pay scale right now, but I'm a patient girl."

"You kind of have to be, don't you? Being married to Adam and all?"

"Oh, he's not so bad. Whenever I have something critical I need done, all I have to do is park him in front of the television and do it."

Mitch was out of the shower and staring at the two hysterically laughing women with a look of bewilderment, so they both stopped laughing and stared back with stern looks and knives in their hands. Mitch, guessing he was in trouble for something, just grabbed the newspaper and sat on the couch, Salt hopping to his lap to help.

"So, what are you going to be doing?" Willow asked.

"I'm an assistant to the assistant manager of human resources. I think I'm going to be doing the background checks and arranging drug screens, but he hasn't said for sure."

Willow threw the cucumbers in the salad bowl and Jessie began tossing it. Willow got the salad dressings out and placed them on the table, then got the wine glasses out.

Adam came out and stuck his head in front of his wife's nose. "Smell my hair."

Jessie's head flew back. "You smell peachy. Now get out of the kitchen."

He lifted his arms in front of Willow's nose, "Smell my pits."

"Get away from me, you freak. Go ice the wine and feed Pepper."

∞∞∞

It was a great evening. Great friends, relaxing conversation, good food, good wine and laughter abounded. Mitch's day had been pretty slow, but Mike had gotten knocked on his ass by a ten-year-old when he thought it would be cool to join their neighborhood football game and decided he should be the quarterback. When he told the story, Mitch asked him if he shouldn't be called the quarter sack.

When the conversation moved to the living room, Willow's phone rang. They all watched her stare at the screen, ring after ring.

"What's up?" she finally answered. "With what?" After a few seconds of listening, she got up and pulled paper and pen from her credenza. "Give me the address," she said, wrote it down and then hung up her phone.

"Guys, I have to go. You get to do the dishes. Lock up when you leave."

"Are you going to need help, Will?" Mitch asked, sensing it was serious.

"I have this," she said, closing the garage door behind her.

Birch

Travis felt a small amount of guilt about leaving Barbie at the station without wishing her a good night, or a see you tomorrow, but it was only a small amount. She had treated him like shit all day, constantly badgering him about his drinking and his eating habits.

Screw her! He didn't have a problem. She was the one with the problem. What a bitch! He didn't care what the captain said. Travis knew the only reason the guys hung with her was because she looked like a fashion model. Her personality was not conducive to holding onto friends. No one who talked porn shit, like she had to the killer, was a good person.

Travis pulled into his driveway, locked up the beater and entered his house, sat his keys on the coffee table and went to the kitchen. He opened a cupboard and pulled out a tumbler, then opened the cupboard next to it and pulled out his scotch. He sat both on the prep island, then picked up the bottle, ready to pour, but sat the scotch back down. He'd show her. He could stop anytime he wanted.

He went to the bathroom and relieved himself, and then to the living room and sat on the couch, turning on the television. Channel after channel scrolled through, until he settled on football, and leaned back on the couch.

After the Vikings got two first downs, Travis decided football was better with a drink. He stood and walked to the kitchen, stopping half-way. What the hell was the matter with him? He said he was going to show her he could stop. He walked the rest of the way, put the cap back on the scotch, put it back in the cupboard, along with the glass, and went back to his football game.

Ten minutes later he stood up and walked to the refrigerator, looking for yesterday's pizza, found it, threw a couple of pieces on a paper plate and put them in the microwave. While they were heating up, he looked again at the cupboard with the scotch, walked to it and reached for the cupboard door.

Travis stood there with his hand on the knob and just stared at it. The microwave dinged so he let go of the knob and pulled the pizza out and walked to the couch. After a few bites, he decided the pizza tasted horrible without something to wash it down. He sat it on the coffee table and stared at it. Then he looked at the picture of him, Kris and the kids. He switched back and forth between the pizza, the picture and the football game.

His glance fell to his hands. They were shaking badly. One drink, to steady himself, wouldn't be the end of the world, so he walked to the kitchen, pulled out the scotch and the tumbler, and stood there with the scotch hovering over the glass. A minute later he sat the bottle back down and walked back to the couch. Halftime.

Feeling fidgety, Travis stood back up and walked to the sliding glass door and out to his backyard deck, looking up at the sky. He looked at his uncut lawn, the weeds that used to be his wife's prize flower garden, the swing set and his grill.

Not feeling any better, he walked back in, looked again at the picture of his wife and kids and walked once more to the kitchen, to stare at the scotch. He picked up the bottle and glass and walked to the kitchen table, sat in his chair and opened the bottle again. The liquid called to him, but he didn't want to listen.

He stared at it some more and put the top back on the bottle. Dammit! He knew what he had to do.

Travis walked to the coffee table, picked up his phone and dialed the number. It rang forever.

"What's up?" was the answer.

"I need help," he said.

"With what?"

"I haven't had a drink since I've been home, but it's taking a major effort. My wife left me and took my kids with her. I... I need help... please. Your dad..."

"Give me the address."

Travis did so, hung up the phone and walked back to the table, picked up the scotch and tumbler and put them both away. He paced, sat on the couch, stood up and paced some more, sat at the table, stood up and walked to the deck, walked back in and sat on the couch and repeated the process several times, making a concerted effort not to look at the cupboard.

Finally, the doorbell rang, and he opened the door and let Barbie in.

"Why am I here, Birch? What is it you need help with?"

"I know we don't know each other very well, but you're the only one I know with the experience."

"Experience with what?"

"I drink too much. I need to stop, but it's hard. My wife..." He paused trying to decide if Sturgeon would care about his personal problems, decided she wouldn't, so went back to the basics. "I need to stop."

"So, stop."

"I'm trying, but I can't. It's hard."

"Why?"

"I have personal issues that wouldn't interest you."

"You didn't pull me away from my friends to tell me you're a drunk, Birch. I've been telling you that all day."

"I know. Believe me, I remember. It's not just me being a drunk."

"What is it then, Birch?"

"I'm..." He couldn't say it. "I'm... uh," he tried again, but still couldn't say it.

"You're what, Birch? You need to tell me why I'm here, or I'm walking out that door."

"I think," he started, but saw the look on her face. "I think I may have an alcohol problem."

"Not good enough," Barbie said as she turned and walked toward the door. Fear surged through him that he was about to be left to deal with this alone.

"I'm an alcoholic," he muttered. She stopped and turned toward him.

"You're going to have to speak up. I didn't hear you."

He knew she'd heard him, and he knew what she was doing. "I'm an alcoholic," he said loudly and with conviction. She walked up to him and put her hand on his cheek.

"Come with me," she said and walked to the kitchen and began opening cupboards. She pulled every bottle he had out and sat them on the counter next to the sink, stepped to the side and stared at him. He knew what she wanted him to do, but he didn't know if he could.

Travis stared at the bottles and she stared at him. He walked to the sink, picked up the gin and stared at it. Then he opened it and poured it down the drain.

He followed with all the bottles of whiskey, brandy, vodka and then picked up the scotch, hesitated a moment then poured it down the sink.

"Stash?" she asked.

"Hallway closet," he said. "They're not opened yet, though. I can probably save them and give them as gifts."

"No, Travis. You can't."

He wasn't lost on the heartwarming feeling he got when she had called him Travis. He walked to the hall closet, pulled out the three bottles of scotch, walked them to the sink and poured them down.

"Pack a bag," she said. "You're coming with me."

"Where are we going?" he asked as he made his way to his room, with her following.

"Emberton."

"Oh, no. Sturgeon, I can't go to rehab. The captain will put me on A.L."

"Yes, he will, Travis. Because it's what's best for you. Your career was nearly over. You were backing yourself into a corner. You're coming with me to Emberton, Travis. Your new life starts right now. You have a chance to fix the mess you used to be, and I'm going to be there with you, every step of the way."

"Why? You don't even know me."

"I know you, Travis. I know you well."

He finished packing his bag, looked around his room, and walked out to the living room, looking around.

"Sturgeon?"

"Willow!"

"Willow. I don't have any friends. I've kept mainly to myself. I'm not sure what to do about this place or my car."

"You have one, and I think you'll find that will improve with each passing day. Let's go."

The two of them walked out and Travis locked the door. Barbie held out her hand and Travis dropped the keys into the opened palm. From now on it will be Willow, not Barbie. What an amazing woman. She didn't have to help him. She could have told him to call someone else. She didn't. She came. What a friend she might turn out to be.

When they were on their way, Willow hit the wheel sync. "Call Dad," she said after the prompt.

"Hi, honey."

"Hi, Daddy. How are you two?"

"I'm doing well. Mom's a little frustrated. She's decided she needs to take up crochet work, and it's not going well, so far."

Willow laughed. It was the first time Travis had ever heard her laugh, and it sounded good.

"She will prevail. She always does," Willow said. "Dad, I need your help."

"Oh, I guess he left. This is Walter, his butler."

"That wasn't even funny the first time you pulled it. Listen, Dad. I have a friend who's just realized he's an alcoholic. Is there any chance you can help him get set up?"

"Of course, I can, honey. I can even be his sponsor, if you want."

"No, Dad. I don't want him afraid things might get back to me. No offense."

"None taken. What's his name and where do we find him?"

"We're on our way to Emberton right now. His name is Travis Birch."

"He's in the car with you? Well, you're rude. Hi, Travis. I'm Carl."

"Hi, Carl," Travis said. "I really appreciate your help. I need to get this licked."

"You did that yourself, Travis," Carl said. "Recognizing the problem. I'll meet you at Emberton. It'll take me about a half hour to get there. I'll make a couple of calls, first. I think I have just the guy."

Goodbyes were exchanged, and with Willow promising to keep him informed about the case, Travis checked into Emberton Rehabilitation Facility.

Logan

Chulo was somewhat sorry he'd had Brittany retired. She may, at twenty-eight, have lost her appeal with the clients, but he could have used her in-house. He had been in a foul mood, though, and he let that opportunity slip by.

Not many of the men working for him could afford one of his girls, and Brittany would have been a good morale booster. A perk he could have easily absorbed. He could have made enough from them to keep her in clothes, food, makeup and medical. He just wouldn't have had enough to realize his usual profit.

The most expensive overhead he had was medical and dental. The girls needed to be checked after every new client, which sometimes did get expensive, but he hadn't had any new clients in several months. He couldn't exactly advertise. He depended on word of mouth.

It was pointless to dwell on it. He had made the decision and issued the order. Brittany had been retired. His men were either going to have to wait for another girl to lose her appeal, or they were going to have to come up with the cash, less their ten percent discount.

A rap came at his office door and Horace stuck his head in. "Hey, Chulo. I'm not sure you're going to like this, but Crystal's got some info for ya."

He opened the door and let Crystal slide past him into the room.

"Hi, Crystal," Chulo said. "How was your date last night?"

"Mr. Williams is always good to me, Chu," she said, looking down as the girls always did, and wringing her hands. She looked at Horace and got a reassuring nod, so she continued.

"Mr. Williams asked me if I was going to stay with you or go over to another guy. I don't remember his name. It sounded strange. Not American. I asked Horace if you were closing down and what we were going to do, but he said I should talk to you. I didn't mean anything, Chu. I was just asking. Please don't be mad at me."

"We're not closing down, Crystal, and I'm not mad. Did it sound to you like Mr. Williams knew the man he was talking about?"

Crystal just shrugged and continued to look sheepish. Chulo knew the nervousness was because meetings with Chulo were usually because of a complaint from the client, and he was almost always angry during that meeting.

Chulo stood and walked around his desk, putting Crystal in a warm embrace and kissing her on the head. "You don't worry about this, Crystal. I'll call Mr. Williams and get the information from him. You did very well in coming to me with this. I'll buy you a couple new skirts." Crystal's eyes lit up at that and she finally brandished a nice smile.

Chulo walked her slowly to the door and squeezed her again, and then spoke to Horace. "Horace, get Crystal something to eat." He stroked Crystal's hair as she was turning to leave and then looked at Horace and pointed to the floor. Horace nodded at the order to get back immediately after getting Crystal's breakfast. Chulo closed the door behind them, went immediately to his desk and searched his book for the client's number. He called it.

"Hello," came the response after two rings.

"Hey, Jake. This is Chulo. Do you have a minute?"

"For you, I do. How's my girl? I wish you would stop feeding her so much. She doesn't eat worth a shit."

Chulo laughed. "They're all that way, Jake. They think they'll get fat and their men won't like them anymore. Just keep watching what she eats and doesn't eat. That's what I do."

"I'll give that a try. Are you calling about Aviar? I'm sorry, Chu. By the time I realized I asked, it was too late to take it back."

"What's done is done, Jake. No harm. What's the deal with the guy?"

"Well, if you don't know about him, I would guess he's pretty new in the area. He apparently noticed her and I having dinner last week. He must have read her, because this week, he approached me when she was powdering her nose. He offered a better deal and a better service. He even said I could have the same girl, which is why I asked her if she was switching."

"She's not switching. Did the guy have a card or a number?"

"Yeah," and then after a moment's hesitation, "You're not going to get me mixed up in anything ugly, are you, Chu?"

Chulo laughed. "No, Jake. That kind of thing only happens in the movies. He probably thought she was free-lance. We'll just sit down and make sure we don't overlap."

"Good. Talking is always less messy. She probably didn't notice, but I stuck the card in the side pocket of her purse, guessing you'd need it."

"Oh. Good. Thanks, Jake. If you promise her a tip, there'll be no charge next time."

"You got it. Gotta run. Later, Chu." Jake hung up without waiting for Chulo's goodbye.

Horace had come back in during the conversation with the client and sat on the sofa. Now Chulo threw his hands behind his head and swiveled, looking up at the ceiling.

"New player?" Horace asked.

"Looks like it," Chulo said, continuing to swivel and stare at nothing. After a long minute, he told Horace where to find the man's card, sending him to retrieve it. Chulo began formulating a plan to convince the man that another city would be a wiser decision.

∞∞∞

Four hours later, having called in favors, dug through public records and set up surveillance, Chulo, Horace and three more of his men approached the farmhouse. There wasn't even a gate. Just a dirt driveway leading from the main road directly to the house.

Horace was the only one visible in the van. He drove up to the house and stopped, exited the vehicle, then walked up to the door and knocked. A man answered the door, and Horace began a predetermined conversation, holding up the business card and asking for companionship.

Chulo could read the man's smile. Horace had set this up in advance, and this was where he was told to come and set up an account. Everything looked to be going according to plan. As soon as the man invited Horace in and turned to precede him, Horace threw his arm around the man's neck and stuck his gun in the man's temple.

Chulo's other three men were out of the van and charging the house, ARs at the ready. Chulo followed at a much slower pace, carrying his baseball bat and watching the scene unfold.

When he reached the doorway, his men had two other men face down on the floor and were searching them. His third man was looking toward the back. Horace had his man's head shoved so hard against the wall, Chulo thought it might cave. The wall. Not the head. Everyone was turned to face Chulo.

Chulo stood in the middle of the large room. It was obvious a wall had been knocked out to make the room larger, but there were no obvious seams. A lot of work had been done here. A lot of money had turned this ordinary farmhouse into a comfortable setting.

From the outside, you would never know it. It looked run down. There were no yard birds clucking and pecking and no clunkers with the wheels missing, but other than that, just a family farm in bad need of a paint job and an outhouse.

Inside the front door, three sofas were strategically placed. A bar was built and recessed into the wall to the left. Toward the rear of the room, the floor had been elevated, and another couch and two chairs surrounded an ornate coffee table. Two very expensive looking lamps sat on the end tables on either side of the couch. The right side was all wall, with the occasional two-way mirror built in. Probably where the office was.

Chulo slowly walked toward the bar, tapping his baseball bat on the floor as he walked. He found the Jack Daniels and poured himself a finger in a tumbler, then drank it down. He made a face of disgust, looking at the empty tumbler. "Watered down. Cheap bastards!"

He set the Jack on the bar, facing the wall believed to be offices, took his stance and lined up the bat to the center of the bottle, encouraging Horace to move himself and his man. Once all was clear, he swung with all his might and the bottle flew across the room, bursting through one of the mirrors, setting the glass flying inward.

Still standing at the bar, he spoke, elevating his speech, "Are you ready to come out here and talk to me now, or should I have one of my men shove one of yours through that hole?"

Horace pushed his man towards the others, tripping him so that he fell. He walked past the mirrors toward a far door, opened it and aimed his gun inward. He walked in while Chulo looked around for something not watered down. Some scuffling was heard in the room, and in a minute, a man in a very expensive suit flew from the doorway into the wall opposite, then hit the ground with a resounding thud.

Horace reached to pick the man up by his tie, but the tie was a clip-on and came off in Horace's hand.

"Oh. Hell, no!" Chulo spouted as he burst out in laughter. Horace grabbed an ankle instead and dragged the man to the center with the others. Chulo walked up to the group, tapping his bat. He walked around the four men, tapping them with the bat as he passed. He stopped at the man in the suit.

"You must be Aviar. Nice place you've got here," Chulo said as he looked around. "It's a fucking bordello. Where are the girls?"

The man stayed silent. Chulo tapped him in the chest with the bat. "You. I'm talking to you." The man remained silent. Chulo walked to the nearest man, lined up his bat and swung with all his strength, striking the man squarely. Blood exploded out of the man's eye sockets and all over the suited man. The struck man fell dead.

Chulo walked back to the suited man and wiped the bat on his suit. He went down on his haunches and looked the man in the eyes. He saw anger. He saw hatred. Chulo tapped him on the head with the bat. "Where are the girls?"

The man stayed silent, so Chulo stood and walked to the next man. "What the hell happened to your face, man? Were you playing with a chainsaw?" The man was not nearly as defiant as the others. He looked like he had been in a chick fight.

"They're in the basement," he spouted, before Chulo could line up.

"You have a basement?" Chulo asked, looking around. "Well. Hell's bells! Where's the stairs?"

"There's a push panel behind the pantry door," the man said, eyeing Chulo's bat.

Chulo glanced at Horace, and the man made his way to the kitchen to look for a pantry. Chulo told one of his men to drag the messy body out back, while he and the other two presided over what was left of the pimps.

Chulo tapped Aviar again. This time on the shoulder. "So, what made you decide to start your business in my city?"

"It's not your city," the man said. "It's free enterprise. Just like everywhere else."

Chulo went back down on his haunches in front of the man, reached and turned his head to face the mess being dragged out the back door. Chulo put a questioning look on his face and rubbed his chin. "I'm not sure I agree."

Horace came back out of the kitchen and Chulo looked his way. "It's a fucking squalor, Chu. The girls don't even have a toilet down there. There's shit and piss everywhere."

"What kind of shape are they in?" Chulo asked.

"Awful. They all came barging from their rooms, and I use that term carelessly. They should be called cells. They all grabbed at me wanting drugs. These guys got them pretty hooked. They're messed up."

"Well, shit. Bret, go out to the van and bring the shovels. Then go back to the office, explain the condition of these girls to Crystal and Beth. Grab a vial and a few needles. Bring soap, shampoo and robes. We'll have Crystal and Beth ween them off slowly. It'll be their project. Have one of them bring my car. I have work to do. You guys are going to have to handle this.

"Horace, get into the office and see if you can find a client list, or anything else we can use. See if you can find cuffs for Aviar here. Then look this place over. Find the shower. The rooms they use for entertaining their guests, etc.

"Dave, Phil. Take these boys out back. Have them dig a grave for the unfortunate soul that Aviar made me kill. Once that's done, have them shovel the shit out of the basement."

Chulo looked the place over again. This really was a nice-looking place, but it was set up as a bordello, and Chulo wasn't set up to be an in-house business. In-house tended to drag the price down, but he was not above trying it. He was going to have to find payment stubs and other bills, so he knew whom to pay, but that should be easy enough. He would also need to get passwords and such so that he could pay those bills, but Horace was good at finding that stuff out, one way or the other.

Sturgeon

Willow hadn't had a very good visit with her dad. She hadn't really expected she would. His attention was taken up by Travis and Travis' sponsor. She left them to their conversations and left Emberton, driving back to her partner's house. She bagged up all the empty bottles and cleaned his kitchen, and then drove home.

When she got to her house, she saw the guys had done a good job cleaning up. The only two things left undone were the slow cooker pot, which she found soaking in the sink, and the newspaper, which Mitch had left strewn all over the couch and coffee table. She left both and went to the bedroom, donned her shorts and Tee, climbed in the bed and picked up her copy of Swan Garden. Alice was being taken to the laundries, and Willow wanted to know how that turned out.

When she woke up, she finished cleaning the pot and put it away and grabbed the newspaper, rolled it up and walked to the garage. She dug a roll of duct tape out of her toolbox and stretched a piece across the newspaper, placing it in her front seat. She got into her car and began the drive to work.

When she arrived, she took the paper in with her and went first to the patrol lockers. She attached the duct tape to Mitch's locker handle, tamping it, tightly, on and around the handle. She dragged the rest of the tape across the front of the locker, took out her evidence marker, and wrote 'Forget to clean up something?' along the tape.

She climbed the stairs and went right to the captain's office. He was in conference with a man and woman that were obviously feds, based on their attire. The captain saw her looking through the window and waved her in.

"Where's Birch?" the captain asked.

"He's unavailable today, Captain," Willow said. "It has nothing to do with the case."

The captain was smart enough to pick up on that and asked the feds to vacate the room for a few minutes, after introducing them as Agent Mark Maxwell and Special Agent Lisa Tanner. After the two were out and Willow closed the door, she began.

"Detective Birch is in rehab, Captain. He called me last night and informed me of a medical condition that is covered by the union. I drove him there myself."

"Don't get pissy, Sturgeon. No one's going to fire Birch. Your sergeant told me to assign you to Birch and let you handle it. I had no idea you could work that quickly but thank you. Birch is a good detective and I don't want to lose him. I will have to put him on administrative leave, however."

"With pay," Willow emphasized.

"With pay," the captain confirmed.

"I take it you knew he had a problem?"

"Both partners before you asked to be reassigned. Miller spilled the beans."

"Yet you didn't see a need to intervene? Ask him about it? Get him some help?"

"Two words, Sturgeon. Internal Affairs. Not to mention the hard feelings he would have for Miller. Now that he's in rehab, the door is open for me to provide the full support of the station. As soon as we're done here, I'll go see Lizzy and let her know. She will have to tell me when he can come back."

"I will be stopping in daily," Willow announced sternly.

"I would expect nothing else. I would also wager he will be getting frequent visits by others. Let the agents in. Let's get this done."

Willow opened the door and asked the feds back in, and everyone took a seat.

"Detective Birch is going to be out on medical leave, agents. Detective Sturgeon will give the briefing." With that, he nodded at Willow. The two feds looked her way.

"I'm afraid we don't know that much, yet," Willow started. "We have two bodies, but we believe there are four more. Our first victim had six stab wounds in her torso, and the second body had five..."

"Sorry to interrupt, Detective," Special Agent Tanner said. "Was the second body a woman, as well?"

"Yes, but we have no evidence the other four will be. As far as I know, both bodies are still with the coroner. There were no signs of sexual assault, and the cause of death was not the stab wounds in the torso. Both women had an ice pick shoved through their ear canal.

"Our first victim, Heather Simmons, had a picture of herself and a man standing by a sailboat, but we haven't been very successful at finding out who he is. We do have what we think might be his DNA. The Simmons woman put up a fight and had skin tissue under her nails, so he might be pretty ugly, right now.

"She has a very good friend that we were going to speak to today. I can get you her name when we're done here."

Special Agent Tanner looked at her in a confused manner, then at the captain, then back at her, then spoke directly to her, "Detective, I'm afraid there's been some misunderstanding. We won't be conducting any interviews or interfering in any way with your investigation. We are only here to provide support for you and aid where we can. There is no evidence this killer has crossed state lines, so I'm afraid we can't get involved more than that. I need a little more to go on before I take this upstairs. Most of our time is spent on domestic terrorism these days.

"You tell us what you need and we'll provide it," she continued. "Agent Maxwell will be stationed here as a liaison, but he's all I can spare right now. My cell will be available to you, but this will be your baby unless jurisdiction warrants otherwise. Might I ask a couple of questions?"

"Sure."

"Is there a name on the sailboat?"

"No, the picture's a close-up. Looks like a selfie."

"Is there a similarity between the two victims? Hair color, skin color, eye color, age?"

"I can check on the eyes and age. Both were Caucasian and both were brunettes."

"Caucasian brunettes? That's good. It narrows our possible targets to two or three million. So, as it stands, right now. This minute. You have no person of interest. No murder weapon, and you believe you're missing four bodies. Did either victim have a cell phone?"

"No, but I called the number of the Simmons victim and a man answered. He called me back yesterday and we exchanged pleasantries."

"Whoa! What?" the captain interjected.

"That is actually a good thing, Captain," Special Agent Tanner said. "We might be able to provide Detective Sturgeon with some advice for future conversations."

She then turned back to Willow. "Do you remember the conversation, Detective? I can turn that over to our profilers. Maybe they can give you an idea of who you're dealing with."

"I do," Willow said. "And I heard elevator dings and circular doors in the background. We have Research working on it right now."

"Agent Maxwell can see if any guests match any known people in our database. Was there any sign of narcotics? Any indication they were sexually active?"

"We don't have enough yet from the lab or the coroner about either. Can Agent Maxwell come with me on interviews, so the captain doesn't stick me behind a desk while my partner is out?" Willow asked. She wondered why Special Agent Tanner was concerned with those facts, but she also knew she was new in the detective division and probably would see the correlation as she became more experienced.

"Do your cars have Wi-Fi capability and USB ports?"

"Yes."

"Then yes, he can. He also has software that can trace calls, should the gentleman call you back. He can also start a facial recognition search. It takes a long time, but we may as well get started."

"I may as well go take a nap, since I'm not here," Maxwell said. Tanner patted him on the shoulder with a smile, and then stood and handed Willow a business card.

"If Mark gives you any trouble, call me. Otherwise I would just as soon you go through him for what you need."

"I will do that," Willow said, and stood and shook hands.

Special Agent Tanner left, and the captain had Willow take Agent Maxwell to Birch's desk. He would use that desk until Birch came back. Willow showed him where all the plugs and ports were and then went back to the captain.

"I'm going with you to talk to Amy," the captain said. "She didn't handle the news well, and I don't want her badgered."

"I don't badger," Willow responded.

"I wasn't talking about you. Leave the fed here. Let me know when you're ready."

"I'm ready."

Sandman

Mike shut down his desk and office for the rest of the afternoon. He had already let the boss know that he was on his way to meet a client. He told Michelle to take messages and not forward his calls. The client was Chulo, and Mike wasn't interested in making the visit longer than necessary with interruptions.

He rode alone in the elevator and used the time to enter the address of the meeting into his GPS app. If the information was correct, this would actually take him out of town. He wondered if he had been given the correct info. If he hadn't, then Chulo might have to wait a bit because Mike was going to this location. It was a beautiful day for a drive.

He started up his Mercedes, put the top down, rolled down all the windows and left the parking garage, left arm hanging over the door, sunglasses on and The Eagles blaring on the radio. He was Joe Cool. He would get the occasional old timer looking over at him when he stopped at traffic lights, but he just smiled and waved.

With the traffic lights and the traffic in general, it took twenty minutes to get to the address he was given, and he was more than a little skeptical. It was a farm, for Christ's sake. What the hell was Chulo even doing here? He hesitated before turning in the driveway, unsure.

His hesitation wasn't shared by the BMW that flew around him, turning in the driveway. It was Chulo's BMW but driven by a blonde that definitely wasn't ugly enough to be Chulo. A van followed the Beemer, and Mike turned and followed the van.

The three vehicles drove up the driveway to the house. It was a good two hundred yards from the road, way too set back to make it a profitable farm. Mike's curiosity was peaked. He saw and waved at Chulo coming from the house as he pulled in behind the BMW.

The BMW driver was pulling a box from the back seat, and another girl, just as good looking, pulled a box from the other side. She must have come from the van. The two women carried the boxes into the house, stopping long enough to get a hug from Chulo. They were met at the door by a man that Mike was convinced must have been the giant David slew. He took up the whole door.

Mike got out and walked toward Chulo, who was now digging in his trunk. As usual, Chulo was pulling out his box of goodies, but he only removed an ice pick. As he turned and smiled at Mike, Mike asked the question he was dying to get an answer to.

"What the hell, Chu? You farming now?"

Chulo laughed. "No, man. This is a good set-up, though, and depending on what you have to say, it may be our second office. Let me get this to Horace and I'll give you a tour and tell you what I'm thinking."

"Horace is that man-mountain I saw earlier? Where'd you get him, the NFL? Why does he work for you and you haven't given him any of your freebies yet?"

Chulo laughed again. "Horace is a pussycat. He just has a fetish for ice picks."

Mike looked at the house, surveying possible needs, and there would be a lot of them. What a dump! He couldn't for the life of him figure out why Chulo would want to do business here. His other office was much more attractive. Mike's shed in his back yard was more attractive than this place. Chulo must have guessed what Mike was thinking.

"Not the outside, compadre. We just need some work done inside."

"You called me here for a remodel?"

"Only because I want the best," Chulo responded, clapping Mike on the back and steering him up the steps.

When they passed over the threshold, Mike's breath was taken away. The interior didn't resemble the exterior in any way. Ornate lamps, vases and other lavish décor surrounded very elaborate furniture, and the place was massive. There was a very expensive looking rug in what could only be described as a sitting area. A couch and two chairs sat around the rug, and they were all of the same design.

The place even had a bar, with several stools and three tables strewn around it. The back wall looked a little out of place. It was pretty plain looking and had no windows. Mike looked around. There were no windows anywhere, except what looked like mirrors to the right, one of which had been shattered. He headed toward it, but Chulo grabbed his arm, holding him in place.

"Hold off on that area, Mike." Chulo then walked over to the broken mirror and stuck the ice pick through. He turned back to Mike, "Horace has some cleanup to do and some passwords to locate."

"With an ice pick?" Mike asked, but Chulo just laughed and led Mike down a hallway.

About halfway down, the blonde that had driven Chulo's car stood outside a door and Mike could hear the shower going. He wondered why the two women had come here to take showers. Across the hall from her was the first room. Chulo led him in after introducing him to Crystal. She gave Mike a nice smile and shook his hand. The woman radiated warmth. Mike knew she was one of Chulo's girls.

As soon as he entered the room, the smell of sex nearly gagged him. It permeated from the walls, the bed, even the floor. If Chulo wanted to use this place, he was going to have to do a lot of cleanup. The smell of the room and the condition of the entry solved the mystery plaguing Mike. "Was this a fucking cathouse?"

"Okay," Chulo said, his hands going to his pockets and looking up at the ceiling, as if deciding what to divulge. "I can see this is only going to work if you know the story. Have a seat."

Mike looked at the bed, the chair beside it and the floor, "Uh... no, thanks. Let's go outside."

Chulo looked around the room and nodded agreement. The two walked back down the hall and out the front door. Once outside, Mike listened as Chulo explained about the three girls they found in the basement and what the men here had done to them to keep them in line. The woman that had driven Chulo's car was one of his, and along with one other were going to be working on nursing the three women back to health.

Mike also learned that the farmhouse was indeed used for the business he suspected. It was Chulo's intent to use the farmhouse to store supplies, to house the girls, and as a meeting place. He would leave a couple of men here to help the girls with 'heavy lifting' and other needs they might have.

It was also Chulo's plan to turn the farm into a farm. He would hire the planting and harvesting out, but from the road, it needed to look like a functioning farm. What he wanted Mike for was to turn the interior into something that resembled a farm, as well. There needed to be a living room, a kitchen, a dining room, and the entire rest of the house needed to be bedrooms, including the entire upstairs.

Chulo also wanted a false wall, but he didn't want a cop coming into the farmhouse and noticing. Mike told him that wouldn't be a problem. He could put a bathroom on one end and a tool shed on the other and use the center for whatever he needed the false wall for. Simple paneling could be used to hide the doorway.

"What about the basement?" Mike asked.

"Don't worry about the basement. These men that were here are going to see what it's like to live down there. They're being injected right now with the drugs they used on the girls. At least two of them are. The other one is in a meeting with Horace as we speak. If I need anything done down there, I'll let you know."

"Meeting with Horace?" Mike laughed. "He's in bad need of an ice pick, is he? How do you plan on paying for this place, Chu? You're not exactly the legal owner."

Chulo laughed at the ice pick comment. "Bill collectors don't really care where the payments come from. They only care that they're paid. We'll set up another account and pay the bills on line. It's really not an issue. People do it all the time. This is a farm, so we're going to name the business 'Sunset Farms'."

"Are you branching out? Are you going to have an in-house service for those who can't afford house calls?"

119

"No. There's no money in that, and it's highly dangerous. There's no time to do background checks on the clients before they meet the girls. They could be cops, have STDs, or many other things that we check before setting them up. I take care of my people, Mike. I'm not going to put them in questionable situations."

"You are the man, Chu. The ultimate boss. I guess I'd better get some measurements," Mike said as he popped his trunk.

Gaudier

Missy Gaudier tried several times to get her sister to come out of her room, but Amy wasn't having it, so Missy began making breakfast for her, and her brother. Tony was setting the table, and she could tell he was just as worried about Amy as she was. Just when she was about to crack the eggs, the intercom buzzed from the gate.

"Who dat?" she asked into the mic.

"Chet Carson," came the response.

"Dad's in Italy, Uncle Chet, and Mom's in Oakland. You got a warrant?"

"Missy, you'd better open this damn gate or I'm going to throw you in the pool again."

"I was ten, Uncle Chet. You might find it a little harder these days." Missy pushed the button to unlock the gate. "You want breakfast?"

"Who's cooking?"

"Me."

"I'll pass."

"Now I'm going to throw your butt in the pool. How many?"

"There are two of us."

"Okay."

∞∞∞

The captain explained to Willow about the kindness of the Gaudier family and asked her to eat what she could. Willow drove through the gate and waited for the captain to close it, but as it turned out, it must have been on a sensor because it closed itself. She drove to the front door of the huge mansion. There were no cars in the circular driveway, and she wasn't sure if she should leave the cruiser or find a ditch to drive it into.

What unbelievably gorgeous grounds. Perfectly trimmed hedges provided the border for the lawn area big enough to host a golf course. There were trees everywhere. So many that this enormous mansion wasn't even visible from the road. Probably by design. The pool the captain spoke of was on the south side of the mansion, and you probably could have fit Lake Michigan in it. Two men with massive cleaning poles were working at cleaning it.

Willow and the captain climbed the steps to the front door. Two sets of steps, with sculptures on both sides, at the top. Both were lions, and she didn't think they had been brought in. They looked to have been sculpted right where they sat.

"Wipe your feet," the captain said as he twisted the knob and pulled the door opened without so much as a knock. She found that curious and asked herself why in the world the door would open out.

A man who looked to be in his twenties was walking toward them. He and the captain did the man-hug thing, and the captain introduced him as Tony Gaudier. Before she could react differently, Tony gave her a 'just met' hug and a 'pleased to meet you'. He then led them to a dining table big enough to seat twelve.

The captain walked into the kitchen and hugged a fairly like-aged brunette and asked her where her sister was.

"Still in her room, Uncle Chet," the woman responded. "She's pretty down right now. She won't come out, or even answer her door."

Missy and Tony brought the food out, and the captain introduced Missy. Willow got another hug, but this time was prepared and returned it. The four sat down and began breakfast, with the conversation switching between the reason why Mom was in Oakland, Amy's friend Heather, and the financial situation of the city.

Willow offered to help clean up, but the Gaudier siblings were not having it, so she and the captain climbed the stairs and went to what must have been Amy's room. The captain knocked. The door didn't open and there wasn't an answer.

"Ames, it's Uncle Chet. Will you let me in?"

There was a thump and quick steps coming toward the door. The door opened, revealing another brunette who didn't look all that different from the one downstairs.

"Did you find the guy?" the woman asked.

"Not yet. We have..." The door slammed in his face before he could finish, but he calmly knocked again. "Ames, we have a picture of a man standing with Heather. Will you look at it, please?"

More steps, and the door opened again. Willow provided the picture.

"I've seen this guy," she said. "He was at the harbor trying to get me and Heather onto his puny sailboat. She snapped this with her phone. Where did you get this so fast?"

"The harbor?" Willow confirmed. "Not the marina?"

"I'll answer your question when you answer mine. Where did you get this picture?"

"I found it in Heather's armoire."

"Yes, the harbor. Which is why I pulled Heather away from the loser. Why the heck would he be at the harbor with a sailboat? She must have gone back after I left her. I shouldn't have left her." The woman sniffed and teared, and the captain pulled her head onto his shoulder.

"Miss Gaudier," Willow began, but Amy lifted her tearing eyes and looked at her with a questioning look and then back at the captain.

"Who is this woman?" she asked the captain.

"Detective Willow Sturgeon. She is the lead investigator on Heather's case. She may want to find her killer even more than you do."

"I doubt that," Amy said as she clasped a hug on Willow. "You can lose the Miss Gaudier thing. My name's Amy. There are two Miss Gaudiers here, and we're easily confused."

"Will you sit with her? Talk to her? Everything you say may be a key to finding Heather's killer."

"Okay," Amy said. "Let's go downstairs to the library. I'm hungry."

Amy led the way and, when downstairs, Willow decided Amy was a year or two older than Missy, and Tony about the same amount older than Amy. Amy and Willow went into the library while the captain sat back at the table with the coffee-drinking siblings.

"Do you remember anything about the sailboat?" Willow asked as they sat. "Did it have a name or any numbers that you remember?"

"No. I didn't pay attention, but there was an expensive looking camera on one of the benches at the stern. That's what creeped me out. That and the 'sweets' comment. It looked to be about a thirty-footer. It had a small cabin, one mast, and there wasn't a sail on it. It may have been a Nick."

"A Nick? Sorry, I don't know much about sailboats."

"A Nicholson. I think they're thirty feet or so. Maybe thirty-two."

"He called you sweets?"

"Not me. Heather."

"Do you remember anything about him, at all? Tattoos? Scars? Height?"

"He was taller than us, but not as tall as Tony. I didn't see any scars or tattoos, but judging by his attire, I would start looking for him at thrift stores, if I were you."

"Where exactly at the harbor was the boat docked?"

"The very south end."

"Why were you two there, anyway? Was this a scheduled meeting?"

"Dad had to fly to Italy to meet with his fellow investors, and he asked me to sign for the shipment."

"Shipment of what?"

"Cocaine, mostly, but there were bricks, booze and some meth equipment, too."

Willow smiled and did manage to refrain from laughter. "Okay, so I got a little off topic. I apologize. Have you, since you've known Heather, ever seen her without her phone?"

"Once, when it was too late and she was tipsy. I made her stay here instead of driving home. The next morning, she went into the shower without it. Otherwise, she slept with that phone."

"What day were you at the harbor? Do you know the time?"

"It was Saturday. We'd finished shopping about six, went through the drive-through at Mack and Don's gourmet eatery on Hillshire, probably about 6:15. She had a fat-free Big Mac and fries with a diet soda. I just had a salad. So probably 30 minutes for that. Twenty minutes or so to reach the harbor, so maybe shortly after 7, we got there. I dropped her off at home about an hour after that."

Willow looked up at the ceiling, calculating times in her head. Tony came in with a plate for Amy, and Amy asked him how tall he was. Six-feet even. Amy was five-seven and Heather five-six. Willow noted that.

"All right," Willow began, "I'll put my California math together here. That's about a twenty-minute drive, so we'll say 8 to 8:40. Was that the last time you saw her, then?"

"Yes, but I always text her when I get home, and she usually responds, and this time she didn't. I figured she fell asleep."

Willow calculated again. "It's about fifteen minutes from her apartment to here, right?"

"Some days. I texted her Sunday morning at eight to see if she was coming to church with us. She didn't respond then, either. So, I guess I lost her before that."

"I'm so sorry, Amy. Hypothetical situation for you. When you leave Heather's, she gets back in her car and drives back to the harbor and hooks up with this guy. They go sailing and have a few drinks. He brings her back. She's so out of it, she leaves the boat, forgets her phone..."

"Huh uh!" Amy interrupted. "I was with you until the forgetting her phone part. Heather got so clocked on New Year's Eve that Tony had to carry her upstairs. She still had the presence of mind to ask about and feel for her phone. There's no way she left it on that boat. Is he the guy who killed her?"

"I'm working on it still, but I really would like to speak with him." Willow pulled out one of her business cards, scratched the patrol numbers and wrote her cell on the back. She handed it to Amy. "If you see him or his boat again, call me. Right away. Don't approach him, Amy. Just call me."

As Willow stood and walked to the door to let Amy eat breakfast, she turned and asked, "You didn't happen to notice a knife on the boat, did you? Or why he would call Heather 'Sweets' and not you?"

"No knife that I saw. As for the other, I was trying to pull Heather away from the guy. He probably figured I wasn't interested."

"Okay. Thanks, Amy."

Sturgeon

Willow left the library and signaled the captain she was ready to go. He looked to be having fun conversing with Missy and Tony, but he got the hint and excused himself.

They left the mansion grounds, and the captain asked her what she thought of the 'kids'.

"They seem well-mannered and pleasant," she answered. "They look a little old to be living at home."

"Not so much. Missy's twenty-one, Amy's twenty-two and Tony's twenty-four. Tony has just graduated and has a suiter. He'll be moving on soon, but Missy and Amy are single and still in college. They're only home for the summer. Trevor has told them that when they move out, they will take with them a four hundred-thousand-dollar dowry, which is what he started with."

"So, they stand to lose a lot of money if they move out. Do you know where they stay when school's in?"

"They both have apartments near the school. Missy's just graduated Stanford and is continuing her education at Johns Hopkins this fall. Amy also graduated Stanford, but last year. She is currently going for her Masters at the University of Minnesota.

"Trevor and Lauren raised those kids right. All three will have the same success Trevor did. They are not like other silver-spooners. They are kind, considerate and very mannerly. I will say, though, that Missy could probably spend four hundred K in a month, but she wouldn't. She does love her clothes."

"Amy was very helpful. The guy in the photo is our guy. This photo was taken, went home with Heather, got printed and hidden before she went back. She wanted to know this guy, but she respected Amy's opinion, too. Smart woman, in respect to respecting Amy's opinion, but she wasn't too bright when it came to choosing her men."

"Yeah," the captain said, shaking his head. "I'm a little worried about Amy, though. I'm going to have to call Lauren. Did you tell her you liked the photo guy?"

"Not at all, but she may have picked up on it. She could tell I was interested in a comment he said to Heather. Why?"

"Buster is her dog. He was in the back yard when we were there. He's fourteen now and moving more slowly. When Amy was nine, Buster was just a puppy, and one of the neighbor kids chased him and hit him with a board. Simply because he didn't like Amy shunning him. She got on her bike and chased him down, took his board away from him and proceeded to beat him to a pulp.

"That cost Trevor a goodly sum," he continued. "What I saw in Amy today was mourning. Denial. In a couple of days, that will turn to rage. You need to find this guy before she does. She will kill him."

"Or be killed herself. You need to keep her out of this, Cap. She can really mess things up for me."

"I will call Lauren. As for being killed herself? Maybe, maybe not. If this guy goes up against either one of those kids, he'd better bring his "A" game, and he'd better be packing more than a knife. They are very capable of inflicting harm."

Willow thought on this. She had to admit, every one of the three did look in better shape than Willow, and Amy was totally capable of slipping a little cash to the harbor master to get him to call her when he saw the boat. If she was as vindictive as the captain suggested, she had the money to make the same arrangement up and down the coast. Willow was pretty certain Amy would be asking for the picture soon. Unless she remembered something about the boat that she decided Willow didn't need to know.

Willow was going to drop the captain off and go see Travis. Then she had to make haste to the harbor and make sure the harbor master would be more afraid of what Willow could charge him with than he would be the monetary rewards from Amy.

She also needed to find something for Agent Maxwell to do for an hour or two. He certainly wouldn't be able to go with her to see Travis.

"Let's stop off and see Birch," the captain blurted out, jarring her from her thoughts.

"I'm not sure it's a good idea for you to visit at this early stage, Cap."

"Why? Is he thinking I drove him to drink?"

"No. The loss of his brother drove him to drink. Then he lost his family, which made it worse."

"He needs to know he has my support. You seem to know a good deal about a man you've known for one day."

"I found his wife's number last night, when I was cleaning his kitchen. She gave me the scoop."

"When you were what?"

Willow smiled at the captain and made the detour to Emberton. "Do you think you could find something for Maxwell to do while I run over to the harbor?"

"Of course, I could, but then you wouldn't be partnered, and therefore couldn't go to the harbor."

Willow snickered her frustration and pulled into the Emberton parking lot.

When they got inside, they found Travis right away, without even having to ask. He was sitting in the lobby with Fred, his sponsor, and they appeared to be playing cards. Travis noticed them and brandished a look of shame, dropping his head.

"Hey, Detective," the captain greeted. "This is a hell of a way to get time off. How are you doing?"

Fred excused himself and went to the coffee maker, and Travis stood and greeted the captain, nodding at Willow.

"Sorry about this, Cap," Travis said. "I guess I let it get out of line. I thought I could stop on my own, but I found out different."

"The important thing here is that you found out, and you knew you needed help. I came on behalf of the department and myself, to let you know nothing's changed. The job is still there. You'll have to talk to Lizzy, of course, but it's not as if you shot anybody, so that should be easy."

"At the risk of inflating an ego," Travis responded, "I owe a lot to Detective Sturgeon here."

"Willow," Willow corrected.

"Willow," Travis continued. "She saw me for what I was and badgered the shit out of me."

The captain looked at Willow. "I thought you said you don't badger."

"He's exaggerating," Willow said. "I spoke once about it."

Travis busted out in laughter and Willow poked his arm. Then Travis became immediately stoic, displayed a look of shock and began pressing his hair down and checking his clothes.

"Hello, Travis," the new arrival greeted him.

"Kris. How did you know I was here?"

"I was called last night. Willow something? I'm glad you're here, Travis. I came to give you encouragement, in a way."

Willow tugged at the captain's sleeve. He got the message, and the two of them said their goodbyes. She nodded at the sponsor standing off to the side, watching. She wanted to ask him how things were progressing, but she knew what his response would be, so she didn't bother.

Birch

Kris was a sight for sore eyes. Still as beautiful to him as ever. Her copper-colored skin still unblemished and as smooth as silk. Her hair was new. She had streaks of lighter brown dangling down on either side of her perfect cheek bones. Her brown eyes showed signs of being pleased to see him. She looked healthy. Still trim, but athletic. He longed for her. Now, standing before him, the longing was graduating to desire.

His body temperature was beginning to rise. His knees were becoming wobbly. Travis tried his best to keep his facial features even, but she would have to be blind not to see what he was feeling.

"Please," Travis said, indicating a chair opposite. Kris sat and Travis looked at Fred. Fred got the picture and mouthed he would be back later. He would have to thank Fred at another time. The man was giving up his day to be with Travis, and it had been one visitor after another.

"It's very, very good to see you, Kris. Do you have the day off?" he asked. He knew better, but he could always hope.

"No. I told them I would be late, so I won't be long, but I wanted to talk to you."

"Don't worry. I won't ask the question you probably feared I would. I'm just happy to see you." In truth, Travis was dying to know if Kris was seeing someone, but he also knew Kris. Her moral character would not allow it.

"You know me well enough not to even think it. We're separated, not divorced. At least not yet."

Fear surged through Travis. He wondered if that was the purpose of the visit. Was she about to serve him? Just as he had realized what he was doing to himself and his family, was he about to find things were going to worsen? "Not yet?"

"I'll be honest! I have been considering it for several months."

"Please, no, Kris. Please." He knew as soon as he said it that it had sounded juvenile and full of fear, but he was not above begging.

"Travis, stop!" Kris said, looking around at how close others were. "I wouldn't be here for that purpose. I still love you, Travis, but I can't be with you until I can see that you care about yourself. About me. About the children."

"I know," he said, dropping his head. A certain amount of fear departed his thoughts, but the core remained.

"Travis," she said, digging through her purse and pulling out her wallet. She unsnapped the wallet and turned it to face him. "Do you know who this is, Travis?"

"Yes, Kris. It's me."

"No, Travis. It was you. Look at the confidence in the eyes. Look at how self-assured the stance is. Travis, I'm so very sorry about Charles, but he wouldn't want your life to change so much. This man," she pointed at the picture to draw his attention back to it, "didn't drink himself into a stupor. This man didn't eat pizza and hamburgers every night. This man cared about himself."

"Are you saying if I take better care of myself, you'll come home?"

"No, Travis. I'm saying if you care about us by caring about yourself, we can talk about it. There's a difference between doing it because I want you to and doing it because you want to. You have to want to."

"Why did you come here, Kris? You said you were going to provide encouragement." That was a stupid question. He made it sound like he was impatient and wanted her to get to the point. In truth, he would be okay with her beating around the bush as much as she wanted if it meant more time with her.

"Yes. I'm here to make you an offer." She checked her watch and stood. He stood with her. "If you can show me two weeks of caring, two weeks without a drink, a hamburger or a pizza, I'll bring the kids over for a few hours, while I go school-supply shopping."

"I could just come with you and the kids."

"Slow down, Travis. You and I are more than two weeks away. I have to go to work." She turned to walk away, stopped and turned back. "This is a one-time offer, Travis. If you can't get control, I'll be filing."

"How will you know?"

"I'll know."

Travis watched Kris walk toward the door. She hadn't looked any different than the woman in the photo. She looked the same as the day he'd married her. She was gorgeous inside and out. What had he done? How could he have ruined her life this badly?

"Beautiful lady. Sister?" a man said, walking up to him.

"Wife," answered Travis.

"You're a lucky man. She's very pretty. I'm Dave."

"Travis," he said as he stuck out his hand. The man accepted it. Travis looked back at Kris exiting the building. He set his jaw. Willow was right. Things were going to change for him. He was the one that was going to change them. He would win her back or die trying. Kris set the goal. It was up to him to achieve it. Achieve it, he would.

Having gone a longer amount of time than he had in quite a while without having a drink, he could tell he was thinking better. He was very critical of himself. He was a loser. Not anymore, though. Thinking more clearly, he realized he had gone from being a hard-nosed detective to being the guy who just wanted to get his shift over so he could go home and have a drink.

Life without alcohol looked to be much more appealing. He would have a family again, and he would have a job he loved. All it took was for some snot-nosed kid to slap some sense into him. He knew Willow wasn't a kid, but to him she was.

Now she was out there alone, basically. She didn't have the experience yet to solve this case. She was good, but her talents lay in solving lesser crimes. Murder was big time, and he had left her alone in a chasm of evil.

He needed to get his head squared away. She needed him. It was time for him to stop feeling sorry for himself and get back to his life. He hadn't known Willow very long, but long enough to know that she wouldn't ask for help. She wouldn't fold. She would keep trying. That officer he had talked to about her had said she never quit. 'Oh, well' was not in her vocabulary.

Travis was probably wrong in thinking she wouldn't solve the case. She would, but maybe not fast enough to stop another murder. He needed to get himself fixed and get back to her. He was wrong to think Kris was the sole motivator. She was the catalyst, though. She was his wife, but Willow was his partner.

Sturgeon

When Willow and the captain got back to the station, the captain went into his office and closed the door. She saw him immediately get on his phone while she proceeded to the V.

Agent Maxwell had his head buried in his laptop, so she opened her email. She selected the one from research first and scanned it. There were three hotels with circular doors. She noted the names in her notebook.

The only other email about the case was from Fenowicz about Heather's stomach contents, which she already knew. She looked at her cell and saw it was closing in on 11AM.

"You ready to hit the road, there, Agent?" she asked, trying to not sound like she was rushing him.

"Absolutely," he said. "I was just trying to get a lock on that cell number you gave me, but he must have turned it off."

"I'm sure he only turns it on when he wants to annoy me," she said as she stood. "I want to get to the harbor and check a couple of hotels on the way back."

"Good. I need to book a room anyway."

"Well, good. We can kill two birds with one stone. How do you stand with the Coast Guard?"

"We're the FBI. Everybody loves us."

Willow laughed. "Okay. Scan this picture and send it to them. We have nothing on the sailboat, except white. A witness thinks it may be a Nicholson, about thirty feet, but she didn't sound like she was certain. Ask them to keep their eyes open. The guy is who we're looking for, not the girl. Unfortunately. Maybe we'll get lucky." She waited for him to scan the photo and then accepted it back. "I have to run downstairs and get this photo taken back to the mother. Back in a bit."

With the in-house chores done, Willow and Agent Maxwell exited the building toward the cruiser. When she reached it, she found I.T. digging around under the dash. "What the hell are you doing?" she asked.

"Your computer is gone. You're now working off a tablet. I'll show you the setup in a sec."

"Make it a quick sec, will ya? I'm trying to catch a killer here."

"Gee, no one ever rushes me. I don't know if I can handle this pressure."

"What the hell was wrong with the computer? It was working fine."

"It was stationary. The tablet is portable. Shall we have a seat and talk about the list of advantages, or are you in a hurry?"

Willow threw her hands up and paced back and forth for ten minutes while the dickhead finished setting up cables under the dash. When he finally finished, she glared at him and asked if there was anything she needed to know that would be different than the computer.

"It takes pictures, for one. For another, you don't have to run back and forth to the car to look things up." He showed her how to remove and replace it and then moved over to another unit.

"Criminy," she said as they were pulling out, "what detective would carry a frigging tablet around?" Agent Maxwell raised his hand.

"What happens if your interview bolts?" she asked him. "Do you ask someone to hold it for you?"

"They make a good Frisbee, and they hurt like hell."

Willow didn't know Maxwell well enough to know if he was joking, so she dropped it and turned her attention to the road.

"Have you had any luck with a missing person report on your Jane Doe?" he asked.

"Not as yet," she responded. "Speaking of which, and I'll certainly understand if you don't have access, can you check your database? I'm still looking for four more."

"Not a problem. There won't be much, with nothing more to go on, but I'll do what I can. You want me to stick to the Coastal area?"

"No. I do think the guy might live on his boat. If not, I'm sure it's his preferred place of mischief. Check everywhere with water that connects to any large body of water."

The conversation ebbed and Willow went back to focusing on the road and thoughts of the killer, Travis, Amy, the hotels, marina, and harbor. She needed to get a name for this killer, somehow, she needed to ID the Jane Doe, and find four more bodies.

She also needed to locate the knife and the ice pick, but she needed to find the sailboat first. This could conceivably be a very long investigation. If she did find four more, the challenge would be on to find out when they were last seen and where. She wondered if Heather was killed in the park. Was there enough blood? She could have been stabbed there, but her gut told her both women had been killed elsewhere. Then she thought back to what Travis had said. These women, these victims had to be connected in some way. She needed to find out how.

Her gut had to be wrong, though. Dragging or carrying a body through a city park just to bury it was stupid. There wouldn't have been any suspicion at all of a man and a woman walking together. People wouldn't normally even notice. Heather had met her killer. Maybe Jane Doe had, as well. It was the same man. A player.

More than anything else she had to find out, she needed to listen to Travis. She needed to learn what connected the victims. It had to be something more than just a love of sailboats. Both of these victims were Caucasian brunettes. Were the other four? Had this sicko had a rough relationship with a Caucasian brunette in his past?

Her phone rang. She didn't recognize the number. "Detective Sturgeon," she said into the overhead mic.

"Detective, this is Beth Simmons. Is this a bad time?"

"Not at all, Mrs. Simmons. How are you holding up?"

"I've been better, Detective. I'm calling because I've just received a rather unusual call. I thought you should know."

"Lay it on me."

"Heather's friend Amy's just called and was asking me just about the same questions the other detective did."

Shit. "What did you tell her?"

"About the same answers I gave the other detective, but when I realized she was interrogating me, I told her I had to prepare dinner, so I hung up and called you."

"I appreciate that, Mrs. Simmons. If she calls again, tell her I told you to have her call me. That you're not allowed to interfere with the investigation."

"Okay, I will. I wonder why she was asking so many questions."

"Heather was her best friend, Mrs. Simmons. She probably just wants to know whom to hate. I have to go now, but I have one more question. Did Heather mention any other men in her life besides Walker? Maybe someone she identified as being like a brother or best friend?"

"She never said anything to me about anyone but her friend Amy and that jackass. That's my word, by the way. Not hers."

"Okay, Mrs. Simmons. Amy is not a bad person, but if she calls you again, let me know." Willow hung up with Mrs. Simmons and keyed the mic again.

"Call Captain," she said.

"Carson," came the response after two rings.

"Sturgeon, Cap. Your phone call to Mrs. Gaudier didn't work. Amy just interrogated Mrs. Simmons."

"God damn it!" he screeched and hung up immediately. This was a good thing, because Willow was pulling into the harbor lot. She and Agent Maxwell exited the car and she saw that he hadn't been kidding. As they were walking toward the docks, he was still using his tablet, searching for missing person reports.

Willow looked up and down the docks as far as she could see, but saw no sailboats. Cargo vessels and tugs aplenty, but no sails. She made her way up the steps to the harbor master, with Maxwell following silently. Now elevated, she looked again, but still saw no sailboats. She did see video cameras, though, but they appeared to be focused more on the walkways than the docks.

"What can I do for you?" the man in the office asked.

"I'm Detective Sturgeon and this is Agent Maxwell of the FBI. Are you the harbor master?"

"Yes."

Willow held up the photo. "Have you seen this man or this boat?"

"Several times. He comes in on a Friday. Usually late afternoon. I let him hook up at the end, down there."

"I need to see your log book and video feed."

"What for?"

Willow was getting irritated. "Because I want this man's name and the boat ID."

"It's a sailboat. I don't make him register; it's just a sailboat docked out of the way. He said his name was Mike Sanders, from Charmaine. There's no coverage of the areas on the end. No one ever uses it. That's why I let him dock there."

"In other words, he slips you a couple of c-notes and you look the other way. What can you tell me about him?"

"I don't appreciate the accusation, Detective," the man said, huffing.

"I don't give a damn. I'm investigating multiple murders, and this man is a person of interest. A very strong one. If he turns out to be my guy, I'll be back with bracelets. Should I ask you again, or did you understand the question?"

"I don't know much. He comes in Friday, goes to town, and leaves Sunday. It's only been a couple of weeks. Maybe three. Once in a while, he takes his date out on the boat. I really don't pay that much attention."

"I believe you," Willow said, causing the man to scowl. She held the picture up again. "Was this his date?"

"No. This lady had longer hair, and not so dark. I've seen that girl, though," he said, scratching his chin. "She may be the friend of Miss Gaudier. They came to sign for a shipment last weekend."

"Was there a name on the sailboat? Any numbers that you remember? Size? Type?"

"Honestly, at the risk of another insult, I don't know that much about sailboats. I don't think he does, either. I've never seen a sail on it."

Looking exasperated, she was sure, Willow handed the man her card. "If that sailboat docks, you call me, immediately. You might want to think twice about the greasy palms. I'll arrest you for interfering with a murder investigation, and I'll show up at every hearing. I'll put your ass away for as long as the law allows. So, when Amy Gaudier comes and lays out her charm and that wad of cash, think about what I've just said."

"She already called," the man said sheepishly.

"When?"

"Just before you walked in."

"What did she want to know?"

"She asked when the sailboat usually comes in. I told her Fridays after three or four."

"What was the offer?"

"A thousand dollars."

"That won't cover your bail. I'm not joking about this." She turned and, with Agent Maxwell in tow, she stomped down the stairs.

"The Coast Guard's just found a body," Maxwell said before they got to the car. "Looked like a shark attack. Chewed up pretty good. Female, five-six, brown hair, hazel eyes. Missing her left leg. Too far from shore to be a swimmer or surfer." He kept scrolling but looked up at her. "Definitely one of your victims. Three stab wounds in her torso, and a piece of metal they can't identify right now in her right ear canal."

"Damnit!" she screamed. Willow had held out hope that the idiot just couldn't count, but now she knew. There were definitely more victims. She took a deep breath, and calmly said, "See if they can send divers down to find what she may have been anchored to, or if there are more bodies. How far out was it?"

"Less than a mile, so we're good. This may draw us in, though."

"Bring them up to speed and ask nicely if they want our coroner to do the autopsy. Explain the gravity of the investigation, and the need for speed. They'll decline, but whichever coroner it is will get pissed and be thorough. If it does bring you in, you'll be welcome, as long as no one else dies. See what you can dig up on Mike Sanders of Charmaine. I'm guessing early to mid-twenties."

"On it."

Birch

Travis had been having severe withdrawals since checking in the night before last. He was shaking badly. There was a nurse in his room, taking vitals, and she had told him he had a fever, which explained why he was sweating. She asked Fred if Travis had been displaying any symptoms of anxiety, or if he appeared to have seized at any time. Fred hadn't noticed any, so he guessed his withdrawals weren't that severe after all.

"When can I get out of here?" he asked the nurse.

"Right now," she said as she continued checking his blood pressure. "This isn't a prison. You leave when you want, but you won't be doing yourself any favors, and I don't make house calls."

"Let's do this right, Travis," Fred said. "If you try to speed things up, you'll just prolong the agony. From what you said of the conversation with the wife, I can't blame you for being in a hurry, but you still have quite a distance to travel. Let's make this cure permanent."

"I know. It's not just Kris. Willow's out there alone. Will you take me with you tonight?"

"If you think you're ready. You'll be expected to stand up and announce yourself, and Carl will be there. His daughter works with you. He won't say anything to her, but you will wonder."

"I know what I am. I have no problem announcing it. I need to move forward and not delay. Can I ask you a question?"

"Other than that one, you mean?"

Travis chuckled. "Yes, besides that one. Are you married? Do you have a family I'm taking you away from?"

"My wife, both sons, brother and sisters all said they would leave me if I didn't stop hanging out with you," Fred said with a smile. "They have gone through this with me, Travis. They know how important a sponsor is. Our situation is not all that dissimilar. My wife had left me, as well. I won her back. Will you?"

"You can bet your life on it."

"Okay, I will. Now that she's done poking at you, how about a cup of coffee?"

"I'll be honest. The coffee here's not much better than the sludge at work."

"I was actually thinking of Starbucks. Do you think you can shave and shower without cutting off your nose?"

"I'm with you," Travis said, jumping from the chair and grabbing a change of clothes. He knew this was a test. He knew he would pass it.

"I'll wait for you in the lobby," Fred finished as he left the room.

While Travis was getting dressed, he couldn't help but think about the case. He thought about Willow, basically having to go at it alone because he had been too weak-minded to solve this problem long ago. Brand new on the job, and she had been stuck with a drunk. Thrown right into the fire without an extinguisher. He would find a way to make it up to her.

Travis realized he was making it sound like what'd happened to him was the worst thing possible. It was far from that.

His suffering was minimal compared to that of Mr. and Mrs. Simmons. They had lost a child. There would be no changes they could make in their life that would bring that child back. Unlike Travis.

Someone had killed an innocent young woman. More than one. Travis wasn't kidding himself. He knew there were more, but the key was Heather Simmons and the fight she'd put up. The DNA under her fingernails. That was going to be the key to the prosecution. That was going to be what put this sick bastard away.

He needed to find this guy. He needed to find something to connect the victims besides brown hair and their age and gender. There had to be something. If the bastard was killing everyone he dated, he would really be a hard nut to crack.

Truthfully, they didn't have much in the way of hard evidence. Heather Simmons' fingernails, a bottle of dish soap, a fingernail file and a nail brush. The degenerate hadn't had the time to clean out her nails. The witness had seen the body, and the sicko had been forced to leave his tools behind. His thoughts went to whether any prints had been found on the soap bottle. He wasn't sure either of the other two items were an option for prints.

Travis was dressed within a half hour, he had signed himself out, and he and Fred began the drive to the local Starbucks. Fred had a nice car. A Lexus IS. He had never asked Fred what he did for work.

"This is a nice car, Fred. What is it you do for a living?"

"I don't do anything. I've hired people to do it for me. I own a furniture store. Grayson's."

"Holy cow. That's a pretty big store. That's where the wife and I bought our dining set."

"Well, thank you. You are at least partially responsible for this car."

"Your last name's Whittier, though. How did Grayson's come to be?"

"Grayson was my favorite pet, growing up. A husky. Loved that dog. We were inseparable. I have no reason beyond that."

So, Fred was rich. Travis tried to imagine what would drive a wealthy man to drink, but not having that problem, he couldn't imagine. He knew other things besides money caused excessive drinking, not the least of which was liking the taste. It wasn't money that sent him into the abyss, and he knew that wasn't the problem with Fred, either.

"You don't need one. That's a good enough reason." Travis checked his phone again.

"She still hasn't called yet, huh?" Fred said, noticing the phone.

"No. She said she'd keep me informed of the case, but maybe she forgot. She's kind of busy, being basically by herself."

"Well, don't jump to conclusions. Maybe she doesn't have anything new. Or, she could be the one who's been following us since we left Emberton."

Travis turned around and looked at the car behind. "Yup. That's Willow."

Sturgeon

None of the personnel she talked to at either hotel had seen any scratched-up guests, and none recognized the man in the photo, but she did obtain video footage of the lobbies that coincided with the time frame. She handed the flash drives off to Maxwell and he loaded them onto his tablet.

Maxwell had zoom experience and apparently lip-reading talents. He would use those talents along with her statement of the conversation she had with the man, and he would see if he could single him out. Willow didn't think it would pan out, though. Just about everybody talked and walked. There would probably be too many possibilities at 3:15 in the afternoon.

Now her plan was to drop him off at the station so he could focus all his attention on the video feed. He would need some quiet time, anyway, as he attempted to get Charmaine PD to find Mike Sanders. There were two possibilities in the age range they were looking for. Now Mark was going to call Charmaine and see if they would locate the two and dig a bit. She wanted to go see Travis and give him an update, anyway.

When they arrived at the station, Mark went to Travis' desk to review the feed, while she made a detour into the captain's office.

"Detective," the captain acknowledged.

"Cap, any luck with that Gaudier thing?"

"I called her dad this time. He was in meetings, but said he'd call me back. You may have to put up with it for a couple more hours."

"I hope not. She could really mess up our case and make prosecution harder on the ADA."

"I understand. Amy's not all that interested in prosecution, though. It's probably going to take Trevor to stop her. Obviously, her mother couldn't."

"Cap, I know you have a certain amount of pride in the Gaudiers, but this isn't a sporting event. This man is dangerous. The Coast Guard found number three yesterday afternoon."

The captain looked frustrated and ran his hands through his hair as he leaned back in his chair. "I'll send another team to meet with the Coast Guard. You stay on Heather Simmons. You need to find this guy, Sturgeon, and quickly. I know you think I'm bluffing about Amy Gaudier, but you don't know her. I do.

"I don't think you were listening to what I said," he continued. "She caught that boy and beat him with the same club he used on her dog. She will search for this guy, she will find him, and she will kill him. With his own ice pick. Then I will lose one of my best friends. Because I had to send his daughter to prison for murder one."

Willow turned and walked to the door but stopped and looked at the captain. "If she interferes with my investigation, I will arrest her, Cap. I will." She walked out the door, not waiting for a response, and left the building to go see Travis.

When she reached Emberton, she saw Travis walking out of the building and getting into a vehicle with his sponsor. She thought it was a little soon for him to be leaving, but she didn't know for sure that this trip was permanent. She tried to reach the car before it left the lot, but she had to wait for another car that was backing out.

Willow caught up to the sponsor's car right away, and just followed it. It pulled into a Starbucks and stopped. She pulled in next to it, looked over and smiled at Travis. She got out of the car and opened the trunk, pulling out his laptop that she had picked up from his home the night before, when she had gone over to work a little more on his house.

She wasn't sure she could trust Fred, and she didn't want to get herself or Travis in trouble. As he stepped out, she handed Travis the laptop.

"I thought maybe you would like this while you're at Emberton," she said as she handed it to him. "I know there's not much to do there, and I thought you might want to pass the time playing some games or buying out Amazon. I know that place isn't exactly a hotel." She patted him on the chest, sliding her hand down to his shirt pocket and dropping the three flash drives into his shirt pocket.

She could tell by his eyes that he understood and felt the drives fall into his pocket. She could also tell that he was excited about working the case. In truth, she didn't need him to review the footage. She already had Agent Maxwell working on it, but she did want him to know she was still his partner, and he was a part of the case. She hoped Fred hadn't noticed. Travis was on administrative leave, not restricted duty. He wasn't supposed to be involved at all.

After Travis put the laptop in the car, the three of them entered Starbucks and ordered their drinks. Fred was insistent on paying, so she and Travis thanked him, gracefully, and they all took a seat, waiting for the baristas.

"Why are you out here by yourself, Willow?" Travis asked.

"I'm just coming to see you, Travis. It's not like I'm going on interviews or chasing bad guys."

"You were chasing us. We're about as bad as they come." He looked over at Fred and smiled. Fred nodded, laughed and voiced his agreement.

"What's new on the case?" Travis asked.

"Well, let's see. I think the biggest news was the call we got from the Coast Guard yesterday. They found number three."

"Where?"

"Offshore from Moon Lake Bay. Less than a mile. Maxwell thinks the feds will get involved now, but Cap is sending a team there anyway."

"Any similarities?"

"Caucasian brunette. I don't know all that much yet."

Willow continued to give Travis a rundown on the case, and when she had relayed everything she could think of, she excused herself, grabbed her green tea and left the two of them to their conversation. She pulled out her notebook and made a note to call the hotels to see if they had a Mike Sanders as a guest last weekend. She should have asked when she was there, but she was too excited about the video feed.

Her phone said it was 10 AM. It was time to break some rules. She called Mark and asked him to disappear for a while so the captain would think they were out working the case. He said he needed coffee, anyway, so he would run over to Starbucks. Willow made a left and headed toward the harbor.

While she was driving, she called the downtown Holiday Inn. She got some dumbass from some online booking company instead, which infuriated the shit out of her. You couldn't call a hotel directly anymore. You just got some company promising to save you money, but in the end, usually you ended up paying more. Legalized scam.

She arrived at the harbor and climbed the stairs, cornering the harbormaster. "You know you're in trouble for allowing that sailboat to dock without registering, right?"

"I know. It won't happen again. I promise."

"I promise you it won't happen a third time," Willow countered. "I'm going to let this slide, for now. In return you're going to do something for me."

"Like what?" the man asked cautiously. Willow handed him her card, for the second time, after scratching off the patrol number and writing down her cell number.

"You're going to be one of my confidential informants. You're going to call me if you see Amy Gaudier anywhere near here. You're going to clear the end of the dock down there this Friday night and instruct your staff to avoid the area. In addition, if you even suspect there is any illegal activity going on here, from any ship, you're going to call me.

"In return," she continued, "if you get yourself in any hot water on a misdemeanor crime, you're going to call me and we'll talk. Any questions? Do you understand or would you rather turn around and put your hands behind your back?"

"I understand. I'll call you."

Willow stared at the man long enough to make him nervous. "Put the phone number in your phone. Use the name WS. What's your number?" The man provided it and Willow entered it into her phone under the name harbor. Then she walked him out to the overhead walkway, looked both directions for the sailboat and then looked at the various ships.

"I want you to check with every employee you have who works Friday nights. Anyone who came into contact with the man from the sailboat, I need to talk to. I don't want to hear any 'I don't want to get involved' shit. I don't care if it was just a short greeting. I want to talk to them. Clear the dock. This Friday night. Everything south of that red tug. Make sure it's clear of any pallets or personnel."

"Why? What's going on?"

"Just do it. Are we clear?" The man nodded and she checked her phone. Noon. She walked to her car and left, heading for the Holiday Inn. This hotel was on the opposite side of the street from the other two, but the windows were open, with a clear view. She stopped at Panera, got a salad and a water, and made notes of what she still had to do. She called the man who had found Heather's body and set up a follow-up interview.

Willow didn't know if she was going to find the woman she had originally talked to when she arrived at the hotel, but she needed CIs, and this was her best shot, right now, for the downtown area. The woman hadn't committed any crimes and had no reason to help Willow, so it would be more a matter of asking politely. Women weren't as easily intimidated as men, anyway.

She approached the desk, asked for Vicki, and found she really was on duty. She had to wait a few minutes, as Vicki was assisting a guest, but eventually the woman exited the elevator and the two sat in the lobby chairs.

The conversation was lengthy, as Willow explained her situation, being new to homicide and the trouble detectives had trying to get people to open up, fearing retaliation or being tied up testifying in court. She explained the confidential part of confidential informant, and the need to have one in this area.

There was a lot of conversation back and forth, with questions asked and answers given. There was talk about the scratched-up man, and Willow gave her as much info as she could without damaging the investigation. The conversation stayed cordial and ended with an exchange of phone numbers, and a list of people who had worked last weekend. Unfortunately, no Mike Sanders registered on those dates. However, Willow now had two CIs.

She left the hotel and checked her phone. 2:30PM. She drove to Duncan Avenue, the home of her witness, and was met at the door by a rather handsome man in his late thirties or early forties. He made her wait a moment, staring at him through the security screen, as he walked toward a hallway and called for his wife. Once she got to the door, he opened it, asking her in. Strange.

"Do I look dangerous?" she asked, as she took the seat offered.

"I apologize, Detective," the wife said. "My husband watches too much news."

"What happened to those poor Olympic girls," the man clarified, "is awful, and those actresses... but there are also women joining the movement because someone asked for their phone number. It's out of hand and it will damage relationships, I think. I just choose not to participate."

Willow caught herself from speaking out to this moron, and she needed to see if he remembered anything related to the murder, so she changed the subject.

"I'm just here to see if maybe you can think of anything else that you might have remembered since talking to the officers.

Maybe hearing movement or seeing something out of the corner of your eye. A jogger materializing out of the area. That kind of thing."

"There were a couple of joggers who stopped to look before the police got there, but after they got there, they closed down the path, so none after that."

"What did these joggers look like? Were they dressed for jogging?"

"Hmm. Now that you mention it, the one guy was in shorts and wearing skids. Never saw anyone run in those before."

"Skids?"

"You know. The shoes without laces. Slippers with the anti-slip soles. They're worn a lot on snowy or icy sidewalks up north."

"Deck shoes?"

"Yeah. Like that."

Willow pulled out her phone and opened the photo. "Did he look like this?"

"God, no. This guy had been in a fight. His face was all puffy and scratched up."

"Look closely. Could he have looked like this before the fight?"

"Yeah, maybe. Same hair, it looks like."

"Which way did he come from? Did he leave the same direction?"

"I didn't see which way he came from. He was just there, but he jogged off deeper in the park. Oh. He had a backpack. That was kind of weird, too. It looked empty, except for one of those folding shovels like you see in the military strapped to the outside. I actually thought he might be military and was going to thank him for his service, but he seemed to be in a hurry."

"A folding shovel? He must have had that in his backpack for weight, huh? Was there anything else about him you noticed? Tattoos? Piercings?"

"No. I didn't notice anything like that. Except for the face, he just looked normal."

"What color were his clothes? Did it look like he favored Earth tones? Blues?"

"His shirt was green and his shorts kind of brownish. The skids were brown, too."

Willow gave the man her card and asked him to call her if he thought of anything else. "It doesn't matter if you think it's unimportant. Just call me."

She thanked them and departed the house. Ugh. What a moron!

Four o'clock. Willow called Maxwell and told him she was calling it a day. After exchanging cars, she drove north from the station and came to a stop sign. If she turned west, the road would take her to the Gaudier mansion. If she turned east, home. Maybe if she spoke to Amy directly, the woman would listen to reason. Yeah, maybe. Then maybe the captain would flay her for going behind his back. She turned east. Her phone rang.

"Sturgeon."

"Hey, it's Mark. Just got an email from the Coast Guard. You're going to love this. They already have an identity on the swimmer. I'll email it to you. They agreed to make a dive in the morning. I also got a text from the boss. She said she has some preliminary information for you from the profiler. She'll be in her office at nine, if you want to call her."

"Okay. Thanks, Mark. I'll do that. How do you feel about a walk in the park, tomorrow?"

"I'm game."

∞∞∞

Willow pulled into her garage with no one following her in and climbed the stairs to the kitchen. She opened her freezer, took out four chicken breasts, and threw them in the sink after she had filled it with cold water. She went to her room, changed into her sweats, and unlocked the door as she walked to the exercise room.

After ten minutes on the leg press, the door opened and closed. She heard footsteps climbing to the elevated kitchen area, and shortly after descending them.

"Hey, Will," Mitch said. "I brought a bottle of grigio. Threw it in the fridge."

"You put it in the refrigerator?" Willow asked. "You're such a nimrod!"

Mitch sat on the lat pull, looked at her, stood up and walked back to the kitchen. He returned and went back to the pull, and said, "Hey, Will! I brought a bottle of grigio. I set it on the counter."

"Gee, thanks, Mitch. I appreciate it. I had a friend once who put a bottle of grigio in the refrigerator. It came out tasting like grape juice."

"Wow, really? What a nimrod!"

159

Mitch's day had consisted of mostly graffiti calls. He was certain he had a new gang start up in his district. He went on about his day for about ten minutes, before the door opened and closed again. Willow was now on the treadmill and Mitch had switched to weights.

Jessie and Marci came in and greetings were exchanged. Adam was splitting an extra shift with one of the graveyard guys and wouldn't be joining them. Marci was a second shift patrol officer who spent most of her time with yoga. Willow could probably count the number of times the woman had come over on one hand.

"Day off, Marci?" Willow asked.

"Three actually, she said as she was stretching against the wall. "Came over tonight to see if you were mad at me."

"Why would I be mad at you?"

"Good. What you don't know won't hurt me."

Willow laughed. "Did you ticket my mom?"

"She was doing fifty on Hanson, Will. Didn't have much choice."

"I swear," Willow said, between sobs of laughter, "I'm going to have to take that woman's keys away from her."

"If you think that's funny, you're going to love where she was going in such a hurry."

"Traffic court?" Willow said, and the room erupted in laughter.

"Better. To city hall with a signed petition to have the speed limit on Hanson changed to forty-five." The room erupted again and Willow began to get a little uplifted from her depressing day.

Sandman

Mike closed up his office, waved at Michelle, and took the elevator down and out of Zachary Architecture. He put his papers and briefcase on his passenger seat, started the Mercedes and left the parking lot turning northeast on Sampson Avenue. His routine was the same to and from work. His personal life was another matter.

Tonight, was going to be his second date with Marie. The first had gone well. Tonight, he would up the ante and take her to a more expensive restaurant. He would adjust as time went by, making the changes he needed to make until he noticed any discomfort or confusion on her part. That would tell him when he had maxed her out. Reached a level of expenditure that she wasn't comfortable with.

He'd already found out on the first date that she wasn't a user. He had coyly brought up the topic of a 'friend' whom Mike had to help shirk his dependency. Marie had responded that she never understood why people would do that to their bodies. It had actually created a very nice conversation as Mike took the side of the user and the things that could conceivably get them involved in drugs, and Marie continued with her rebuttal. It had been light and never got heated.

Mike could see this turning into a long-term relationship. He had been impressed with Marie, and since she'd agreed to a second date, he'd assumed he had made a good impression, as well. Marie was perfect, physically. She was just the right height, the top of her

161

head coming up to his eyes, enabling him to admire the curly brown locks. He preferred brown eyes, and hers were hazel, but that was not a deal breaker. The brown hair was the deal breaker. He found blondes too flighty and redheads too fiery.

His obsession with hair color had started in high school. At that time, he had been interested in a particular blond fellow student in his chemistry class. That had lasted an entire two months before Courtney was already seeking greener pastures. She had a very warm smile, which was what had attracted him to her, but the longer they were together the sooner her eyes began to drift. He had found it too difficult to keep her happy.

She eventually moved on, and he wasn't sorry for it. He was struggling, trying to find the words to break it off himself, but she decided to end it herself via a text message. He had really been pissed that she had resorted to breaking up with him by text, but the anger lasted less than five minutes once he realized she had done him a favor.

Mike had spent the rest of his sophomore year hanging with the guys. He didn't want rumors circulating that any girl he went with would be getting him on the rebound, and he needed the break, anyway. So demanding, she had been. Always wanting to party.

When school was out, he went to do some work with his dad. He drew some pay that kept him in some things he liked, such as video games that the parents wouldn't buy for him, and the rest he would save up to buy himself a car.

His dad was in construction and Mike loved building things, so it worked out well. On one after-work get-together with the team, they gathered at the house of his dad's assistant. That was where he'd met Miranda. Like her dad, she had the red locks of their Irish heritage. He and Miranda hit it off right away. She didn't go to the same high school, but that was okay with him.

They had gotten together several times, hanging out at the mall, Starbuck's, or the arcade. Miranda had a great personality, the cutest freckles on the bridge of her nose, and a body that would cause many guys to do a double take. He had liked her a lot, because despite the admiration of others, her eyes were only on him.

Mike had enjoyed this relationship much more than that of Courtney. He and Miranda had a future. He could feel it. That was until he tried to feel them. She slapped his hand away from her breasts and glared at him. They had been seeing each other for over a month. It was time for exploration. He didn't understand her reluctance.

The glare lasted for nearly ten seconds before she asked him what the hell he was thinking. He explained himself honestly, saying they had been together for a while and she should be flattered that he was interested.

For the next ten minutes she released barrage after barrage of insults and obscenities with her face no more than six inches from his and twisted in fury. Her dad was a construction worker so some of those obscenities embarrassed him, and his dad was in construction, too. Miranda left no doubt in his mind that he should keep his hands on his dick and off her breasts. She stormed away and left him feeling berated, belittled and confused. And that was the end of Miranda. She didn't call him and he didn't call her.

So, his experience with a blonde was a dud, and his experience with a redhead was even more so. Michael Sanders wasn't someone who defined a person by their hair color. At least he thought he wasn't. The summer ran on without any further ass chewing or text dumping. He hadn't made enough money to buy a car, and it would have done no good, anyway, since the upcoming school year would find him in the junior class and unable to drive to school.

Riding the bus turned out to be a good thing. On his first day back to school, he had the good fortune to sit next to an absolutely stunning brunette on her first day in her new school. Her name was Beth, and her smile was mesmerizing. Luck was with Mike, as she accepted his offer to show her around and help her find her classes.

Unlike his two previous relationships, he and Beth hit it off and became an item. They stayed together, not only through their junior year, but all through the summer and through their senior year, as well. 'Mike and Beth' became a frequently used term at school and when out and about. Her eyes never strayed. She never blew up at him, even when he copped a feel. It was obvious she didn't like it, but her reactions were calm and deliberate, not a total freak-out.

They had talked freely about sex. Beth wouldn't take any chances of becoming pregnant in high school. She wasn't totally sold on condoms, saying they weren't fail-proof. She said her first time was going to be with him, but it wouldn't be until after she graduated. Also, she didn't believe in kissing in public, and his hands needed to stay off her breasts and ass.

When they were alone, though, it was a different story. When her parents were gone, or his, the make-out sessions became intense, and his hands were busy. The way she caressed his neck and cheek during a kiss was exhilarating.

Then, with about a month left in their senior year, they were once again alone at his house, and after about a half hour of sucking the breath from each other, she pulled a condom from her pocket, unzipped his pants, and began slowly caressing it over his manhood, stroking as she did. Disaster struck within three minutes of her caress. The two of them laughed long and hard, but he could tell she was disappointed.

Disaster struck again on the last day of school. Beth's parents were divorcing and she was going to live with her dad in Atlanta. She was going to enroll in Georgia Tech. 'Mike and Beth' were no more. It had been heartbreaking, but that was what had made Mike judge women by hair color. Blonde, no; redhead, huh-uh. Brunettes all the way.

When he arrived home from work, he checked his mailbox and found, among other things, a business card. The name on the card was Detective Josh Thompson, Charmaine Police Department, with a phone number and extension. He closed his garage door and entered the house, setting the card on the end table of the couch.

He turned on the shower and got the clothes out that he would wear tonight on his date with Marie then walked back into the living room and glanced again at the business card. He left it sitting there and proceeded to the shower.

When Beth had left him, he talked about it to one of his dad's construction workers, and how he felt like he had wasted two years of his life. Eighteen and going to college, still basically a virgin. The man had given him the number of one of his friends. Mike had called the number, and that was how he obtained his first supply of roofies. No more waiting two years to get laid. Now the woman either put out, or he would ease her inhibitions.

Had he been caught? Was that what the detective wanted him for? There was nothing on the card. No explanation, no questions. Was that a detective's ploy? Drop off the card and see if he gets a call, or if the person tries to dodge it? An innocent man wouldn't dodge. Had one of his exes ratted him out?

This night was about Marie. He would call the detective in the morning. There was nothing on the card that indicated it to be urgent. That's not dodging.

Thompson

Josh sat his homework from last night down on his desk and went to get a cup of coffee. Eric wasn't in yet, so he would have a few minutes to review the case they were working on, check his voicemail and email, and get the interviews planned out. Hopefully, one or two of those voicemails would be the Sanders guys.

It wasn't unheard of but tracking down persons of interest for another department wasn't his favorite part of the job. This particular person of interest, though, was a different story. Not only was there a murder involved, there may be six. He would love to be part of the team that nailed this psycho.

There were only four voicemails and six emails. Pretty calm. Two of the voicemails were from the Michael Sanders guys. He decided to save them for last. He opened the emails, perused their contents and attached them to their respective files. Except the one from the company wanting to sell him copy paper. That one he dumped. Idiots!

He opened the voicemails, read the one from his daughter, and learned she was ready for her driving test and new car. As if. Cute of her to leave a voicemail, though, instead of bringing it up at breakfast. The next voicemail was from Eric, saying he was going to be about a half hour late. Figures. That left the last two. He opened the first.

---"Hi. I'm calling for Detective Thompson. My name is Michael Sanders, and I guess you left your card at my house last night. My sister was not very helpful in whatever message you left her, which is standard. I'm currently in Haiti on a mission..."

Josh stopped there. Those missions took a lot of time, so probably not his guy. He saved the voicemail, just in case. It had a number to talk to him direct, along with an area code that had to be Haiti. He opened the last voicemail.

---"Top of the morning to you, Detective. I'm Mike Sanders, and you left a business card in my mail box last night. I would have called you last night, except for two reasons. One, I actually work for a living, unlike you coffee-drinking, donut-eating detectives; and two, I had a date with a woman who I'm sure is much better looking and better company than you are. Feel free to give me a break from work this morning...

By the time Josh made it all the way through the voicemail, he was laughing his ass off. This guy was hilarious. He had left a number to his office, and Josh wrote it on a sticky and stuck it on the back of one of his cards. He opened the email from the fed dude and downloaded the picture of the perp to his phone.

Eric ambled in and asked if he had by any chance been late enough that Josh had finished up the paperwork.

"Yup. As usual, I finished your work. Let's hit the road and stop off for coffee and donuts."

"Coffee and donuts? Are we doing donuts now?" Eric asked.

"Not this guy. I'm up for the coffee, though. Take a look at this voicemail. This guy had me laughing so hard I thought I would choke. You'll get the donut part."

After Eric finished the voicemail and they had their laugh, both the detectives loaded up their gear and made for the cruiser. Getting this out of the way quickly would get them back on their normal routine. With Eric driving, Josh called the Sanders number.

"Zachary Architecture. How may I direct your call?"

"Mike Sanders, please," Josh answered.

"One moment." The elevator music was supposed to make the wait less strenuous, but it wasn't doing anything for Josh.

"Sanders."

"Mr. Sanders, this is Detective Thompson, Charmaine P.D. Is this a good time?"

"As good as any. What can I do for you, Detective?"

"We're doing some grunt work for another department. They're looking for someone named Mike Sanders as a possible witness to a crime. We've eliminated all of our Mike Sanders's except for you. Would there be a good time soon for you to come down and talk to us, so that we can put this to bed and move on with our own cases?"

"I'm pretty busy. I can do without the drive time. Is there any way you can pop up here?"

"Absolutely, since you invited us. When is convenient?"

"If it's quick, anytime you like. Otherwise, I'll have to pencil you in."

"Five minutes tops."

"Good enough. I'm on the fifteenth floor, suite 1507."

"We'll be there in a few. Thank you."

"No hesitation at all," Josh said to Eric after he hung up. "This ain't their guy. Head over to Zachary. Let's get this done."

While they were ascending in the elevator, both detectives studied the picture on Josh's phone so they wouldn't need to pull it out during the interview. They ignored hair color, which could be changed, and focused on eyes, ears, nose and bone structure in general.

They reached the fifteenth floor, got off the elevator and proceeded to suite 1507, opening the door to a young and attractive receptionist with a magnetic smile. They introduced themselves and asked for Mike Sanders. She announced their presence on her intercom and another door opened immediately.

"Detectives," the man who looked nothing like the photo announced, "Please, come in." He turned and walked back into his office with Josh and Eric looking at each other and shaking their heads. "So! I understand I may have witnessed some malfeasance?"

"Only if you were in Carpel last weekend. Were you?" Eric asked.

"No. Sorry. Guess I'm not your man."

"When was the last time you were there? Do you know?" Josh asked.

"Oh, geez," Sanders said looking at the ceiling. "Maybe five, six months ago. What happened? Robbery?"

"Oh. No," Josh answered. "Just looking into a no pay at the marina there. Do you own a boat, Mr. Sanders?"

"Used to. Sold it about a year ago."

"We have a feeling the man you sold it to didn't register it and used your name at the marina. Do you still have the registration info? Bill of sale?"

"I'm sure I do, but it would be at home."

Josh pulled out his business card and handed it to Sanders. "Would you see if you can locate it and fax it to that number? We'd appreciate it."

"No problem. I'll look that up as soon as I get home. I don't have a fax at home, so I'll fax it tomorrow."

"That'll be great. Thanks a lot," Josh said, sticking out his hand for a handshake. Sanders took it and Josh and Eric turned for the door. Josh stopped and swung around, looking into the eyes of the man he'd just shaken hands with.

"Just one more thing, Mr. Sanders," Josh said pulling out his phone. "Is this the man you sold the boat to?"

Sanders studied the picture. "Boy. I'm just not sure. It was a year ago. It might be. I don't think the woman was there, though."

"Okay. Well, fax that stuff to us, and if you can think of anything that might help, don't hesitate to call."

"Will do."

Josh and Eric made their way out of the office and down the hall to the elevator. Eric looked to see if anyone had poked their head out of the office after they left and then asked his partner the question.

"Well. How was the handshake?"

"He's full of shit. He knows something or has done something."

"Let's get back to the cruiser and run him, then," Eric said. "You're going to have to teach me how you do that some time."

"I have magical powers. Whenever someone's lying to me, the lie permeates through the hands and imbeds in my mind."

"Well," Eric said as they stepped onto the elevator, turning back to face the doors. As the doors were closing, Eric stuck his hands in his pockets. "Sanders isn't the only one that's full of shit, then."

Sandman

Mike realized he was pacing and the door to his office was open. He didn't want Michelle to see he was nervous after the detectives left so he walked to his easel and placed both hands on it to calm himself. Shit! What a dumbass. Mike would need to call the prick. He couldn't do that from his cell or his office, in case the detectives checked his phone records. He would need to use a burner.

He had planned on using his break time to score some more Special K but he would have to put that on hold and make the call instead. Fuck. What a dumb shit!

Now he was going to have to find a different supplier. The detectives would probably be watching him. He was going to have to change everything. Where he got his coffee. Where he ate. Where he took Marie. God damn it! Shit! There was more to this than a no pay. Detectives wouldn't have even stood up for something like that. They had him, and he was going to implicate Mike.

Mike certainly didn't need Michelle to say she noticed anything unusual in the event the detectives returned. He waited what he thought was an appropriate time for the detectives to leave and then put on his best face and exited his office.

"Hey, Michelle. I'm going to grab a coffee. Do you want one?"

"Oh. No, thank you, sir. I'm on a diet. Thank you for the offer, though."

Same answer he always got from her. No matter what he offered, there was always some reason to decline. Whether it was bringing her coffee, picking her up something for lunch, or even a snack from the vending machine. It was almost like she knew how he got his jollies, but he was certain Michelle's upbringing prevented her from being an imposition. What a sweetheart. She was a babe, for a blonde, but she was a blonde.

Mike smiled and then left for the elevator. As he was descending he formulated in his head the words he was going to have to say to the dumbass. He made his way out the front door to his car and drove to Walmart, bought the phone, followed the directions and made the call.

"Who's this?" came the answer.

"You need to get your ass out of town, man. No. Better yet, out of the country," Mike said.

"Calm down. What's got your nuts all crunched?"

"That chick you said was dumber than a bag of rocks. Wasn't. The cops got your picture standing right next to her. What's wrong with you? How could you let her take your picture?"

"There's no way. I have her phone. How did they get the picture? She just ran home to change her shoes."

"She wasn't as enamored with you as you thought she was. She loaded it on her computer or something. They have it."

"Doesn't prove anything. It just proves we were at the harbor together."

"Harbor? Not the marina? The cops said there was a no pay at the marina. Shit. They were baiting. Why didn't you just get rid of the body, man? Detectives wouldn't have handled a no pay. They have you, man. You need to split."

"A jogger was coming. I hid, but he saw the body. I should have just taken him out, but he was a guy, and it would have messed up the numbers, anyway."

"Numbers?" Mike blurted incredulously. "This personal vendetta you have against her is going to get us both thrown in prison for the rest of our lives. Well, me, anyway. You, they'll probably inject."

"The picture bitch was number six. The seventh unit is all I have left. She fucked me over. Now I'm going to fuck her. Then I'm going to kill her. Then I'll split. Not until then."

"Get rid of the fucking boat. Get rid of everything you have that connects me to you. Take my name off your phone. Eliminate me altogether. Don't call me. Stay out of Charmaine. If I see you again, you won't get to seven."

Mike hung up and smashed the phone to pieces. He looked around for a coffee shop so Michelle wouldn't wonder, found one and bought a small cup. Then he proceeded back to his office. On the way, he stopped at the community restroom in the hall of the fifteenth, checked himself over to see if he was flushed from his anger, ran some cold water and washed his face, took a deep breath and left for his office.

Birch

It was officially his third full day sober. The nurse this morning told him his fever had broken, and he did feel considerably better. He had no headache either. He was still shaking a bit, but not nearly as bad as he had. The nurse told him she had seen worse withdrawal symptoms than his. She felt he hadn't reached critical consumption, yet. Probably due to the fact that he worked and hadn't got to the point where alcohol was more important than income.

Travis knew most of it was due to him only drinking in the evening, but he also knew he made up for not drinking during work by drinking himself into a stupor every single night and all day on his days off. He wondered how he found room in his stomach for food.

He also knew whom he had to thank for where he was. Not only Emberton, but where he was in life, as well. There was a very good chance he would get a second opportunity to win over the love of his life. All he had to do to see the kids was to stay sober and take better care of his body, but he knew Kris wasn't going to be that easy.

Willow had done so much for him already. He wasn't sure if he wanted to ask for more, but that woman was a hell of a physical specimen. If she wouldn't let him use her equipment, he had no problem hiring a physical trainer at one of the local fitness clubs. He was going to win Kris back. He would do what he needed to.

He was determined to make Kris proud of him, and he was just as determined to show Willow that her effort to make him see himself for who he was, was the right thing to do. He was done losing partners. He knew now, although he would never say anything to them, that his previous partners had lost confidence in him. They had requested to be reassigned. He couldn't blame them. He may have done the same.

After he was cleaned up properly, Travis made his way to the lounge area with his laptop and the flash drives that Willow had snuck into his pocket. He poured himself a cup of coffee, declined breakfast, and parked himself in a corner chair. While the drives were loading, he began to think about what they had so far.

They didn't know who this guy was, other than he had a sailboat and called women 'Sweets'. They had a picture, but even that was nondescript. He was young, maybe mid-twenties, but his name or where he was from was still a mystery, unless he told the harbor master the truth, which Travis doubted.

About the victims, they so far had knowledge that they were all women, all Caucasian, all brunettes and all early to mid-twenties. There didn't seem to be any correlation regarding length of hair. Heather Simmons had hair down to the middle of her back, but the two Jane Does were shoulder length, at best.

The man was not only a killer. He was sadistic about it. He killed these women by sticking an ice pick in their brain, and then numbered them with stabs in the torso. A real sick bastard. He was obviously strong enough to hold the woman with one hand while he inserted the ice pick. At least one of those women had clawed him up pretty bad, but according to research, not bad enough for an emergency room visit.

The last victim, Heather Simmons, was found on August second and believed to have been murdered on August first. They wouldn't be able to determine when this spree started until they found number one. Travis didn't think this man was just out to kill women for sport. Travis was certain the man had a specific target in mind. Either he had already killed his target and was using the others to cover his tracks, or his target was still out there.

Travis thought the man's target would be whomever his last victim turned out to be. He didn't think it was Heather. Heather Simmons had one hiccup in her life, and he had been in custody during Willow's phone call. He wasn't their guy. There was at least one more victim to come.

He thought back to the phone call Willow had received from the guy and was repulsed once again by her language and topics, even though he knew her motive for doing so was to make her alluring enough that the man may follow up. So far, he hadn't. At least Willow hadn't mentioned that he had. He didn't think she would keep that from him. The man may have been calling her from the lobby of the hotel he was staying at, so he began to focus on the footage.

Travis scanned, paused and made notes. Scanned, paused and made more notes. This was going to be a difficult way to nail this guy. Nearly everyone walking through the lobby or sitting in the lobby was on their cell phone. Using his zoom feature, he was able to narrow it down to the men who looked most like their guy, but that was still a lot of them. There was a geek convention this week, and every one of the geeks stayed at these three hotels, it seemed. Since the time frame indicated the convention's afternoon break, the lobby was packed.

After he had scanned the footage of each hotel several times, he switched to his email. There were a bunch of well wishes from officers and detectives, which made him feel good, but embarrassed at the same time. Once he was through all of them, he switched to the ones he thought had to do with the case. There was one from the coroner, and he opened it.

The doc noticed bruising in the jaw area of Heather Simmons and believed the killer had cupped her jaw from behind. The pick had been inserted in her right ear canal, so he determined the killer was right-handed. Simmons, not being able to see what she was scratching, probably got his neck or arms. The killer would have been dodging the flinging arms around his head, so he thought Birch and Sturgeon should be looking at the arms.

The toxicology screen came back negative. There were signs of mild alcohol consumption. Wine, to be exact, but no signs of known drugs, so there had either been no attempt to weaken the mind of the victim, or she declined the drugs, causing the fight. The killer seemed to be enjoying the challenge. There were no other obvious signs of a struggle. No other bruises, no other broken bones other than the knuckle or lacerations, and Simmons had at no time been choked.

The second victim had been identified through dental records. The woman's name was Chessly Brassard of Clovis. She had been reported as a missing person on July 27. Her last known location had been Santa Cruz. Her boyfriend, who had filed the missing person report, had been under surveillance the whole time, so was no longer considered a person of interest. The cadaver was not conducive to finding bruises, but once again the right ear canal was the place of insertion. There was no sign of a struggle. This time, however, there were feint traces of heroin and fentanyl.

He closed the email and opened the one from Agent Maxwell. That one had been sent to Sturgeon, the captain and Travis. It was short, just informing them that Special Agent Tanner had ordered all information regarding the case entered into N.C.I.C. However, the body the Coast Guard had found had also been identified. Geri Ann Blankenship, a missing person from San Francisco. Missing since July 23rd. Eight days before the death of Simmons. Travis knew they were running out of time.

The next email was from research, copied to him, but directed at Willow. Her request to have any and all information about the second victim gathered had been approved and sent by Santa Cruz P.D. and Clovis P.D. They further indicated there were no posts or links or private messages on any of Heather Simmons' assorted social media sites that indicated having a relationship with anyone, including Randy Walker.

Apparently, he was being kept out of the loop on some things, because those were the only three emails relating to the case. He was on A.L. though, so he wasn't too surprised. He was actually surprised he got those three.

He sent an email off to Lizzie requesting a return to duty meeting, closed his laptop and walked it and the three flash drives back to his room.

Sturgeon

When Sturgeon got to the station, she found Agent Maxwell already at the desk and, as usual, glued to his laptop. She was convinced there were three priorities in the man's life. His laptop, his tablet and his phone.

"So, why did I need to know about Special Agent Tanner and the N.C.I.C. thing?" she asked.

"It's just a heads-up," he replied. "That usually indicates she's going to become more involved."

"We're going to have to clean off another desk?"

"No. In reality, you'll probably never see her. There are too many resources she has access to at the headquarters. No offense, but she would be handicapped here."

"None taken. I am aware." She sat to begin with her email, when she heard Maxwell's phone ding. He laughed and turned the phone toward her.

[Please have Detective Sturgeon call me when you see her. Thanks]

Willow saw the text was from SALT. Special Agent Lisa Tanner. "Mark, I need you to switch lanes. There has got to be something that connects Simmons, Brassard and Blankenship. We know Heather worked at Southwest Airlines. Dig up what you can on the other two. Anything that connects them to airports. Taxi driver, travel agency, baggage claim. Anything. Brassard lived in

Clovis, and that would have been a hell of a commute. Maybe she was a shuttle driver. Can you do this?"

Mark gave her a thumb up. She pulled out the business card and dialed the number. The phone rang twice and was answered. "Special Agent Tanner."

"Good morning, Special Agent. This is Detective Sturgeon."

"Good morning, Detective. Please call me Lisa. I think we'll be talking more in the future, and I'd like to do away with titles if it won't cause too much culture shock."

"Not at all. It's Willow. What can I do for you?"

"First, I would like to give you my email address. I'd like you to copy me on any info that you get on the case. I don't need victim information, just whatever you get that might be related to the person of interest. I'm assuming we're still thinking about Mr. Sailboat?"

"He's my number one, yes," Willow answered. She entered the email address in her contacts and related hers to Lisa.

"Also, I see that the Brassard victim from the park had traces of heroin and fentanyl. If you could keep me informed on any evidence you might come across that would indicate where the killer obtained that, I'd appreciate it."

"Oh? Is that important? Does it link to other victims?"

"No. Not at all, but that usually is a good income for people who funnel money to domestic terrorists."

"Ah. Gotcha."

"I have the profiler ready with a prelim," Lisa continued. "Do you have a minute, or would you prefer to call back?"

"I am so ready. Let me put you on speaker so Agent Maxwell can hear."

"Okay, I'm transferring now."

The most annoying music Willow ever heard played during the transfer, causing Willow to look at Agent Maxwell with a raised eyebrow, but he assured her he hadn't picked the music.

"Good morning, Detective," said a woman's voice. "This is Agent Whitlock."

"Good morning. You are on speaker phone. I'm here with Agent Maxwell."

"Oh, I'm so sorry for you," Agent Whitlock said with sadness.

"That's very funny, Gemma," Maxwell shot back.

"Detective," Whitlock continued, "first of all, let me explain that profiling is not a perfect art. Are you familiar with the process?"

"Yes," Willow said.

"Okay, then I'll skip profiling 101. Here is who I think you're dealing with. Your killer is a male. He is a sociopath, probably in his early to mid-twenties. He distances himself not only from people, but from civilization in general. In all likelihood, he lives on his boat, or a houseboat, or a shoreline, or even a small island. He may come to shore on occasion to re-supply, but mainly he stays away.

"If he receives mail, I would guess it would be through a Post Office box. You can't get a Post Office box anymore without an address, but that won't help you unless you know the city and box number.

"This man is on a mission. The numbers indicate that he has a final number in mind. I believe the spree he is on is caused by being rejected in his past by a Caucasian brunette. That could have happened at any time in his life, even as an adolescent, and the shame that he felt festered until it manifested itself into its current state. Even if the woman is now a blonde, his mind tells him she's a brunette.

"Sailboats aren't cheap, so we're not talking about an hourly employee here. I don't believe he works at all, based on his social problems. He is probably a son of a wealthy family or has gained an inheritance of some sort. There's also a possibility that the boat's not his.

"The ice pick indicates to me that he either makes his own ice or he buys it in blocks. Maybe he lives too far from shore for cubes to be practical. He could have purchased the knife for a variety of reasons, including cleaning fish.

"His victims, thus far, have all been met by him either on a beach or a shoreline city. There is no indication, and I don't believe there ever will be, of any victims found inland. I don't believe even river cities will be visited. He is an ocean man. The fact that all three victims were found on the central coast area tells me the other three will be, as well. That said, the rejection he suffered also happened there.

"I believe this man wants the woman who rejected him to know what she caused, but I don't believe he wants to be caught. If that's the case, he will need to make himself known and make her known, but he won't do that until he is secure that it will do you no good to have the knowledge. She will be his final victim. He will find a way to make her aware of those he killed, before he kills her. My guess is you will get a phone call or letter telling you where to find the bodies when he has her.

"There is a possibility that the pick and the ear have a deeper meaning in his mind. It's a stretch, but the possibility is there that he got into a huge argument with the rejecter and she may have told him that she 'picked' another several times, and then asked him why he didn't 'listen'.

"Gemma," Maxwell interrupted, "what triggered this now? Any ideas? If it could have happened in his youth, why wait until now?"

"Could be a lot of reasons for that, Mark. Not the least of which is the possibility that he's been institutionalized until recently."

"What's the significance of the numbers?" Willow asked.

"Clueless," Whitlock said. "That could be a lot of things, as well. Length of time they were together. Number of dates. Their ages at the time of the rejection. Until there is a final number, or I have more info, I'm not going to be able to help with that. I will need a correlation between victims. Something other than physical appearance. There must be something that connects them to each other and the final victim."

"Mark's working on that. Sorry for the interruption. Please continue."

"That's pretty much all I have for now, Detective. As we get more information, I might be able to narrow him down better. Sorry."

"Don't be. That's more of a help than you know. Have a great day," Willow finished and hung up. She looked over at the captain's office and saw him alone. She excused herself, stood and walked to, and in, the office. Then just stood there, thinking.

"Detective, are you trying to decide if I need a new interior designer or are you at some point going to tell me why you're here. You're interrupting my coffee."

"Cap..." she started but wondered if she should. Then she decided she would, so she sat in a chair. "Captain. You told me the story of Amy Gaudier having shunned that boy. Shunned, how?"

"What's this about, Sturgeon?"

"Bear with me, Cap. The boy was shunned by her and beat her dog because of it. How did she shun him?"

"He was ten, she was nine. Every boy in school wanted to know her. She was just as gorgeous then as she is now. He wanted her attention, and she told him her dog was better company than he was."

"What color was her hair then?"

"Same as now, and just as wavy."

"So, she 'picked' her dog over him? What kind of damage did she do to the boy that cost her father so much money?"

"Several swings of the club hit the boy in the head. Trevor had to pay a lot of medical bills. He also paid the parents a goodly sum for their silence. He didn't need the bad publicity. He also set up a 2 million-dollar trust fund for the boy. Where are you going with this?"

"Just a sec. What kind of medical bills?"

"She broke his right arm, his left clavicle, opened a gash in his head, broke his nose and busted an eardrum."

"Which ear?"

The captain looked like he'd just come upon an epiphany. "There's no way, Sturgeon. That family moved long ago. The father was transferred to Hawaii."

"Amy was very concerned where I got that picture, Cap. She recognized him in the photo, and she recognized him at the harbor. That was why she was pulling Heather away. She wasn't thinking the guy was trouble. She knew it. She knows who this guy is. She just doesn't know where to find him. Did she know they moved to Hawaii?"

"No. Trevor kept her totally clueless about the family, so as not to bring up bad memories. He had been pretty hard on her, and she was pretty despondent for a long time at being a disappointment to him."

"I don't think Heather was a mark, at first. When he saw her with Amy, though, it was too good to pass up. I think he may have recognized her, too. The profiler believes all the victims are somehow associated with either each other, or his final victim. I need to find out if Amy knew Brassard or Blankenship.

"I think we're going to have many more victims. Maybe one for each year that's passed. I also would bet a month's salary on who the last two will be, since they're a year apart, both brunettes and Caucasian. He'll target Missy for the sole purpose of causing Amy even more hardship. When would that boy have had access to the trust fund?"

"He would need to provide a four-year college degree. The major didn't matter."

"Well, he's one year older than Amy, so..."

The captain picked up his phone, but Willow pushed the button back down, earning her a reproachful look.

"How do you plan to handle this, Cap?"

"I'm going to call Trevor and get the man's name, and you don't want to be hanging up my phone on me, Detective."

"Hear me out."

The captain hung up the phone, folded his arms across his chest and stared at Willow, leaning back in his chair.

"You have said yourself that those kids can take care of themselves. If you want to keep them out of prison, then we need to be coy about our questions. Right now, Amy has no clue where to find this guy. If her dad warns her of impending danger, she will spend her days walking around the marina and harbor, making herself available. Right now, she's spending her time making phone calls and offering rewards.

"If we ask to station officers at the mansion, they're just going to laugh at us. What I need, captain, is to know who this man is, without Amy knowing I know. She has a good deal of money and can buy her way to him. As it stands now, she is focusing that money on the shoreline. If her dad tells her where the family moved to, she will adjust that focus."

The captain waited patiently for her to finish, and then spoke, "There's one problem with your theory, Detective. Missy. If your suspicions are correct, this guy will save Amy for last, which means Missy will be targeted before her. Missy Gaudier goes shopping with her friends three or four times a week.

"I have watched those kids spar in their gym. Sometimes Amy wins, sometimes Missy. If he attacks Missy, she will defend herself to the death of the man. We need to know where those other bodies are, to give their families closure. We need this man alive. The time has come to bring the Gaudiers into the loop.

"Yes, they have money. Trevor will have no problem offering rewards, but those kids? Those kids will be looking for revenge. He killed Amy's best friend. Tony called me yesterday asking for a copy of the picture. I naturally declined, but it did tell me it's now a family affair. We need to talk to those kids and get them to back off if we're to find him alive."

"We know they're targets," Willow interrupted. "Can't we just put them in protective custody? Take them off the street?"

"Pointless. We can't force people into protective custody, and they'll refuse. Even if they agreed, it will just force Tony to step up the pace to get them out. We need to get them to want to help us get those families closure. Anything else we try will just create laughter at the dinner table.

"With your permission, Detective, since I seem to need it, I'm going to call Trevor first, and then their mom. I will get those three kids in the house at the same time. Then you and I are going to visit. Get to work."

Willow didn't even make it back to the desk before her phone rang.

Birch

"I need a ride," Travis said into the phone.

"Geez, you're a pain!" Willow replied.

"I know, right? I called Lizzie, and if I can get there before 10:30 she'll see me."

"You don't think you're rushing this?"

"Nope. I have a shot at getting my life back together. All it's going to take is a better diet. One that doesn't include scotch, among other things. I'm going to miss my pizza, but not so much that I'll let it cost my happiness."

"All right. I'm on my way."

"Thanks, Willow."

Travis hung up and finished packing. He didn't need rehab. The thought of Kris and the kids was all the rehab he needed. Everything he had fit into the one overnight bag he had brought from the house. The only thing left to do was to get his keys from Willow.

Even if Lizzie held him back, he still wasn't coming back to rehab. He would spend every minute he had available working on the house and Kris' garden. Serious weeding was needed there, along with the rest of the yard. The house was far from clean, so that would take some time, too.

He threw the bag strap over his shoulder and began walking to assorted rooms as well as the lobby, shaking hands and wishing the friends he had made swift recovery. He signed himself out, went to the outside benches and called Fred.

The conversation with Fred only lasted five minutes. Fred had been busy with his store manager, but he did agree with Travis that he didn't need to be at rehab anymore. Fred thought the Thursday meetings would work better for Travis, but Travis wanted to go to the Tuesday meeting. That way, if something happened and he couldn't make the Tuesday meeting, then he could make the Thursday one.

Willow made good time. She drove up no more than twenty minutes after he had hung up with her. He threw his bag in the back seat and got in the passenger seat. He guessed Agent Maxwell must have been left at the station. Travis asked for and received his house and car keys, and Willow drove out of the lot toward the station.

"What's the latest?" he asked.

"I think Amy Gaudier and our killer have a history," she replied and then began telling him her thoughts, her conversation with the captain, and her briefing by the FBI profiler.

"It's a possibility," Travis said, "but it sounds like a bit of a stretch. It's worth checking out, though. Did you call five-oh?"

"Why, no, Dan-o. I didn't. I've just found out this morning. I have no idea which city. Plus, I had to pick up your dumb ass."

"If you happen to have to leave before Lizzie is finished with me, I'll grab a taxi. I have a lot of work to do on that house, especially the yard."

"You need a carpet cleaner," Willow said. "I cleaned the kitchen and living room, but that carpet smells like booze. I'm guessing you dropped some."

"You cleaned my house?" Travis asked, a little too loudly.

"No. I cleaned your kitchen and living room. You never listen to me. I didn't clean bedrooms, and I ain't touching that hell hole you call a bathroom. Did you ever use the toilet sober?"

"You didn't have to do that, Willow," Travis said, astonished. He did know the house was a mess. He hadn't cleaned it in quite some time. The last time being just before it became obvious to him Kris wasn't coming back.

"You're an amazing woman, Willow Sturgeon."

"Oh, I know," she replied, looking over at him with that beautiful smile that he'd never seen that first day.

"If I might make a suggestion? Even if it's not okay, I'm going to anyway. You might want to rein in the assumptions and conclusions a bit. Feelings are good, when it comes to the gut instinct, but we work on hard evidence. Never settle. Be certain."

"I appreciate the feedback. I've caught myself thinking the same thing, but this Amy thing sticks in my craw."

"See. That might be your gut. Not your craw, but you have to be sure. Work it."

He exited the cruiser and thanked her for the ride. She went toward the desks and he turned toward Lizzie's office.

He walked into human resources and continued past the cubicles and interview rooms to the rear. Lizzie's door was closed. He checked his phone and saw that he still had a little time before 10:30, and he wasn't sure if he should just walk in.

Travis felt stupid just standing there and looking at the door labeled 'Elizabeth Drake, Ph.D., Behavioral Analysis'. He looked around for the nearest HR rep, trying to decide if that person would know if she was in conference, and when no one caught his eye he decided he would just call her and see if she was busy. He was nearly jolted from his skin when Lizzie slapped his shoulder from behind.

"Oh," Travis said, "I wasn't sure if you were in."

"Watch this," Lizzie said with a warm smile. She raised her hand and knocked on the door. Travis smirked and nodded; he should have tried that. The two walked in and Lizzie urged Travis to a seat.

"Not that one," she said in a raised voice, causing Travis to halt his descent half-way down. She smiled again. He snickered and continued to lower himself into the chair.

"Would you like a cookie, Travis?"

"Oh, no, thank you," he said, patting his stomach.

"Good, because I don't have any," she responded. "So, you would like to return to duty."

Lizzie was the best there was at loosening up people who had to meet with her. She had a great sense of humor, was very pleasant to look at, and always had a nice smile. Lizzie was also nonjudgmental. The downside was you could talk to her all day about how great you were feeling and how ready you were, when you really weren't, and she would see right through it. She would simply tell you to hit the bricks and come back and see her when you could be more honest.

"I'm sure. I'm okay. I have new motivation. I wasn't sure how long I would be on A.L., the captain never said."

"You're not on Administrative Leave, Travis. It was submitted that way, but I changed it to medical leave, per the union mandates. Tell me about this motivation."

Talking about his personal life to Willow or Fred was one thing. Talking about it to someone who could flush his career down the toilet was something else. Lizzie waited patiently while he processed the request.

"I have been given hope. All I need to do is watch my diet and stay away from alcohol."

Lizzie, who had been leaning forward in her chair with her forearms on the desk, sat her pen down, leaned back in her chair and locked eyes with him.

"How about if we just sit and stare at each other for a little while? I don't have any appointments until 10:30. If you haven't told me what's going on with you by then I'll deny your request."

"I'm not trying to be evasive," Travis said. "I have a hard time talking about my personal life. I know nothing leaves this office, but it doesn't make it any easier."

"Life isn't supposed to be easy, Travis. If it were, you wouldn't have a job. Quit with the shame and tell me what's going on."

After several seconds of battling his inner demons, he opened up. "I lost my brother three years ago. He was a forest ranger. Shot by a hunter. I didn't handle it well and took to the bottle. Things just got worse from there. My wife put up with my drinking for over a year. Nothing she said could get me to stop and she finally took our kids and walked out the door. My answer to that was more alcohol.

"My partners kept being taken away from me, and last Monday, I was assigned a new partner. For seven solid hours, she berated and belittled me because of my drinking. I was determined to shut her up and vowed to end my drinking, that night. I realized after about three hours, it wasn't going to happen unless I had some help.

"I called her, that night, and asked her for help, because she had already gone through it with her dad. She came to my house and made me pour out all the alcohol and then took me to rehab. Her dad met me there with a sponsor from A.A. and they walked me through the process.

"Tuesday, my wife came to see me and told me that if I stayed away from the alcohol, I could see my kids again. She also gave me hope that she may be available to rekindle our relationship if she could see that I was taking care of myself. That is my motivation. She will see that I can. Will you clear me? If she sees I'm back to work, she'll loosen up a bit."

"No."

"No?"

"It's one thing, Travis, to stay away from the alcohol at rehab, when you're surrounded by others. It's something quite different when you're alone at home. You stay away from the alcohol for the remainder of the week and come and see me Monday, and we'll talk. Spend some time with your partner. What's her name?"

"Willow Sturgeon."

"Spend some time with Willow, just shooting the breeze, but not too much time. I need to know how you do when you're alone. You need to make an effort for some alone time to fight those demons."

"I will. I can lick this. Nothing thrown at me can deter me. I will get my family back. I will."

"Good. Prove it. Now get out. I have things to do."

Sturgeon

Willow was bored out of her mind. The captain had been on the phone with Trevor Gaudier for some time, and she wasn't leaving until she knew where to find her person of interest. She was eager to get this guy in custody. She was certain he was the killer.

Maxwell was indifferent to the wait. He continued to search his database, looking for more victims, while at the same time checking to see if Heather's phone was active. He searched the web for sailboat designs, trying to line them up with the one in the picture. He web-chatted back and forth with his cohorts at the FBI, asking for this info or that info. He searched for similarities between the victims. Willow felt she should be doing something, too, but she wanted to know, right away, the gist of the captain's conversation.

"Hey, Willow. Can I get a ride home?" Travis asked her as he walked up.

"Can you wait? The captain is talking to Trevor Gaudier, and I want to know where our guy is."

"No problem," he said, pulling up a stolen chair next to her. "Lizzie offered your services. She won't clear me, but if I have a good weekend, I can come back and see her on Monday."

"She offered my services, how?" Willow wanted to know.

"She wants me to spend some time alone to see how I do, but she also wants me to spend time with my partner, when she's available, to break up the desire. If there is any."

"That's kind of her. I'm not going to be available tonight, Travis. I won't get home until very late."

"Friday night dates. Aw, yes. I remember those."

Before Willow could respond, she saw the captain hang up and bolted for his office. He was shuffling papers and looking like he was about to leave.

"What did Mr. Gaudier say?" she asked as she crossed the threshold.

"It was a good try, Detective, but the boy Amy thrashed is not your guy. He is in Italy with Trevor and has been for two weeks. Trevor is working with him on investing techniques."

Willow's shoulders slumped. She was back to square one. Travis was right. She was too assuming. She had a sudden feeling of insecurity. Maybe she wasn't cut out to be a detective. "That's a pretty firm alibi," she said. She mentally slapped herself to shed the insecurity. She could do this. She knew she could. "I still think Amy knows who this guy is, Cap. It eats at me."

"I'll give her a call and ask her if she'll fess up, but I don't want you going out there and pressuring her. Let me rephrase that. I don't want you going out there."

Willow's frustration mounted, but she left the captain's office and told Mark she would be back after dropping Travis off.

"Bingo!" Mark blurted. "Every one of the victims went to Stanford. They all graduated this year."

"Amy graduated last year, but that doesn't mean anything. She's his target. I can feel it. Get me everything you can, Mark. Majors, friends, everything they will tell you. We'll get a court order, if necessary. I'm driving Travis home. Then I'll come right back."

When she returned, she shared with Mark the conversation she'd had with the captain, and then she and Mark left for the park. On the way, she explained that she was looking for a backpack or anything else they could find that might be evidence.

She was going to show the picture around the marina again, as well, but this time she was going to try to get someone with knowledge to see if they could determine the type of vessel based on the limited view they had, though she didn't think she was going to be successful.

For the next two hours, she and Mark canvassed the entire park and marina and talked to every boat owner they could find, from sailboats to speedboats, to fishing boats, and they came up empty. There just wasn't enough of the boat visible in the photo for anyone to even hazard a guess. All they got when they asked if it was a Nicholson was 'maybe'. They found nothing at the park, either.

"Maybe we're going about this all wrong," Mark said.

"I'm listening," offered Willow.

"There must be a boat dealership around here somewhere, right?"

"Oh. Good idea, Mark. Taylor Boat Sales is not too far from here. Someone there has to be able to recognize something in this photo."

She and Mark stopped at Noodles and More for lunch and then proceeded to Taylor Boat Sales and, once again, split up and began talking to salesmen, managers, and potential customers, and, once again, came up blank. All they got when they mentioned or asked if it was a Nicholson was a bunch more maybes. This was a hollow lead. The boat was a lost cause, and she would have to focus on the man.

"Any luck with the security footage?" she asked as they were driving back to the station.

"Nah! They were too crowded. I am convinced, though, that no one talks to anyone, anymore. They can't get off their phones long enough."

Willow and Mark next went to the airport. They talked to employees, assorted executives, baggage claim, flight attendants and pilots. No one had seen the man before or knew of any enemies Heather had. No one knew the other two victims, either.

It was late afternoon when they got back to the station, and Willow made her notes in the files, read her email, sent one off with the details of their miserable day to Lisa, and then began cleaning her area, mind still swirling. She kept trying to figure out this photo. How did this photo get taken, printed and stuffed in the Armoire in the little time there was after Amy left Heather? Was this intentionally done? Was this Heather providing a person of interest before she went back to meet the guy? There had been a printer at Heather's.

Willow called the coroner.

"Coroner. This is Jack."

"Hey, Jack. It's Detective Sturgeon. Is the doc handy?"

"No. He left. Maybe I can help. Or... you know, if you just want to talk."

"Jack. Was Heather Simmons wearing a swimsuit under her clothes?"

"No. Red bra and pink thong with black trim."

"Okay. Thanks, Jack... and, Jack? Do you know what LGBTQ is?"

"Yes."

"I'm the L."

"Oh," Jack said with sadness.

"Have a nice weekend, Jack."

"I never would have guessed that," Mark said after she hung up with Jack. He continued to pack his gear.

"I'm not. I just don't date co-workers and I've found it saves them a lot of time and effort coming up with new lines, and it saves me a lot of energy fending them off."

Mark laughed as he made his way down the stairs.

∞∞∞∞

When Willow got home, she pulled into her garage and closed the garage door. She opened her trunk and pulled out the bags from her shopping outing, and went into the house, leaving the front door locked. Everyone knew Fridays and Saturdays were her personal time, so there wouldn't be any workouts tonight.

Willow went into her bedroom, stripped down and began pulling out items from the bag and removing tags. She donned the skin-tight jeans and a blouse that exposed as much as she dared with a hem that fell just below the waistline. Next, she tied up her hair as tight as she could and pulled out the brown wig, donning it as well, tucking in the loose blond strands. She checked herself out in the mirror, attached her off-duty to her hip and made her way back to her car.

Birch

Travis finished cleaning his bathrooms and made the decision he would start tomorrow morning on the weeding of Kris' garden, and the yard, in general. He went to the refrigerator and cleaned out all the old pizza and removed the ice cream from the freezer, sending both down the garbage disposal. After dark tomorrow, he would clean the refrigerator.

Chores done, he went to his room and changed into the most comfortable clothes he could find, attached his nine to his hip and climbed into his beater. He drove to the harbor, intending to watch for the sailboat and end this problem. Hopefully he would be able to repay Willow's kindness with an arrest.

When he reached the harbor, he parked and took a few minutes to look around for a place close to where Willow had said the boat docked. Close enough that he could reach the boat while the man was tying it off, but not so close that the man could see him and bolt back out to sea.

The area directly south was wooded and the dock butted right up against those woods. How convenient was that! Travis locked up the beater, grabbed his 'cuffs, made sure he had his badge and ID and began the walk, changing direction several times to get past the buildings and rail units.

He got to the woods and worked his way toward the dock area and began searching around for the clearest view. It was obvious this was some sort of hideout for the dock workers, because it was littered with empty beer cans, cigarette packs, plastic wrappers and rags everywhere. Travis moved, studied, moved and studied until he was sure he had the ideal spot.

He was out of sight, but still had a clear enough view to see the boat angling in, the pier, the benches on the pier and the access way. One of those benches had a brunette sitting on it with her feet curled under her, reading a book. She would look up on occasion and stare out to sea, but mostly she was engrossed in her novel. Travis wished he was closer to warn her away, but it would be just his luck the boat would pick that time to slip in. He made the decision that he could get there before any harm came to the girl.

He spun his head to the right. Had he caught some movement? He stared and listened but guessed it must have been an animal. Nothing was there. He looked back at the pier. The benched brunette had put her novel away. It was getting too dark for her to read, and the lighting on this end was poor.

An hour passed. Then two. The bottle of water Travis had brought was expended, but he kept vigilant. He was troubled by the brunette. She still sat there. Unmoving. Staring out to sea. Was she waiting for the same man Travis was? Was this a pre-arranged date? Had he inadvertently stumbled on the perfect bait? He felt a certain amount of glee; suddenly certain the sailboat was coming. The brunette sat up, straightening and looking hard at the horizon. Travis heard it first. The nearly silent humming of the motor. Then he caught sight of it. A white sailboat, slowly making its way in.

His sailor would be focusing on the brunette, so Travis began to slowly edge forward, checked his off-duty, his badge and his ID. He looked again at the brunette. She was now sitting back, with her arms stretched along the bench, her legs crossed, and a flippant look on her face. Travis looked hard at the woman. Did he know her? She looked vaguely familiar.

The man tied off his boat and began to secure items on the deck. Travis began walking with determination toward the pier.

A black streak flew past him, headed right at the sailboat. Completely black. Head to toe. The figure was moving fast and Travis knew he wasn't going to be able to catch it. He thought of shouting for the figure to stop, but he wasn't ready to out himself. He began running after it. The figure hit the pier and was full-out, charging the slip the boat was docking at.

The brunette noticed the figure and was up, running at the boat to warn the man. She reached in her back pocket, but the figure was on her, sweeping her feet from under her. The brunette went down with a thud. The black figure didn't miss a beat and continued her charge, but the brunette was up and chasing.

The man on the boat had heard the commotion and was frantically trying to untie his ropes. He had already restarted his engine. Travis needed to hurry. He would have to deal with the other two later. He needed to stop this boat.

The brunette caught the figure and bulldogged it to the wood of the pier. The figure elbowed the brunette and her head flew back. The figure twisted and delivered a blow to the face of the brunette, but the brunette dodged most of the punch.

Travis ran as fast as he could, but he knew he wasn't going to make it. The man was already at the controls and the boat was backing out. Travis ran down the slip, trying to decide if he could get close enough to jump on the boat without falling in the drink. It was a lost cause. The boat pilot made eye contact with him as he was backing away. He brandished a wide smile. It was too dark to get the numbers and facing the wrong direction to get the name. Travis reached for his phone and quickly snapped a picture.

He turned back toward the pier and saw the fight was still going strong. The brunette had the mysterious figure in a full nelson, but the figure threw both arms straight up and both feet flew straight out, pulling right out of the nelson. Its right foot came straight up and caught the brunette flush under the chin, and she flew flat on her back. The figure jumped up, but the brunette's left foot swept the other's feet and it went down with a hard thud.

The brunette was on it, knee to the neck and gun to the head. Travis saw the glitter of handcuffs on the brunette's belt. He reached the two combatants and put his weapon in the temple of the brunette.

"Police officer," he said. "I'll take that gun."

"Thanks for the help, Travis," Willow said, sending a shock through Travis. "Will you cuff her, please?"

"Her?" Travis asked as he placed the cuffs on the prone figure. Willow holstered her weapon and stood the figure up. She removed the black head covering, and Travis was staring at yet another brunette.

"Amy Gaudier," Willow said, between huffs and puffs, "You're under arrest for interference in a felony investigation, and battery on a police officer. You have the right to remain silent, so do so. Don't answer any questions until your attorney arrives."

"What the hell kind of Miranda was that?" Travis asked.

"Special circumstances," Willow stammered out. She handed Gaudier over to Travis, and bent over, taking several deep breaths, then walked over to the bench and sat, still sucking air. Travis walked Gaudier over and sat her on the bench, too. She didn't seem to be breathing at all. Willow dialed her phone. Travis knew she was calling for transport.

"Hey, Cap. Sorry to bother you at home. Travis and I are at the harbor. We were waiting for the boat. It did come in, but before we got to it, Amy interfered. What do you want me to do with her? You were right, by the way. She kicked the shit out of me."

After a short pause, she continued, "No. I only asked him along for a second set of eyes. He didn't partake in the investigation, and he didn't get the shit kicked out of him."

Another pause. "My mouth is bleeding, I have a knot starting on my head, I took several blows to the ribs, but I don't think any are broken. Did I mention she kicked the shit out of me?"

Another pause. "Okay. I'll wait right here. Right in this spot, sitting on this bench. Right here." She hung up her phone, leaned back, took several deeper breaths and looked over at Amy.

"Uncle Chet seems to be a little pissed off with you, Amy. He's coming and bringing your mom with him."

Amy's eyes went from passive to aggressive. "You arrested me. You have to take me to jail."

"Yeah," Willow said. "I'd rather go to jail than face my mom, too. Too bad, so sad. She's on her way.

"Were you able to get anything?" Willow asked Travis.

"Not much," Travis answered. "I got a picture of the boat, but it was pretty far away and dark. Maybe your FBI friend can do something with it."

"What's his name, Amy?" Willow asked.

Amy hung her head and stared away from them toward the other end of the pier. She was obviously weighing her options, but after several seconds, came to a decision.

"Blake Manning."

"That wasn't Mike Sanders?" Willow nearly screeched.

"Who the hell is Mike Sanders?" Amy asked.

"Who is Blake Manning to you?" Travis asked.

"A nobody. Something I scrape off my shoe after walking through a pasture."

"If you would have been up-front with me," Willow said, "he would already be in custody, the fear of him striking again would be gone, and you wouldn't be in this position. It's a distinct possibility that it's you he's after, considering all the victims so far are Caucasian brunette Stanford graduates. If he's as evil as I think he is, he would have gone after your sister first, though. You would have had a hard time living with that."

"He already tried that. It's not me he's after. Maybe you should have shown that picture to Missy."

"I need the story, Amy," Willow continued. "I need to nail this guy."

"He tried the date-rape thing on Missy at college. She saw his reflection and left. She put a notice up at school. He was kicked out. It effectively ruined his life. He swore revenge, yada, yada, yada."

"Was he arrested?"

"Nope," Amy said, looking at Willow and showing disgust. "That's not how the law works, Detective. By the time the Palo Alto police got their warrant, the evidence was gone and it was her word against his."

"If there was no evidence, how could the university kick him out?"

"Stanford doesn't give a rat's ass about police policies. They have their own investigation. They have zero tolerance for that shit. Not to mention who the complainant was, who her dad is and how much money he has funneled into Stanford. He killed Heather, Detective. You have your restraints and policies. I don't. You need to stay out of this and let me handle it."

"That's not going to happen, Amy. I know you're angry, and I am truly sorry for your loss, but this isn't a vigilante society. You need to stay out of this and let us handle it."

"Well, you're doing a bang-up job. She's been dead almost a week, and what do you have? Nothing."

"What would we have if you had been forthcoming in the first place? Stand up. I don't want your mom seeing you in handcuffs."

Travis was listening intently and soaking all the information in. He made notes on the man's name, Palo Alto, Stanford and everything else that was said. He had no idea why Willow was being so passive about the ass-whooping she'd taken, but he guessed she would tell him if she had a mind to.

He felt he must be missing something. Procedure was procedure. Amy Gaudier should be on her way to the lockup. He and his fellow detectives and patrolmen didn't care how rich someone was. You do the crime, you do the time. Period. He had a feeling Willow liked the woman or had some future plan to gain her trust and get her aid in finding the guy.

Willow didn't look all that much like a fashion model right now. She had taken off the wig and unfolded her curls, and they were all disheveled. Her mouth was bloody, despite her attempts to clean it. She had a shoeprint in the middle of her blouse, and Travis thought she was going to have a nice shiner in the morning.

He gained a lot of respect for her, though. She stuck with it and corralled the woman.

Travis saw the captain approaching with a woman he didn't know, that he guessed was Amy's mom. The captain slowed, but the woman charged on. Amy started to stand, but the woman just pointed at her and Amy sat back down. The woman walked past Amy, past Travis and stopped in front of Willow, looking over the injuries.

"Do you need medical attention, Detective?" the woman asked.

"I'll be fine," Willow answered.

"If you'd like to file charges against my daughter, I will guarantee you a guilty plea."

"Mom," Amy said.

"Shut up!" the woman replied angrily.

"I would rather have a guarantee that Amy's interference will stop," Willow said.

"You have it," the woman finished. She walked over to her daughter, pulled out her phone, paged through a couple items and held it up for Amy to see.

"No, Mom," Amy screeched, and began sobbing.

The woman walked back to Willow. "Heather's funeral is at 10 tomorrow morning, Detective. Then we are having a little get-together at the house. I would like you to come." She hadn't waited for an answer, but instead turned and walked to Travis. "Who are you?"

"Uh... Travis Birch, Detective Travis Birch."

"Are you injured?"

"No. I wasn't involved."

"You should have been," the woman said, "I would like you to come, as well." Once again, without waiting for Travis to gather himself for a response, she turned and walked to her daughter, instructing her to stand up, which Amy did. She walked Amy over to stand in front of Willow, crossed her arms and stared at her.

"I'm sorry for my behavior, Detective," Amy said. Willow looked stunned and didn't know how to respond, but there wasn't time to consider. The mother grabbed her daughter's arm and ushered her toward the parking lot.

"We'll talk about this unannounced action at the wake," the captain said angrily. He followed Amy and her mother, leaving Travis and Willow wondering what had just happened.

"Cap, what was on that phone?" Willow asked.

"Three words. 'On my way'."

Sandman

Mike laid his pencils down on the easel and turned toward his desk. He looked out the window as he did and noticed those two detectives walking through the parking lot toward the entrance. Now what? He had faxed a bill of sale. What the hell could they want with him now?

He walked out of his office and past Michelle to the railing overlooking the vast lobby. The two walked in the door but didn't turn toward the elevator. Instead they made an abrupt right turn and entered Human Resources, one of them pulling a paper from his jacket.

Shit! Court order. Fucking hell! He darted back into his office just as Michelle was answering the phone. He grabbed his jacket and turned to head back out.

"Just a minute, sir," Michelle said to him, but he ignored her, exited his offices and turned right toward the staircase. He wasn't going to use the elevator, which would deposit him in the lobby. He would use the staircase, which had an exit to the parking garage and his car.

"DEA! Stop where you are."

What the hell? Michelle was DEA? Shit! He bolted through the staircase door and rapidly jumped down the stairs two and three at a time. He heard the door open behind him as his beautiful, passive, may-I-get-you-anything secretary was running after him. Bitch! Good luck catching me in those heels.

He was hit in the head as he turned down the next flight by one of those heels, then by the other. He heard her stockinged feet closing behind him. He had a lot of flights to go and he knew he would have to turn on her soon. She was faster than he was without her heels.

When he reached the next landing, he found himself unable to move as she had jumped the rail and wrapped herself around him like saran wrap. She was slamming her heel into the back of his knee, trying to collapse his leg, forcing him down. He fell to one knee but forced his superior strength against her and shoved her hard into the wall. He heard the air leave her lungs, causing her to loosen her hold.

Mike forced his hands between his torso and hers and pried for all he was worth. He was free. He lifted her head and slammed it into the wall, then stood and began again down the staircase, but she kicked his foot and he tumbled down that flight, landing hard on the landing floor. He looked back up at her, but she was trying to shake herself alert, so he jumped up again and raced down the stairs, now with a painful limp.

After several more flights, he finally reached the garage door, barged through on the run and charged at his car. The door flew open again behind him and he heard the padded feet on the cement closing fast. He knew he wasn't going to make it into the car before she caught up. He would have to end the chase here. He unhooked his belt and pulled it free, turning on his secretary.

Pain... excruciating pain... make it stop. Make it...

Mike woke face down on the garage floor. He had no idea how long he had been out, but apparently not that long. He heard a conversation going on, but he couldn't make out the words. His arms were behind him and something was on his wrists. Handcuffs? Was he in handcuffs? His eyes began to focus, but he could only see two things. Wires on the ground. Thin wires. Stocking feet, and the stockings were shredded.

He still couldn't make out the words, but the conversation continued. His brain was jumbled. Jurisdiction. That was it. Michelle and the detectives were arguing jurisdiction. Cars were coming. SUVs. Black SUVs. Two of them, and they stopped when they reached him. More arguing. They were DEA and they were joining Michelle against the detectives.

∞∞∞∞

His life was over. Mike knew that now. He had been in this cell for nearly a day. Zachary naturally refused him counsel. He would need to get his own. In the meantime, he was waiting for the court-appointed guy fresh out of law school. His mind couldn't register a way his future could look promising. No job. No girlfriend. When he had called Marie to get bail, her questions were endless. When he finally told her he was arrested for drugs, basically, she had simply said, "See ya."

Footsteps outside the cell drew his attention as he sat on his cot. A very tall and broad corrections officer stopped at his cell, looking in at him. The door opened and he was instructed to stand up and turn around, which he did. He was handcuffed and taken from the cell to another door.

He was walked through that door to a cacophony of noise, mumbled conversations and laughter. Uniformed officers, among others, were just standing around drinking coffee or water and talking. Something he may never get to do again. Manning. *If I ever get out of here, I'm going to kill you.*

Mike was led to a room with a table and chairs and a camera, sat on one of the chairs, and had his hands uncuffed and re-cuffed to the table. The corrections officer then left the room, leaving him staring at a pasty looking wall.

The door opened and closed behind him, and he turned his head to see a middle-aged man in a very nice suit. The man introduced himself as Mike's court-appointed attorney, and Mike was a little surprised. The man looked confident and knowledgeable. He explained that the prosecuting attorney was on the way and he went over some basic do's and do not's. He explained that he had seen their evidence and they had a proposition that he should consider.

Before he could get the proposition out, the door opened and closed again, and his attorney joined him on his side of the table. A suited man and woman walked to the other side and sat facing him.

"Mr. Sanders, my name is David Sounter and this is Special Agent Darcy Stanton, with the DEA. I believe you know her as Michelle. Before we get started, can we get you anything to drink? Non-alcoholic, of course."

Mike shook his head. "I'm good."

"Okay, then. We're recording now," Sounter said as he pushed a button on a remote.

"Mr. Sanders, have you been read your constitutional rights?"

Mike nodded, but his attorney explained he would have to speak, so he did. "Yes."

"Do you understand the charges against you, Mr. Sanders?"

"Nope," Mike answered.

"Seven cases of sexual assault, fleeing a federal agent, assault on a federal agent, and six cases of accessory to murder."

"What the fuck are you talking about? I don't know anything about any murders." After a slight hesitation, Mike saw a way he could walk away from this. "On the other hand, maybe you should offer me something and then maybe I can tell you who your killer is."

His attorney cupped his face with his hands, and Sounter just smiled.

"I appreciate your candor, Mr. Sanders. However, Blake Manning, the name you were going to give us, is nowhere to be found and can't corroborate your story. Let's start at the beginning." Sounter pulled seven 11x7 photographs from his bag and laid them out in front of Mike, facing him. He recognized them all.

"Who might these ladies be?" Mike asked. "Are these the murder victims?"

"Let's not get cute, Mr. Sanders. You know very well who they are. These are the seven women who have accused you of drugging them and assaulting them. We tested them all. All seven showed traces of fentanyl-laced heroin. The exact mixture, in fact, that we found this morning in your home.

"Special Agent Stanton is ready to testify that she ordered you to stop and you didn't. She also has quite a few photographed bruises from when you shoved her into a wall.

"The FBI has corroborating testimony that your boat was docked at the Carpel Harbor and this bill of sale that you faxed to the Charmaine police department is bogus. It's not even signed by a notary, and there is no such person in the FBI database."

He leaned forward. "Are you done being stupid? Are you ready to talk to us? Because if you're not, you should know, I'll ask for the death penalty."

"What do you want from me?" Mike asked.

"Your supplier and where to find him," Sounter said.

"Along with the password to your phone," added Stanton. "So that we can check if you really do know someone named Blake Manning."

"What do I get?"

"I take the death penalty off the table," Sounter answered.

"Not good enough. He'll just have someone inside kill me. There's no way, with those charges, you're going to get the death penalty. I'm not stupid. I want a walk. Protective custody."

"I thought you said you weren't stupid. That is not going to happen. I can ask for seclusion."

Mike asked for and received a few minutes alone with his attorney. The recorder was switched off. When the suits came back in he was still not overly confident, but his attorney did the talking, with the recorder back on.

"My client can offer you even more information than you're asking for. In return, we want all the accessory charges dropped and a guarantee of a twenty-five-year maximum sentence in a minimum-security facility."

"No dice. If the information is good, I'll drop the accessory charges, and if he signs a confession on the rest, I'll ask for a maximum of forty years in a protective wing. That's all you're going to get. Take it or we'll see you in court."

"How about this? Suppose my client agrees to testify in both the cases. His life will then be in serious danger. You guarantee him immunity and protective custody and he'll guarantee you two convictions."

"If he signs a confession," Sounter replied, "we'll present it to the judge."

"You present it to the judge and we'll talk about the signed confession," Mike answered.

"You're not really in a position to make demands, Mr. Sanders. You write it up and sign it. You give Special Agent Stanton your password, and I'll speak to her on your behalf about her charges. You're in the deep end of the pool, Mr. Sanders. Are you ready to swim?"

Sturgeon

Willow wasn't certain she wanted to do this. She had never met Heather Simmons so going to the woman's funeral just seemed wrong. She'd wrestled with it all night last night, and through breakfast this morning. The deciding factor was the very remote possibility that her suspect would be there, with Missy out of the mansion.

Missy was the final victim. Willow was sure of it. Blake Manning had been seven units shy of his degree when he was kicked out. If all he cared about was getting his revenge, he wouldn't care how many people were around. With Missy dead he would probably just give himself up. His revenge would be ended. Willow just needed to stay close to Missy, without anyone having a cow about it. Missy would be the seventh victim.

Willow sat outside Travis' house. The two of them were going to ride together. She felt she had waited too long, so she picked up her phone and sent a text.

[What the hell, Travis? You said 5 minutes].

She wasn't sure how the pick figured in, but that profiler sounded fairly certain it played a part. Perhaps he was placing the drug in a mixed drink and Missy had brought the ice pick. If he had killed these women with Missy's pick, he would consider that all the sweeter. There was nothing in the Palo Alto report about it, but at that time it would have hardly been relevant.

The investigation had been intense. Palo Alto had interviewed ten other women known to Manning and they had performed every trick in the book to get the guy to confess, without coercing, but he had an attorney at every interview. They even had one of their more attractive officers strike up a relationship with the man but had no luck.

Travis finally came out the door, and despite his bulk, Willow thought he cleaned up rather well. She was impressed. A black suit that was obviously a rental, since he couldn't have anticipated the need with his most recent frame. She picked up her scarf from the seat, and he climbed in.

"You look nice, Travis," she greeted him.

"I wish I could say the same for you. Can you even see out of that eye? Do you want me to drive?"

"No. It's ugly, but I can see."

"Hopefully, there won't be any kids there. You might frighten them. No offense."

"Gee. How could I possibly take offense at that?" She held up her scarf to show him she had it covered.

"How are the ribs?"

"Sore, but not broken," she answered. "Listen, Travis. I know I didn't say so last night, but I appreciate your attempt to stop the guy. I was a little occupied."

"We know who he is, now. It won't take long to track him down. I called Palo Alto this morning. They're going to try to find the detectives who handled the case and see if they have a last known."

"Just so we're clear, in case the captain asks. This was a joint effort. Neither one of us went there without backup."

"No worries. He probably won't think to ask, since we were both there, but yeah. I'll let him know you were smoking a joint."

She swatted him across the chest, with an attempt at a smile, but even that facial movement was painful. Travis looked over at her, and she knew he was about to criticize her choice of wardrobe, but it was all she had that was black. It was a knee length dress, which was fine, but it was way too chesty for a funeral.

"What?" she asked, letting him know she noticed.

"Not that I want to sound like your dad, but are you looking to get the attention from all the men there?"

"I know, but it's all I have."

"Well, I'll be sure to stand next to you so I can keep an eye on things."

"You just keep your eyes off my things. You know I still have Kris' number, right?" she asked, and he laughed heartily.

"Besides," she said, once again holding up the scarf. "Did you remember to get a card?"

"He reached into his jacket pocket and pulled out an envelope. "I brought a few bucks for the kitty. She'll have enough cards to send thank-you cards for. Besides, I seriously doubt she's paying a penny for this funeral."

"Well, that's true enough, I guess."

When they arrived, a good deal of people were already standing about. They were broken in groups of three or four, mostly. The casket was hovering over its final resting place, and this was no pine box. This was an elaborate casket, and Willow knew Travis was right. Amy was footing the bill.

Willow draped the black scarf over her head and adjusted it to cover as much of the ugliness as she could, and tucked the balance into her exposed cleavage, pulling it as wide as it would go. She adjusted her rear view and thought she was as decent as she would get, and the two of them exited her car and walked to the groups.

Amy and Missy were sandwiching a tall man who she guessed was Trevor Gaudier, and they were talking to the captain and another man she didn't know. She searched the rest of the groups and found Mrs. Simmons surrounded by four or five people offering condolences. Lauren Gaudier was standing beside her and shaking hands with the well-wishers. She nudged Travis, and the two of them walked toward the mother.

Lauren Gaudier busted from the group to head her and Travis off. She clamped a hug on Willow, and then Travis, looking back over her shoulder at Mrs. Simmons.

"Detectives. I would consider it a personal favor if you would refrain from informing Mrs. Simmons of Missy's involvement. Missy hasn't been told, herself. She would come unglued, and we don't want a scene here."

"That's not a problem, Mrs. Gaudier..." Willow started.

"Lauren."

"Lauren. Please call me Willow. We won't be offering any names. Even of the suspect."

"Thank you, Willow. After you offer your condolences I would like to introduce you to my husband. How are you feeling?"

"I'm fine, Lauren. You don't need to worry about me. If you'll excuse us for a moment?"

Lauren stood aside and Willow and Travis went to Mrs. Simmons.

"Have you found my daughter's killer yet, Detective?" Mrs. Simmons sobbed out.

"Mrs. Simmons. I do have news for you, if you wish to call me tomorrow. Today, we have come to pay respect to Heather. We are not on duty, and don't have our files."

"I'm sorry," Mrs. Simmons responded through her tears. "I appreciate you coming and I know Heather would, too." Willow gave her a hug and Travis patted her shoulder, then the two went back to Lauren Gaudier, who walked them toward the family. Willow realized the man she didn't recognize from behind was Tony.

"Trev, honey," Lauren said, "this is Detective Willow Sturgeon and Detective Travis Birch."

"Detective," Trevor said, shaking hands with Travis. To her surprise, he repeated the greeting to her. What? No hug? He did pay a lot of attention to her face, especially her eye. Willow didn't miss his casual glance at Amy. Nor did she miss the shame Amy felt at the glance. After Tony and Missy slapped a hug on her, Amy walked up and hugged her.

"I'm really sorry, Detective," she said.

"Willow."

"May I have a word?" Trevor asked, sticking his arm out toward her. She walked under it, so as not to be rude, and he walked her away from the group.

"You knew that my wife would have bailed Amy out within the hour last night. That doesn't detract from the kindness you showed in calling Chet. I want you to know I appreciate it. Amy has decided she needs anger management therapy."

Yeah, Willow thought. *I'll just bet she's the one who decided that.*

"Chet has agreed to find some sort of community service she can perform. I would like you to know that we are at your disposal to help find this gentleman. Amy has offered to use her considerable funds for rewards that lead to conviction, and I'm offering my influence to find him. I'm afraid Amy will have to perform her function from the house, via phone and wire transfers.

"I, on the other hand, am at the department's disposal. I have many resources available, not the least of which is a yacht."

"I really appreciate that, Mr. Gaudier, but..."

"Trevor. Mr. Gaudier died twenty-two years ago."

"Trevor, we have resources ourselves, and, in the event you were unaware, the FBI is also involved. I do appreciate the offer, though."

"I understand. I'm not Amy. I'm not going to hire a hitman to take the gentleman out, but our family doesn't ask for help a lot. So, when we do, that help comes hard and fast. Amy has found a sailboat. It has been abandoned a little south of here in San Pablo Bay. She has people disguising themselves as fishermen, anchored on all four sides. I am asking you to be my friend, Willow, and come for a short cruise on my yacht after the wake. Chet is okay with it as long as you don't ruin the evidence. It's not in your jurisdiction."

"I would love to go for a ride on a yacht. Would I be able to bring my friend Travis along?"

"You may ask anyone along you like, except Amy."

Birch

Travis had been to several funerals in his life, but he couldn't remember any that had the number of people attending that this one did. Willow had asked him to help her by keeping his eyes open for a cocky killer. She was certain he had only one more victim in mind, and she didn't think he would care if he was caught, after the fact.

According to the information Amy had provided, the man's life had been destroyed by Missy. There wasn't much left of his dreams and aspirations. Watching for him, though, had been nearly impossible with all the attendees.

Catching the man would only be half the challenge. They would still need to prove he was the killer and getting him to volunteer his DNA for a match with Heather Simmons' fingernails would be difficult, and even then, that would only prove that Heather had scratched him. The ADA certainly had her work cut out for her. That wasn't his problem. His problem was catching the guy.

Now he stood in the living room of the Gaudier house and calling this place a house was a good laugh. Three stories high, twelve bedrooms, four of which were masters, six baths, a library, a den, two living rooms and a kitchen that he could fit his bedroom in. Not to mention a basement that had been turned into a gym. The dining room was as big as the bedrooms and had a rather elaborate table that looked like it could be adjusted to handle the entire detective division.

That was just inside. He hadn't yet been given a tour of the grounds, but they were huge, as well. Travis had seen the largest swimming pool ever, plus what looked like a guest house. Saving Mrs. Gaudier from insanity was a pool company, a landscaping company and a housekeeping crew, all of which were once weekly. Travis thought if he worked hard and kept his nose to the grindstone, he might be able to afford the toaster.

The house itself was very intimidating. He was surprised, though, by the manners and kindness of the Gaudiers. That much money would normally turn the family into a bunch of greater-than-thou assholes and spoiled brats, but that wasn't the case here. Every single Gaudier passed out hugs like they were candy and could never be seen without a smile. Unless they were in the process of kicking the shit out of detectives, of course.

There were close to a hundred people in this house, right now. Travis kept his eyes on the captain as often as he could, but his main focus was on Willow. She moved around a lot, but not really due to socializing. He never saw Willow more than five feet from Missy, even following her around like a puppy dog.

Tony was on the back deck entertaining several guests, Amy and Missy were running back and forth from the kitchen, with Willow's help, passing out goodies, Trevor was usually seen near the captain, and Lauren never strayed too far from Mr. and Mrs. Simmons. There was certainly nothing dysfunctional about this family.

When the party reached the three-hour mark, people started filing out to go home, including Mr. Simmons, who would be handling some attendees at their own house. Lauren convinced Mrs. Simmons to stay the night, and the two of them were stationed at the door, thanking the attendees as they left. Amy, Missy and Willow were beginning to clean up, with Tony handling the deck. Trevor and the captain were both on the phone, and he wasn't sure what to do with himself. He decided to go help Tony.

It was a little after two in the afternoon when he heard a helicopter. He looked up and saw it descending onto the backyard area. Trevor, the captain and Willow came out of the house, gathered him, and they all began walking to the landing mosquito. Trevor climbed up front with the pilot and the rest in the back.

"I want to make myself perfectly clear," the captain said. "You touch nothing with your hands. I'll give you 30 minutes on the boat, and then I'm calling it in. If you need to open drawers, don't use the handles. Understood?"

"All we need is the knife, the pick, or any reference to Missy or the victims," Willow said, and the captain nodded his understanding.

Travis was in awe once again at Trevor Gaudier's fortune. His own helicopter and pilot, his own yacht, that was big enough to land a helicopter on, but he really failed on one thing. The helicopter and yacht were piloted by the same woman. What a cheapskate.

"Why are we even doing this, Willow?" Travis asked.

"I have to know if this is his boat. If it's not, then we're still looking for a man and a boat. If it is, we're looking for a man. The registration will tell us where to find him."

"He abandoned the boat. He'll know we're coming and he'll take up residence somewhere else."

"Maybe, but we'll have enough for a warrant, and we can tear that house apart. Don't take any pictures. We do this old style."

Trevor and the pilot lowered a ramp down onto the sailboat. Willow borrowed a pair of gloves from the pilot and Travis a pair from Trevor. Just as they were about to descend, the captain stopped them.

"If you plant anything on that boat that ruins this case, I'll fire you both." Willow took off her scarf and handed it to the pilot and then held her arms out, looking at the captain and indicating her attire. Travis laughed and the two descended onto the sailboat.

Travis found the registration right away and began writing down everything that was pertinent. The name on the registration was Michael Sanders. Willow was walking and searching outside the cabin, looking for and finding several bench cabinets. Travis left her to it and went inside the cabin. It was obvious, based on what he found, that this man was going to report his boat stolen. There were no personal items, but items needed for sailing were out in plain sight.

He had only got through the second drawer when he heard Willow's excited call from outside. He walked out to see her one good eye was bulged and she had a huge smile on her face.

"Get off the boat," she said, hurrying to the ramp. Travis followed her and climbed behind her back up the ramp. When they were both back on the yacht, she began pulling on the ramp. With it retracted, she said to the pilot, "Move us out about a hundred yards," and then to the captain, "Call whoever's water this is. We've got him." Then she started waving at Amy's friends, telling them to vacate the area.

"What's going on?" the captain asked.

"I pulled the life jackets out of one of the bench cabinets, Cap. There's a zip bag under them with pictures of Heather and five other women, along with Missy and her friends at a mall, and a very nice camera."

Within a half hour, the patrol boat arrived, made a pass around the sailboat, looking in, and then motored out to the yacht.

"Are you the ones who called this in?" the officer asked.

"We are," Travis said. Willow walked up beside him and the officer grimaced.

"What happened to you?" he asked, looking at Willow and then, suspiciously, at Travis.

"I fell off my high horse stopping a murder," Willow answered, flashing her badge. Travis offered his, as well.

"What makes you think that boat's abandoned?" the officer asked.

"We don't know it is for sure," Travis said, "but it looks very much like one we're looking for in a murder case. The ice pick case."

"No shit!" the man exclaimed, looking back at the sailboat.

"We are the detectives handling the case," Travis said. "With your permission, we'd like to assist you in finding out if it is. You'll get all the credit for what we find."

"Let's go take a look," the officer said. "If there's someone in there, sleeping, you're leaving unless you have a warrant."

"No problem," Travis said as he swung the ladder over the side. Then he said to Willow, "You're wearing a skirt. I'll go over first and keep his eyes on me."

"You're the one who was going to keep your eyes on my things," she said as she swung herself over the side. Travis followed, and the patrol boat eased toward the sailboat. The officer and his partner anchored to the boat and then the original officer climbed onto the sailboat, did a cursory search and then waved them on. They were about to lose their light. It was getting late, and Travis knew they couldn't go right to the evidence.

Travis and Willow began looking around as if they hadn't been on the boat before, and Travis kept watching the officer peering under his brows. The officer went right away to the registration and pulled out the papers.

"Do you have a person of interest yet?" the officer asked.

Willow looked casually around and then said, "We have two. Mike Sanders and Blake Manning." Then she and Travis looked at the officer, who was holding up the registration. "Michael Sanders," he said pointing to the papers.

"Okay," Travis said. "We're going to need this craft impounded and processed."

"No problem," the officer said. He walked to the edge and said to his partner, "Call a tug, Arch."

"Do you mind if we look around a bit?" Willow asked.

"Absolutely, I do. We'll let ya know what we find. You're looking specifically for a knife and an ice pick, right?"

"Or anything that might link him to Missy Gaudier or the victims," Travis added.

"Who's Missy Gaudier?"

Willow pulled out her phone and showed him a picture. He took the phone and sent the picture to his phone. "Is this one of the victims?"

"No." Travis said. "At least not yet. We believe she's the one our guy is after and the reason for the killings."

The officer nodded, then as if coming upon a realization, looked at the yacht and then back at them, "Any relation to Trevor Gaudier?"

"Daughter," Willow answered.

The officer looked around at the boat and then walked back to the side. "Arch, take the detectives back to the yacht and then come back and get me."

With Travis and Willow staring back toward the officer on the sailboat, the patrol boat began the short trip back to the yacht. Travis was hoping the officer would start searching the bench cabinets, but he just walked back into the cabin. He looked his disappointment over at Willow, but she was still watching the sailboat.

"I'm proud of you, Travis," she said.

"Well, that's good to know," he said, laughing. "There wasn't much I could do short of leading him by the hand to the cabinets."

"No," she said, looking into his eyes. She ran her hand up and down his arm. "I'm proud of you for your courage. Your will-power. For the charging you're doing toward your new life."

"Oh, that," he said. "There is a reward waiting for me at the end of this tunnel, Willow. It is something I will not be denied."

Sturgeon

Last night was the first time Willow had ever been on a yacht. Despite the fact that they weren't able to dig for evidence, she'd had a lot of fun. She was sad for Mr. and Mrs. Simmons and Amy, but the Gaudiers had turned a somber occasion into a pleasant experience.

She was getting everything set up for dinner. Jessie and Adam were coming, along with Mitch, and Travis had been there since ten that morning. He had boasted about his grilling expertise, so she was going to put him to work. She had pulled steaks out of the freezer earlier and was now preparing a marinade for the shrimp.

She had done all the exercising she needed to do today, earlier, when she was working with Travis. She had him work for fifteen minutes, rest for ten, change machines, and continue the cycle. The man had a plan, and he was committed to it. He was still down there, now.

A knock came at the door. Neither Jessie, Adam nor Mitch would have bothered knocking, so she knew who this was. She checked her frightening face in a picture on the wall and went to the door. When she opened the door, a ten-year-old boy and a nine-year-old girl sandwiched the woman. They all recoiled at her appearance.

"My God, Willow. What happened to you?" Kris asked.

"Got into a little tussle trying to stop a crime. It looks worse than it feels. I'm so glad you came. Please, come in."

Kris looked around, saw the coast was clear and voiced her concern, "I'm not sure about this, Willow."

"I know. I understand the hesitation, but like I said on the phone, he is a totally different man than the one I was partnered with my first day. You're the reason. You and these two." She smiled at the children, but they were still unsure if they wanted to look at her. "He has hope, now. A desire that drives him to be better. I know things will take time, but any encouragement you wish to share, I will appreciate greatly."

"Okay," Kris said cautiously. "Where is he?"

"Working on his weight, down the hall." Willow showed Kris the hallway and then went back to her kitchen. She put the marinade in the refrigerator and pulled out and began washing and forking the potatoes. She was going to have to stay close to the door. When the others came, they would just charge into the weight room, and she wanted Travis to have some alone time with his family.

She finished washing, forking and seasoning, so she wrapped the potatoes, placed them on a platter and walked them to the deck, setting them on the patio table that she had set up in the event Kris and Travis didn't want to join a mixed crowd. When she turned to walk back in the house, Kris and the kids were standing inside the sliding glass door, looking out at her. She couldn't believe it had gone that badly that quickly.

"Macy has decided her dad needed a shower. I hate to ask this, but do you have any books? I forgot to bring theirs and they have reached their television limit for the weekend. I would like to have a few minutes alone once he gets out."

"Absolutely," Willow said gleefully. She led them to her spare room that she had turned into a reading room and showed them her bookshelves. Macy plucked The Talents of Bet off the shelf right away, and after a few minutes, the boy, Ashton, chose a magazine on guns, which Kris snatched from him. She perused the shelves, chose Huckleberry Finn, and regardless of the available seating, both kids were soon face down on the carpet, reading.

Kris followed Willow back to the kitchen and asked if she could help with anything, but before Willow could answer, three loud and obnoxious people burst through the front door, laughing. They all stopped and stared at Willow's face. Jessie gasped, but the boys asked in unison, "Who did that to you?"

"Calm down," Willow said. "It happened in the line of duty." She spent a couple of minutes introducing Kris and explaining the kids, and then the three newcomers headed down the hall. She and Kris went back to the kitchen, and the two began working on the salad ingredients.

"What would the kids prefer to have for a vegetable?" Willow asked.

"Surprisingly, they like everything except Brussels sprouts, but this isn't about the kids, so whatever you have would be fine."

"I have broccoli, or I have canned corn and green beans."

"Broccoli is fine," Kris said. "If you have some butter and garlic, I can even prepare a sauce."

Willow showed Kris where to find things and then went back to the salad. "I know I don't need to say this, Kris, but he really loves you."

"I know," Kris said, without stopping her prep, "and I miss him. Even with the heavy drinking, he was good to us, but I have to

234

think of the kids. They can't grow up thinking that kind of bingeing is okay. I wish I could shake this fear that a relapse is coming."

"I wish I could promise you it won't, but that's just not realistic. I don't feel it will. He has a lot of help, now. A sponsor. The meetings. My dad."

"Along with a very good friend and partner," Kris finished. The rest of Willow's face turned the same color as her eye at the compliment.

She was about to reject the credit, but Travis walked into the kitchen and stood across the prep island from her, puffing out his chest and patting his boiler.

"What do you think?" he asked.

"It doesn't work that way, Travis," she laughed, looking over at Kris. "You're not going to lose that paunch in one day." Willow did notice that his eyes were looking better and the discoloration was leaving his face. She hadn't noticed his hands shake all day.

"I know," he said, becoming serious. "I was wondering if you could handle one more after-work guest. I can get a membership if it's too much trouble. I have my meetings on Tuesday, so not that day."

"Nonsense," she said. "You're welcome anytime. Just don't make me stop what I'm doing to answer the door."

"Thanks," he said, and despite Kris' presence, he put his arm around her and squeezed her to him. "Where's the taters?"

"On the deck."

Travis walked out, started the grill and strategically placed the potatoes, with Kris watching him all the way. Willow detected hope in Kris' eyes. Once he had every potato exactly where he wanted it, (OCD much?) he walked back in and began looking all around.

"Down the hall," Kris said. "First door on the left past the weight room." Travis walked that direction to say hello to his kids.

Willow finished the salad and pulled the steaks out of the refrigerator, flipped them over once, and then stacked them on a plate, covering it with a piece of wax paper. She lifted the tray and poured the marinade in a bowl, set the brush in the bowl, and then walked the steaks and the marinade to the deck, setting them on the table and pulling the table cloth over both.

Back inside, she reached into the cabinet and pulled a bottle of Merlot out and set it on the prep island. She dug out her ice bucket, set the wine in it and filled it with ice, setting it back on the island. Kris looked at her with trepidation.

"I've learned from my previous experiences," Willow explained. "One of the worst things we can do is change our lifestyle to accommodate him. It will make him feel guilty and unworthy. Besides, wouldn't you like to know how he does? You need to regain that confidence in him, Kris. You're not going to do that by hiding his weaknesses from him. He is a strong man. He will prevail."

"I sincerely hope you're right, Willow. I really do."

Willow heard the shower start, so at least one of her friends was done. Travis also walked by, without a word, went outside and began flipping the potatoes, using the same intensity he had when he'd first put them on. He then walked over to the swing and sat, admiring Willow's back yard.

Kris gathered the plates and headed for the table, so Willow made the offer. "I've set up the patio table for four, if you would rather. I know you don't really know any of my friends. You might be more comfortable."

"No, thank you," Kris answered. "Our family doesn't separate ourselves from our host. I appreciate the offer, though."

Willow watched Kris and had a hard time stifling her laughter. Kris made a lot more trips walking past the patio door than she needed to, in setting the table. She hadn't gone to the extreme of walking one fork out at a time, but it was close. As she set the table, she made a concerted effort not to look at Travis, but he made no such effort. His eyes were on her, every trip.

After a while he grabbed the steaks, so Willow took out her marinade and added the shrimp. She thought about smiling and winking at him, but with only one functioning eye it wouldn't have had the desired effect. Kris had been setting the table for nearly ten minutes now. She had placed a wine glass at every setting.

As the workout freaks emerged, Willow sent them to the living room to sit on their hands while she and Kris finished in the kitchen. She gave Kris a pan, and the broccoli out of the crisper, then she skewered the shrimp and left them on the island, and then went to the living room, turning the kitchen over to Kris.

Willow joined the conversations, but also kept her eye on Kris and Travis. He would walk in, grab the shrimp and walk back out. Walk in and get a bottle of water and walk back out. Walk in, take a paper towel off the roller and walk back out. Willow was trying so hard not to laugh that her eye was watering.

Soon it became time to take to the table. Willow sat on one end, with Jessie and Adam on her left and Mitch on her right. She couldn't wait to see how the remaining four chairs were handled. Her heart spiked when Macy and Ashton were ushered by mom to the chairs next to Mitch. That left the two chairs. Kris took the seat next to Jessie, leaving the end seat to her left empty.

Travis began hauling the goodies in from the grill and when he had everything on the table, took the chair next to Kris. Willow pulled the wine from the bucket, opened it and poured herself a half glass. Mitch reached for it, but Willow passed it to Adam, instead. He poured for himself and Jessie, and the wine was passed to Kris. Travis snatched it and poured a half glass into Kris' glass.

He stood and walked the wine past his family, handing it to Mitch. He walked to the kitchen refrigerator, took out the milk and poured some for himself, Macy and Ashton, and dinner was on. Willow's heart swelled again. Those two were madly in love with each other, and she wouldn't be surprised if they left at the same time.

The dinner conversation was light, jovial, and free of any work-related talk with the exception of a comical story from Jessie about a man with a fraud conviction totally unable to understand why her company couldn't hire him. She had tried to explain that people with fraud convictions couldn't work in the banking industry, but no matter how much she explained, he just couldn't understand the dilemma. His conviction wasn't related to banks.

After dinner, Adam and Jessie handled the dishes, Mitch cleaned the grill and patio, Travis and the kids were putting books away in the reading room, and Willow and Kris sat the couch, watching the action.

"You weren't very coy setting that table, you know," Willow offered.

"I know. I tried to be, but I kept wanting to walk out there and say something."

"What was it you wanted to say?"

"If I knew that, I would have gone out there," Kris said as she covered her face with her hands and rubbed her temples. "I hope he doesn't ask me to move back home."

"He wants that more than anything, but he also knows things take time. I think you're safe."

"Good, because I would. The kids have been on me about it, too."

Willow was stunned. Happy for Travis, but stunned. "It's going to be your call, Kris. Whatever you do. Don't threaten him. That would be really bad. He understands he has made a mess of things. He told me yesterday he wouldn't be denied. He's determined to get you back. When you're ready, give it a try. If it doesn't work out, at least you gave it your all."

Thompson

Josh and Eric sat in the back of the SWAT van watching the monitors as they displayed the actions of the SWAT team approaching the farmhouse. It was Monday and two in the morning, so everyone inside was expected to be sleeping, but that wasn't always a given. According to Sanders, there were bodies on this farm. Murdered. This was a DEA case, as it stood, but if there were indeed bodies, then it would fall to Josh and Eric.

The view on the monitor bobbed up and down as the agent he was watching charged toward the house. There was sound available, but none was being made as the agents were silent in their approach. His man hugged the side of the house near a window as his camera panned back and forth between the window slats and the agent working his magic on the front door.

In just seconds the door was opened and the agents began filing in. Still being silent. The man whose screen he could see now had his rifle at eye level as he entered. He saw three agents in front of his man heading up a staircase to his left, and two more angle off to the right. His man took a position alone in the kitchen, and his rifle and camera were focused on the pantry door. He stood silent and still.

He really wanted to see more of the screens, but the DEA commanders were huddled around them, watching, and their frames were considerably taller and wider than his. He would have to be content with the top right monitor.

The volume erupted as shouts came from the speakers. Then two shots rang out. His man's head began switching from the pantry door to the staircase in rapid succession, but the gun stayed on the pantry door.

One of the switches to the staircase caught two of the three agents escorting several women in various looks of disarray, along with one man. They were all forced to the floor, and his man went back to the pantry view, but raised his rifle. Another agent stepped up to the door and, standing aside, opened the door and yelled down that he was DEA.

He proceeded down the stairs, and Josh's man followed. He saw many boxes, and some items on shelves that he couldn't make out. There were no people hiding. They climbed back up the stairs and it looked like all the agents except one were now congregated around the floored occupants. Then he heard the leader.

"We're clear."

Josh and Eric departed out the van door. Then the van started and began toward the farmhouse, pulling up in front, with everyone climbing out and proceeding into the farmhouse. Josh and Eric followed in their own car.

Before they went in, he saw an ambulance and crime scene unit turn off the road and approach the house. As they went in, Josh saw one of the agents turn his weapon over to one of the commanders. That told him the missing agent was standing upstairs with the person this agent had taken out.

Josh and one of the commanders canvassed all the rooms and gathered all the cell phones they could find. The two of them sat and began going through the assorted phone books on each. They came up with two numbers that were the same on each phone, one of which was the same as the one he got from Sanders.

Chulo. The other was a man named Horace. Eric went into the offices to see what he could find.

Josh saw out the window two black-and-whites along with an SUV drive up. They would be transporting the prisoners. The ambulance was leaving. There had been nothing they could do for the man upstairs. The crime scene unit were getting instructions and directions from one of the other DEA commanders.

With the DEA having things well in hand, Josh began looking around for any signs of bodies or indications of any violence. There would be something here that would tell him where that evidence would be, in the event DEA wasn't able to extract it from the prisoners. He intended to find it.

He started at the dining room table area and moved toward the kitchen. It was something else that caught his attention, however. He stopped his inspection and stared out the window, to the back of the farmhouse. The DEA commander that had been helping him stood and walked toward him, joining his stare.

"You see something?" he asked.

After a moment's hesitation, Josh answered. "That's an awfully small garden for a farm. Wouldn't you agree?"

He and the commander stood silently, staring at the eight-foot by eight-foot area of toiled soil. The commander broke the silence. "More of your victims?"

"Possibly," he answered, as he was dialing the FBI in the hopes that they would be willing to supply more cadaver dogs. When he hung up, he exited the back door and walked to the area, trying to picture the event that would have led to a burial. He didn't think these were more of Manning's victims, but he was fairly certain this was a gravesite. A gravesite that held the bodies of the previous residents of the farm, was his guess.

"This will change things, Dave," Josh said. "We're going to have to wait here for the dogs. You'll have to take the office without us."

Josh moved around the soil in a circular pattern, looking for he wasn't sure what. Clothing. Personal documents. Jewelry. Anything indicating what was buried here. He knew it wasn't a garden. Something had been buried. Even if it was an animal, he needed to be sure.

"We're leaving," said the commander. "So are the black-and-whites. We thought one of the women would break, but it turned out to be the guy. The office is downtown Charmaine. Disguised as a travel agency, believe it or not. According to him, the girls doubled as travel agents. What a ride, huh?"

Josh just rolled his eyes at the misplaced humor. "Anyone talking about this place?"

"We haven't asked, yet. We want to try to hit these places before sunup and the bustle of activity."

"Understandable. I want the head of the snake, though. The Chulo guy. He won't be the first one in to work. My guess is he doesn't even work there. Probably the Horace guy. He's not going to be able to answer my question, but he might tell you where to find Chulo."

"Just exactly what is your question, Detective?"

"Who did they get this farmhouse from and where are they?"

Josh didn't want to add their scent any more than they already had, so he encouraged the commander back into the farm house. Josh and Eric spent the next hour going through drawers and cabinets, finding nothing of value that would lead them to Chulo, even if that was his real name, which he doubted.

Shortly after they had all but given up, the dogs arrived and Josh walked the handlers out to the area. His suspicions were correct. There was definitely a body buried here. The dogs were both reacting loudly. More than one body? Josh called the sheriff's office for assistance and gave them the low-down. Then he called the coroner.

Logan

When Chulo got the call from his contact of the impending raids, he put everything into motion. He collected all his 'banks', packed his bags and destroyed his burner that he used for his side business. He kept the one he used for his contact and, at least temporarily, the one registered to Charles Logan. In the event a call came in related to that phone, he could continue to act as if nothing was different.

It was midnight now. The raids were scheduled to start at 2AM. He slipped cautiously out of bed, so as not to wake up his wife. He stood beside the bed, looking down at her. She had been a good wife. He was going to miss her.

He tiptoed out of the room and down the hall to his son's room, opening the door enough to slip in. He just stood there staring. He'd always known this day would come, and he thought he had prepared himself, but his eyes began to tear nonetheless.

He made his way downstairs and into his den, opened the drawer below the bookcase and pulled out his clothes and shoes, and got dressed. Then he slowly walked through the house to the garage, taking in all the family pictures and knick-knacks they had picked up along their journey together.

He got into his car, backed out of the garage onto the street and stopped, staring once more at the life he was leaving behind. Then he slowly made his way down the street towards his new life, wiping away the tears of his old one.

He drove through the city to the storage facility, entered the code and passed through to container number 121. He unlocked the container and opened the door. Chevy Cruze? Really? The keys had been left in the ignition, so he got in, started it and drove it out. He popped both trunks and moved the suitcases from the BMW to the Cruze. He backed the BMW into the container and did a once over to make sure he had gotten everything out last night.

Satisfied, he closed and locked the container, and slipped the key under the door. He got into the Cruze and reached into the glove box, pulling out the envelope. Driver's license, credit cards, birth certificate. Everything appeared to be here. Wilson Preston put the car in gear and drove out the gate.

He made his way through the city, sticking to the speed limit. The gas tank was full, so there was no reason to stop. He did run into a couple of stop lights, but for the most part the city of Carpel was dead. He took the ramp onto 29 and turned north. He guessed it would take two or three days to reach his destination.

As he drove, he fiddled with the controls, getting adjusted to the car, and at the same time reflected on what he had left behind and what was yet to come. He was going to miss Horace. That big galoot had been a handful, but he was as loyal as hell.

He was surprised, but he had a feeling he was going to miss his girls, too. He had been careful not to become emotionally involved with them, and touching them in any way sexually would have been horrible for business, but they all had great personalities. They were good people. They just didn't give it away.

Sanders, though. He had liked the man, but now he was going to have to make arrangements. Sanders was a dead man walking. His contact was going to keep him informed about the man's protection. Chu... Preston still had friends who owed him.

This was going to be a process. He wasn't in custody, and with the help from his contact he never would be, so there wasn't a hurry. Sanders would get his, though. Witness protection or no. Preston was going to find him. He wasn't all that sold on killing him. Cutting out his tongue so he couldn't talk and his hands so he couldn't write might be a better option.

Birch

Travis was even more nervous, now, than he had been the last time he was here to see Lizzie. He sat in the waiting room, hoping to get her blessing to return to duty. He had already knocked and gotten no answer, so he just sat and waited. It gave him time to reflect on his mannerisms last night.

Willow was a wonderful woman. He couldn't even come up with words to thank her for the marvelous surprise she gave him, so he just hugged her when he left. Inviting Kris and the kids provided him with the best day he'd had in over a year. Kris had been very kind and nonjudgmental. The kids were great, as well. They had wanted to come home with him, but he had told them they would be able to do that soon. As soon as he'd had said it, worry flowed through him that he had just put Kris on the spot, and he apologized to her several times.

When she and the kids left, he didn't get any affection from Kris, but the kids hugged him a lot. He knew he had a long way to go yet, but he could be patient. The end result would be worth it.

Before he left, Willow had given him the rules of the house. Friday and Saturday, she referred to as 'me time', but any other day, he was welcome to work out or come for dinner, or both. She would just need a call, so she knew how big of a dinner to make.

He already saw her workout regimen, so he had asked her of her diet. He had been more than surprised at her answer. Willow was in very good shape. She was athletic, but not overly muscular, and her waist and hips would put a good deal of women to shame. He had thought, at first, she had been joking, but she had insisted she wasn't. Willow Sturgeon had not dieted a day in her life. She said she controls her weight by three basic rules. One, three squares and no snacking. Two, reasonable portions; and three, a minimum of fifteen minutes a day on the treadmill.

The conversation had told him what he needed to do. Now he just needed to do it. He didn't think the alcohol was going to be his biggest problem. Not eating until he bulged would be. He was used to heavy portions, no treadmill and snacking every fifteen minutes. Regardless of how hard it was going to be, Kris was his motivation.

"Well, look at you," came Lizzie's voice, nearly jolting him from his reverie. "No twitching and clear eyes."

"Morning, Lizzie."

"Come on in. Let's chat," Lizzie said, and Travis followed her in her office and took a seat across from her desk.

"How did the weekend go? Can you tell me what you did?"

"Friday, I went out to the harbor and watched the water awhile. Just a calm, relaxing night. I met a couple of people and had a good conversation. Saturday, I went to a victim's funeral and wake, provided what comfort I could, and then had a nice ride on a yacht, if you can believe it. Sunday, I went over to Willow's and worked out and had dinner with her and a few of her friends. It was a very good weekend."

"Well, good. How are you feeling? Any tightness in the gut? Headaches? Insatiable desire for a drink?"

"I'd be lying if I said I hadn't thought about it, but the need I have for my family will always outweigh any other desires. There was alcohol at the dinner table, last night. Willow had invited my wife, who was also there. She's a smart woman, Willow. She put two things in front of me and made me choose. It was no contest."

"I'm glad to hear that, Travis." Lizzie stared at him for endless seconds, boring through his eyes and into his mind. "Where do you think we should go from here? If you were me, what would be your next step?"

"I would send a memo to the captain, saying his detective is ready to be part of the team, ready to help solve this case, should be promoted to Detective One with a substantial raise, have his own office and a healthy expense account."

"No harem?"

"No, but a magic wand would be nice."

"I only have the one. Sorry. Are you okay with me talking to the captain and Willow? I would be asking them to rat you out, basically."

"I'm not afraid, Lizzie. I've got this. Talk to whomever you want."

Travis watched Lizzie stare at him and tap a pencil on her blotter, even though Lizzie never used a pencil in her work. It was obviously a tool she used to try to shake up her interviews. Travis wasn't falling for it and stayed stoic and on her eyes. She looked past him, out her door.

"I'll call the captain and give him my recommendation to return you to duty. The rest of your demands, you'll have to earn. Now get out."

Travis thanked her and left the office. He needed to get to Willow before she left for the beginning of her day, so he quickened his pace, taking the stairs two at a time. When he turned the corner into the bureau, he saw Willow still at her desk and Agent Maxwell at his. He glanced toward the captain's office and saw him on the phone. The captain noticed him and waved him in, so he assumed the phone call was Lizzie.

"Don't screw this up, Detective," the captain said as he was hanging up the phone. "If you even look like you've been drinking, I'm calling her."

"I understand, Cap. There's no chance of that happening."

"Get to work. This has gone on long enough. Wrap it up. I've got other cases."

"Will do." Travis left the office and went to the V, finding Willow now on the phone. He smiled at Maxwell. "You're in my chair, Agent. I'm back on the job, so you're going to have to find a new home." He helped the agent to the closest empty desk, and then returned to his as Willow was hanging up the phone.

"Hey, Willow," he greeted her. "Can you give me a couple of minutes to check my mail?"

"You bet. I want to call San Pablo and see if they have anything on the sailboat yet. Hopefully, that's where it was taken, or I'm going to have to start digging."

Travis had a plethora of emails. There were a lot of notices about meetings, training, and volunteer requests, which he ignored. He started with the autopsy report on victim number three.

Willow was totally incapable of sitting at her desk when she was digging for information. She paced around the desk, through the bureau, to the stairs and back. She chewed her nails or scratched her temples or rubbed her forehead. She watched her feet as she walked, stared at the ceiling, or admired her fingers. What a fidget.

When Travis was on his fourth email, Agent Maxwell walked up to him with his laptop. He sat the laptop down on Travis' desk and turned it to face him. He had a map site opened and the San Pablo Bay area and adjoining roads displayed.

"I've just got a call from Lisa," Agent Maxwell started.

"Who's Lisa?" Travis asked.

"Special Agent Lisa Tanner. She said a man fitting Blake Manning's description was stopped by The Vallejo P.D. this morning for speeding on Porter Street. The officer ran the plates and approached the car to issue a warning. When he was half way to the car, the driver booked. The officer ran back to his car and found the plates came back to a stolen car. A chase ensued and the driver abandoned the car at a Motel 6. The officer lost him in a foot pursuit.

"Vallejo searched the area for about a half hour but couldn't find him. About an hour later, they got a call of a carjacking at gunpoint at Sonoma and Magazine. He escaped Vallejo and was heading this way, but then the car stopped. CHP found it abandoned just south of here."

"How did you know he was headed this way?" Travis asked.

"Gotta love Lojack."

Travis saw that Willow had finally hung up the phone, so he called her over and gave her a rundown, including the part about Manning being armed. She shared her phone conversation with the two of them. They had found the photos and had also found DNA.

"With all the work this guy has done at keeping himself hidden," Willow laughed, "he's going to be done in by the fact that he lived on his boat. He's going to be tried, convicted and executed because of a simple invention. Your ordinary, everyday, 99-cent disposable razor. They are running the DNA, and when it's done, they'll forward it to our lab for comparison."

"I'm amazed that he just didn't toss everything overboard as he made his way to the bay," Travis offered. "He's definitely stepping up his game, though. He's graduated to firearms."

Willow announced that she was going to call the state and see if Manning had any firearms registered to him and then run downstairs and pass the picture around again, so Travis said he wanted to check in with the coroner and began the walk downstairs.

When he got there, the first thing he asked was if there were any new developments on the case, specifically whether the doc could determine if there was any indication that Brassard's fingernails were exceptionally clean. There was no indication of it, and when Travis kept digging for information, the doc became annoyed, so Travis headed back upstairs.

When he arrived back at his desk he loaded his email right away. Willow wasn't back yet, but it didn't look like waiting for her would be a problem. There were a lot of emails. Most had to do with the Manning cases, but a few from Thompson in Charmaine had just come in while he was downstairs, along with one from the DEA.

He left the ones from the Manning cases and went right away to the one from Charmaine. They had conducted raids overnight and arrested several people on drugs and other related charges. It was Thompson's belief that all three caseloads were related. Sanders had said Manning got his date rape drug and ice picks from Sanders and Sanders got the stuff from a guy by the name of Chulo.

That was all they had to go on. Chulo. There were two people still outstanding that were needed before the DEA could go further. One of the names was the Chulo guy and the other was a guy named Horace. Horace was an enigma, but Thompson believed he was Chulo's right hand. Maybe his enforcer. One of the girls thought Horace had killed her friend. A woman by the name of Brittany. She had not been one of the bodies dug up at the farm, however.

Thompson also wrote that there were search warrants in the works for the phone numbers they had on Chulo and Horace, but the phones were probably burners. If not, they should have addresses by the end of the day. They both had to know, by now, that the farm and travel agency had been raided, so they were probably on the run.

Thompson was asking Birch and Sturgeon to get the word out. Chulo drove a black BMW and Horace a white delivery-type van, without markings. There were no plates available.

One of the girls picked up at the travel agency was only fourteen, so there were going to be trafficking charges added to the case. Kidnapping, probably, as well. The man who had done most of the talking said she had been brought in by someone he hadn't seen in a while. That was probably Horace's doing. Another murder.

At some point Willow had returned and was leaning on his shoulder, reading along with him. "They've helped us a lot with the Manning case. We have to do what we can. Why don't you print that up and I'll run it down to the sarge before the briefing of the morning shift. He can have the guys watch for the cars. Not a lot to go on, though."

Travis printed the document and Willow left for the printer. Travis went back to the email. According to Sanders, Chulo worked for one of the ice companies, but he didn't know in what capacity. Thompson and his partner were going to check out Spielman Ice, and he was asking Travis to check out Mitchell Ice. He and Willow would check that out, first thing. There were no murders to investigate presently, other than the existing Manning case. They had a few more things to do, but Mitchell Ice shouldn't take long.

The DEA email was pretty much the same thing as Charmaine, so he saved it for later, as well as the others. Willow returned, and the two of them headed for the cruiser. Travis briefed her during the walk.

"I talked to the sarge and to social to get the car descriptions out there. Social said he needed more or people were going to call whenever they saw either, even if an old lady was driving. As far as Mitchell, they're probably just going to make us get a warrant before they'll give us employee info," Willow said.

"Maybe. Maybe they will be very ready to tell us anything we want," Travis said, looking over at Willow. "Wow. The eye is looking better today. Is that healing, or makeup?"

"It's feeling better, but it's mostly makeup. Why are you so concerned about my appearance, there, Paunch?"

"It's not concern, there, Shiner. It's being happy for your agent friend. Before long, he won't have to be embarrassed being seen with you."

"Uh oh!" Willow said quietly. "Here comes the captain."

Travis looked and regretted it immediately. While his attention was diverted Willow delivered an elbow to his stomach.

"Ugh," Travis exclaimed, holding his stomach. "MEDIC!"

Travis got in the squad and started the engine, switching the sync to his phone. Willow loaded the info onto the computer... i-Pad... tablet thingy and they were off. Mitchell Ice was on the outskirts of the city on the way to Charmaine, so it would be a bit of a jaunt, but now that he and Willow were actually getting along, the time would go fast.

"Where do you think we should go for lunch?" Travis asked.

"It's 9:30 in the morning, Travis. Can we wait to see what part of town we're in at lunch time, first?"

"I feel like a burrito."

"You look like one, too. No burritos. Maybe a salad or soup and sandwich at Panera, if we're near."

"Yum. Tasty." Travis spent a lot of time bantering with Willow, but he wouldn't trade her for the world now. Despite the reluctance he had shown when they were first partnered, he knew if he hoped to patch things up with Kris, he would need Willow to stay on him. He didn't expect the relationship he had with her to be perfect every minute of every day, but the good would greatly outweigh the bad.

"Remind me to call Trevor when we're done here. I want to see if he can keep Missy home today. With this guy in the area, I don't want to take any chances. Hmm, just got an email from Thompson. Phones are burners."

"Yeah, I was expecting that. So was he. We'll go with what we've got. Send him a note that we're two minutes out of Mitchell. Then send yourself an email reminding you about Gaudier. I'm not your secretary."

"No. You're my own personal asshole. Now, here's another one. From a coroner in San Francisco. The body from the ocean had a shaft of a pick stuck in her brain. Partial writing on the shaft is 'tchell Ice. Looks like it's us. I'll let Thompson know."

"They work pretty fast in Frisco," Travis said.

When they arrived, they entered and found a man working the front counter. Travis approached him.

"Good morning. Is the boss around?" Travis asked.

"I'm the manager. What can I do for you?" the man replied.

Travis pulled out his badge and ID, "We're looking for one of your employees. Goes by the name of Chulo."

The man looked disgusted, took off his eyeglasses, and pinched between his eyes. "You know what... I don't know if this is some new game going on or what, but you're the second person to come in looking for this mysterious Chulo. We have no Chulo. Let me see that badge again."

Travis showed his badge, "Who was the first guy? What did he look like?"

The man looked past Travis and Willow out the front window. "He looked like that. The big dude."

Travis looked at the man walking toward the white van. The huge man. "That guy?" he asked incredulously and the manager nodded.

Willow was out the door, running hard, and Travis was on her heels. "Yo!" she screamed. "Hold up a minute." The man glanced at the running detectives and bolted for the van. Travis knew they weren't going to get there in time, so he changed direction and headed for the cruiser.

Sturgeon

Willow was gaining ground, but she didn't think she was going to make it before the man sped off, and she wasn't sure, with the man's size, what she would do if she did. This guy had to be close to seven-foot tall, weigh in at three hundred and looked to be in very good shape.

She gave up and came to a stop, turning to Travis, but he was already in the cruiser. The van started up and sped off, tires squealing. Travis was speeding at her. She keyed her mike.

"610, control. We are attempting to overtake a vehicle. White van. Partial California 7K1. Stand by."

"610," came the acknowledgement.

Travis stopped, she climbed in, and they were speeding off in the same direction the van had taken. So far, still in sight.

"610, control. North on Sage, approaching Broadway. Request backup."

"610. David twelve, David three, copy."

Both units acknowledged and Willow pulled the binoculars from the glove box in an attempt to see the plate.

"Buckle up," Travis said. "This is going to get nasty."

The chase was a little harrowing, sitting in the passenger seat. Willow wasn't in control of the vehicle, but Travis was using good sense following and not racing the fleeing suspect. The speed was something she was used to from her patrol days, but she had been in control, then. Travis was maintaining the speed of the van. Near 100mph. She keyed her mike. "610. We are in pursuit."

"610," control acknowledged. "All units ten-three."

Willow sat the binoculars on the dash and fastened her seat belt. The radio became a firestorm of activity. Both black-and-whites had caught up and were taking the lead. The captain came on and told Travis and Willow to back off and let the units handle the pursuit, which Travis didn't do, naturally, but Willow acknowledged him, anyway. David three told dispatch to notify CHP and Charmaine. Willow looked at the dash and saw the speeds were in excess of 110. She put the binoculars away and dialed Thompson.

"Thompson."

"Hey, Detective. This is Detective Sturgeon from Carpel. A few of us are headed your way. We're in pursuit of a white van with Paul Bunyan at the wheel. How do you get along with your traffic division?"

"They owe me a favor. You coming in on Sage?"

"So far. Just so you know. This is a big man. He won't be going down easy."

"Bring the coffee and donuts. Got it. See ya in a bit."

She hung up and looked again at the dash. Pushing 120. The van driver was doing everything he could to shake David twelve, but David twelve was Marci, so he was pretty much screwed. You don't shake Marci. Luckily, there wasn't much traffic this time of day, so bouncing someone else's car at her wouldn't work, either.

The van swerved onto the shoulder, kicking up dirt and rocks, but Marci flew over to the median and accelerated, avoiding them and pulling fairly even with his rear bumper. The van swerved at her, but she slowed so that it missed, and then she darted forward, connecting with the rear bumper, nearly causing the van to flip.

Willow was nearly startled out of her shoes when, at 120 miles per hour, two CHP interceptors passed the cruiser quickly on each side, taking over the pursuit. One of the interceptors climbed up to the back-left quarter panel of the van and connected. The van swerved, tipped on two wheels and then toppled over on its right side, sliding down the highway. All the units, including Travis, hit the brakes, so as not to be caught up in the crash.

"Well, that's the pits," Travis said as he pulled up with the others.

With weapons drawn, two detectives, two patrolmen and two CHP officers approached the van. Nothing moved, except the left side tires. Marci was taking aim through the windshield and Crocket was right beside her. Crocket must have been satisfied with what he saw, as he holstered his weapon, pulled his nightstick and climbed up the van to the passenger door, breaking the window.

Willow was silently cautioning the rookie. That didn't appear to be a jolting enough crash to render a big man unconscious. She no sooner got the thought formulated when a huge hand came out of the window, grabbed Crocket by the shirt and threw him over the roof of the van. Marci fired twice through the windshield, but the man was climbing out and jumping to the ground.

Marci had hit him. There was blood coming from the wounds, but it hadn't fazed him. Two CHP officers went down as their attempts to subdue him just resulted in him shouldering them, causing them to tumble and roll. The man turned on a charging Travis and simply threw him like a rag doll. Then he turned toward Willow.

Willow holstered her nine, pulled her Taser and fried the bastard. He went down like a ton of lead, twitching and spitting. After everyone was in position, Willow released and went to the cruiser, opened the trunk and pulled out the XLs. Standard cuffs wouldn't work on this guy.

Travis had the guy's head twisted almost backwards, the two CHP officers were twisting his arms behind him, and Marci and Crocket were laying across his legs. Willow cuffed the wrists. Someone had thought to call rescue as the fire truck arrived along with an ambulance and two black-and-whites from Charmaine along with one of their detective units.

She walked toward the Charmaine cruiser with Travis following, picked the guy she thought might be Thompson and asked him where the donuts were.

"Sorry. The smell got to us and we ate them. I'm Josh. This is my partner, Eric. Are you Sturgeon? What the hell happened to your eye?"

"That's a story for a different day. I'm Willow Sturgeon. This is Travis Birch. I think this might be your Horace guy."

The four detectives walked to the stammering and twitching mountain and Josh pulled the wallet from the man's back pocket, paging through assorted cards, and settling on a California driver's license. "Horace Carter," Josh stated. "Well, now there's only one to go." He walked around to face Horace.

"Say, Horace. You wouldn't happen to know where we could find Chulo, would ya?"

"Mmft trzzts."

261

"Still a little out of it, huh? Well, we'll just ask you later. We need to get you booked into the hotel, first. You don't need a Jacuzzi, do ya? Because those rooms are filled currently."

"You guys got this, right?" Travis asked. "We kind of left Mitchell unfinished and we want to get back."

"Do you mind some company? We'll stay out of it. Just tag along."

"That's fine. See ya there."

Travis' leg hurt from when he was thrown, so Willow drove the distance back to Mitchell Ice. When they arrived, the same man was at the counter, and he didn't appear happy they had returned.

"Look, Detective, I still don't have any Chulo here. What's the big deal with him, anyway?"

"We just want to talk to him," Travis answered. "Why are you curious? Let's see some ID."

"While you're talking to the detective," Willow interjected, addressing the manager, "why don't you show me where I can find your employee records?"

"You know how this works, Detective," the man said. "I need a warrant."

"Do you know how this works," Travis asked, looking at the man's ID, "Robert? Do you really want us to get a warrant? Let me see. It's August. For at least three months the temperatures have been pushing triple digits, so my guess is you've stepped up the production. Maybe added a few undocumented to take up the slack. They're not up to speed on health codes, are they? We get a warrant. The health department notices. Immigration notices. Production slows. The city of Carpel notices when it's time to renew that license. What a mess, huh?"

The man looked disgustedly at Travis, then at Willow, then back at Travis. "Fuck this!" He walked to an office door and opened it, looking at Willow. She walked in the door, shadowed by Josh and Eric, and the man unlocked a stack of filing cabinets. "Good luck," he finished, walking back out to Travis.

"Dibs on this one," Willow said pulling the drawer free from the cabinet. She parked herself on the floor and began paging through the files. "Two people come here looking for a guy named Chulo, and this manager can't put that together."

"Yeah," Eric said. "We might not have to look through all of these, though. Chulo was passing out samples of stuff, so he may be a salesman. I'll check and see if they're all in the same cabinet."

Birch

Travis held up the questions, watching Eric walk toward him. Eric asked the manager who would be passing out gift samples of ice buckets, picks and decks of cards, etc.

"The only ones authorized to do that are me and my assistant," he answered.

"Is he here?" Travis asked.

"Nah. He's off today and tomorrow."

"You got a phone number for him?"

"Why do you want to bug the man on his day off?" the manager answered.

"Get me the fucking phone number or I'm going to arrest your ass for impeding a murder investigation," Travis spat out. "Now!"

That shook the man. He fumbled through his rolodex and pulled out the card, handing it to Travis. Travis took the card and compared the number to the one he had on Chulo. They matched, but he already knew it was for a burner. He also knew it wouldn't be answered if he called.

"Let me see your phone," he said to the manager. The manager just looked at him, slack-jawed. Travis stared back and the man handed over his phone. He looked at the name on the card.

Charles Logan. He found the number in the manager's phone book and hit send. There was no answer, so he hung up.

"This is evidence," Travis said, pocketing the phone and rolodex card. So is your employee file. He pointed at the office and Eric darted back in.

"You're taking my phone?"

"Like I said. It's evidence. Besides, we wouldn't want you tempted to call him."

Willow, Josh and Eric came out of the office carrying a paper file. Willow took the manager's ID, laid it on the counter and snapped a picture on her phone.

"What was that for?" he asked.

"Just in case we find out you warned him," she answered, "We want to know where to find you. Have you ever heard the name Mike Sanders or Blake Manning?"

"No, I haven't. Are you going to tell me they work here, too?"

"Nope. I'm not going to tell you that," Willow answered, pulling out her phone and showing the man the picture of Manning. "How about this guy? Look familiar?"

"No."

Willow handed the man her card. "We'll be talking again, the first chance I get. You're going to be my eyes and ears here. You feed me good info, I reward ya. Questions?" The man didn't answer. He just stared at the card.

"I'll take that as a no. I'll be back." She made her way to the group.

Travis pulled out the rolodex card from his pocket and looked it over again, as they were walking toward the cruisers. "This is your guy. They found part of a pick in the victim from the ocean. The engraving indicates Mitchell Ice, so I think you can skip your ice company. Plus, this guy's name is Charles Logan. Chuck Logan. Chu...Lo... Do we have an address?"

"1727 Lincoln Street," Willow said, paging through the file.

"Wide open. It's going to be hard to sneak up on him," Travis said, scratching his chin.

"We can take the back," Josh said. "If you'll tell us what street that is."

"Do you have enough to assist on this? Horace was your killer, right?"

"He was responsible for most of the bodies, but there was one that the coroner said died of blunt force trauma. The impression was one of a large pipe or a baseball bat. One of the guys picked up at the travel agency said Chulo keeps a bat in his trunk. So, we're good."

"There is another option," Eric said. "The DEA wants him for drugs and the FBI for trafficking."

"Hell, no!" Travis said. "They'll just mess it up with their SUVs and SWAT teams. There's four of us. We have three and a half sets of eyes. We can do this."

Willow smiled at him. "Hopefully, he won't run. Then there will only be three of us."

Travis smiled back. "Okay, we'll meet in the Walgreen's parking lot on Hanson and develop a plan. We might need to tie up a couple of squads to block the road."

∞∞∞

With Josh and Eric sitting on Market Street, Travis and Willow pulled up to the front of 1727 Lincoln Street. There were no cars in the driveway, but there was a garage, so any vehicles may be in there.

"A lot of time has passed since this operation started, this morning," Willow said. "I think Horace was at the factory, because he either figured it out, or someone tipped him off. He was there looking for the boss. Probably because he hadn't answered the phone. It's possible Chulo booked. Maybe he knows, too."

"Maybe," Travis agreed. "Let's go find out."

Travis and Willow approached the house. The blinds were open, but no one was visible through the windows. Travis checked the side of the garage before proceeding and then both the detectives walked up to the door. The door opened before they could knock and they were faced with a woman who looked to be in her late twenties, wearing jeans and black shirt, and staring at them through the security screen.

"Can I help you?" she asked, looking somewhat annoyed at their presence.

Travis looked past her but saw no one. "We're looking for Charles. Is he around?" he said, showing his badge.

"He's at work. I'm his wife. What's this about?"

"We just want to ask him a couple of questions. May we come in?"

"No. I told you. He's at work, and you guys don't exactly have a spotless reputation, lately."

Travis smiled at the dig. "Where does he work? We'll try him there."

"You still haven't told me what this is about," she said, folding her arms across her chest.

"There's not a lot we can divulge right now, Mrs. Logan, but there's been a murder and we think your husband has information that will help us find the killer."

The woman continued to stare back and forth between the detectives. "You're full of shit. You think my husband killed somebody, don't you? He's as gentle as a lamb. He won't even discipline our son. I would like you to leave. Come back when you have a warrant."

She started to close the door, but Travis spoke up, "We can do that, but unfortunately that's going to mean involving the patrol division, which means squads in front of your house for the neighbors to see."

"Don't try to intimidate me, you weasel," she blurted, opening the door fully. "You bring all the squads you want."

"Mrs. Logan," Willow interjected, "I apologize for Detective Weasel. We have been to Mitchell Ice and he wasn't there. Does he have a second job?"

"He wasn't?" She looked surprised. "No. That's his only job."

"Will you just tell me if we have the right phone number? He doesn't seem to be answering." Willow read off the number, and the wife said that wasn't his number.

"What happened to your eye, Detective? Did the weasel hit you?"

"No, ma'am. Line of duty. I wonder if I could ask you if you wouldn't mind calling him and asking him if we could meet him somewhere."

"You seem nice," she said with a smile. Then, frowning at Travis, "But no. I'm sorry. I'm not comfortable with this whole situation. I'll ask you again to leave my house."

Travis wanted to tell the woman he was sorry, but not for what he had said, for the likelihood that she would never see her husband again. The situation was moot, however, as she slammed the door in their face.

When they were back in the car, Travis called Josh and told him to meet them back at the parking lot of Walgreens. He and Willow drove the short distance in silence. Travis was sure she had the same feeling he did. Both units arrived at the same time, and Travis began the briefing.

"He's not there. The wife believes he's at work, but we know that's not the case. I'm afraid this guy might get away from you. We don't have the resources to park someone on the street and wait for him to show up. I don't think he's coming back. She was a little shocked when we told her he wasn't at work."

"Well," Josh responded, "our captain sure as hell isn't going to let us sit on the house. It's not even our city. This is going to be a DEA affair. If they catch him, we can charge him with murder then."

"I feel sorry for her," Willow said. "And for their son."

"She appears to be a strong woman," said Travis. "I don't believe she knows anything about his side business. If she did, I think she would have left him."

"Maybe," added Eric. "A woman's love goes a long way, though."

"Willow has an in with the FBI," said Travis. "Are you guys going to bring the DEA up to speed?"

"We will," Josh said. All the detectives got back in to their respective vehicles. Josh and Eric left for Charmaine, and Travis and Willow for the department.

"Someone's on the take," Travis said out of the blue, once they were on the road.

"You have my attention. What are you thinking?" Willow asked.

"Think about it. It's possible that this Horace guy just stumbled onto the raid, turned around and booked. I don't think he had forewarning or he wouldn't have been looking for Chulo. Chulo, though, is nowhere to be found. If he would have gotten a call from someone at that travel agency, his first call would have been to Horace.

"Chulo had plenty of warning, and if he would have warned everyone, the police and DEA would have been suspicious. To him, the raids needed to happen. It was imperative to him that his informant wasn't outed."

"If that's the case," Willow said, "it would have to be someone at Charmaine. Both offices were there. Both raids were there."

"Not necessarily," Travis added. "Highly unlikely, in fact. The Police don't get a lot of heads-up time before those kinds of operations. I think the DEA's got a bad apple in their basket."

Willow pulled out her phone. "I'm going to call Josh."

"He knows, I would bet," Travis said.

"Hey, Josh. This is Willow," she said into the phone, which she had switched to speaker.

"Mole?" Josh answered.

"That's what Travis was saying. He thinks it's DEA."

"Maybe. When I called the guy at the DEA about Chulo, he hesitated too long. My guess is that's the first thing he thought of. I'm not sure how many people had knowledge, but it's not us, I don't think. Eric and I had a whole half hour to get there."

"Hmm. Well, I know who it's not. Our department was in the dark. Good luck with it."

"Thanks. Later."

Willow hung up the phone. "What if it's not the DEA? What if it's some other department and we're going to run into the same problem with Manning?"

"We'll have to sail that boat when we get there," Travis said.

Gaudier

Missy and her friend Ali grabbed their bags and left Macy's. They weaved their way in between cars through the parking lot and eventually reached the Lexus. Missy told Ali she needed to call someone, so she opened the trunk and placed her bags inside, leaving it opened for Ali. She looked through her contacts for Uncle Chet's number to see if he was coming to the party and found it. As she turned around, she saw a look of fear on Ali's face. At first, she thought another one of Ali's twisted jokes was on the way. Then the trunk closed.

Standing behind Ali with a gun stuck in her side was the worst excuse for a human being she had ever had the misfortune to meet. Blake Manning. He had the gun in Ali's side and his other hand around her shoulder. Anyone in the lot would think they were a couple.

"Stay calm, Ali," she said stoically. "He won't hurt you."

"Pretty sure of that, are you?" Manning commented.

"Of course, I am. Because if you do, then it will just be you and me. I wouldn't give you a plug nickel for your chances in that case. What do you want, Blake? What happened to your face? Were you trying to force a kiss on a badger? On second thought, it's actually an improvement."

"Open the back door," Manning ordered, and she opened it.

"Throw your phone on the seat on the other end." She complied. "Open your door and get in." She did as she was instructed.

"Now, miss Ali. I'm going to slide onto this seat and you're going to slide in with me. One fluid motion. If you do anything else, I'm going to put a bullet in the back of your friend's head. Do you understand?" Ali nodded, and the two slid into the car.

"Missy, put both your hands on the steering wheel." Missy complied. Manning picked up Missy's cell phone and scanned it, making sure it wasn't on a call. Then he demanded Ali's. She handed it to him. "Let me see your keys, Missy. With your left hand." Missy handed him the keys. He checked for a GPS attachment and handed them back.

"Start the car." Missy started the engine. "Disable the GPS." Missy flipped through the dash options and turned off the GPS.

"There's a drive-through across the street. You're going through it. You'll order three items. You'll pay and hand me the bag. Ali, I'm going to dump out the bag and put the cell phones in it. Missy will drive up slowly and you'll throw the bag in the trash. Does anyone have any questions?"

"I do," said Missy. "You want fries with that?"

"I'm glad you're finding humor in this, Missy. I hope you can maintain it when your friend here is popping maggots. Slip the seatbelt behind your back and attach it. You do the same, Miss Ali. Behind you." Manning attached his properly. "If you decide to ram anything, Missy, you and your friend here go through the window. I'll step out of the car and put a bullet in each of your heads for good measure, even if the airbags keep you in the car. Drive."

Missy did what she was told. Everything went as the asshole directed. She was driving her car she didn't know where. Manning was making her take residential streets though town, and now back roads out of town. She had long ago lost her recognition of where she was, but her internal compass said she was going north. She had been driving over an hour when Manning directed her onto a dirt road. The road led deep into a wooded area that opened unto a cabin.

She had to think of a way out of this that wouldn't cause Ali to come to harm. This wasn't Ali's fault. She was only in this situation because she was a friend. Ali was the most passive of Missy's friends. The easiest going. Missy had known her since high school. They went their separate ways after graduation, Missy to Stanford and Ali to Oregon State, but they had stayed in touch and even got together on breaks.

Now Ali was in trouble. There was a good chance this psycho bastard was going to kill them both. Missy needed to find a way to be the only victim. It wouldn't do any good at this point to bargain with him. She should have thought of that earlier. Now that he had reached his destination, there was no way he would release Ali. Missy needed to come up with a different plan.

Manning wanted something or he would have killed them already. He had something in that twisted little noodle of his that was the reason they were still alive. She needed to find out what that was and use it to her advantage. He had tried a date-rape drug on her and failed. Maybe that was the plan. Maybe he wanted to succeed.

He had a fistful of Ali's hair, directing her out of the car, with that damn gun still in her ribs. He backed away from the driver's door and told Missy to get out. She complied, and he told her to walk to the cabin. He told her where to find the key, and she opened the door, backing into the cabin, as instructed. He and Ali followed and he kicked the door shut, Ali now in tears.

"Do everything he tells you, Ali. Everything's going to be okay," Missy said, trying to calm the poor girl.

"You listen to her, sweets!" Manning said. "You do everything I tell you and you might live through this. You're not really part of the plan. I hope that doesn't hurt your feelings." Manning instructed Missy to sit with her back to the support beam, and she did. He walked Ali over to his cot and forced her to the floor. With his eyes on Missy and his knee in Ali's back, he began digging through his nightstand.

"Oh, now!" Missy exclaimed. "Doesn't that figure!" She watched as he handed the sex cuffs to Ali, lifting her from the floor. Missy knew, if she didn't come up with something before she was cuffed, it would be over for her. She shifted her weight to her left foot. As he got closer, she would bolt from the floor. He may get a shot off, but she thought she could get help here before Ali died. Her plan was foiled right away.

"Turn around," he said to Ali, which she did. He pressed the barrel to her sobbing lips. "Open," he said, and when she shook her head, he pulled hard on her hair causing her to cry out. He forced the barrel into her mouth and her eyes bulged, certain she was about to die. Missy's chance was gone.

With the gun in her mouth, he forced her to the ground behind Missy. "Hands behind your back, Missy. Either side of the beam." She did so and he instructed Ali to apply the cuffs, which she did. He then walked her across the room and sat her on the floor, removing the gun from her mouth. With the fear flowing through her, Ali was emotionally spent, and was soon tied to another beam with a nylon cord.

"Now, you two, sit tight. I have to go drive that pretty car into the drink. I shouldn't be more than a few minutes. Try not to miss me too much." He left.

"I'm sorry, Missy," Ali sobbed out. "I didn't know what to do."

"Everything's okay, Ali. Listen to me. We don't have much time. I messed him up at Stanford. It's me he's after. Not you. Stay as safe as you can. I think he's going to rape you, Ali. I'm sorry. I think he's going to do it and make me watch. You need to come to a decision to go with it and convince him you liked it, or you need to fight it and then act like you fainted. Either way, he is going to come after me, afterwards. I will use whatever I can think of to hurt him or hold him. You need to use that opportunity to run, Ali. Promise me you will run as soon as you can. I'll be okay if I know you're safe. Think, Ali. Think on how to get away and only how to get away. No heroics. Go for help."

Missy could tell the thought of being raped had just about ended any resolve Ali had left. She could only hope that by forewarning her of the possibility, it would make it less traumatic. She really needed Ali to stay focused and watch for an opportunity, but Ali was messed up emotionally. Missy knew that if she could get even one opening, she would kill her first human being. Hope flowed through her that the opening would come.

She looked past Ali into the kitchen to see if there was anything near that Ali could use to cut her bindings with, but she saw nothing. "Ali, feel behind the post. See if there are any nails or screws sticking out that you can use to saw the cord. Check the floor, too. It's wood, so maybe."

Missy really wished she were more erotic than she was. She knew nothing about sex cuffs. Wouldn't there be a release, somewhere? Was it possible one person could trust another that much? She used her fingers to inspect the cuffs, but found no button or switch. She worked one of her hands over the other and tried to determine whether she could pull them apart, but had no success on that, either. She stood and twisted around the post to see if she could find anything to use, looking up and around, but she saw nothing and resigned herself to the fact that she, at least, was trapped. When she was once again facing Ali, she began looking around her to help find something Ali could use.

Manning came back from his excursion.

"Why are you standing, Missy? Does your butt hurt?"

"It does. Would you kiss it for me?" Missy didn't look at Manning. She did look at everything else, in case an opportunity arose that she would have a moment's freedom. He kicked her legs from under her and she went down like a rock. Everything hurt. Her hands and arms from scraping the post. Her head from bouncing off the post, and now her butt really did hurt. She sure wasn't going to let him know he had hurt her.

"So you can't get a date to save your life, which is understandable with that face. Did you have a fight with a cheese grater? You have to resort to rendering women unconscious to gratify your sexual needs. What else has been going on with you, Blake? Besides those callouses on your palms, that is."

"Ah, Missy. You know me too well. Enjoy your insults while you can, but think about who might have the last laugh here."

"Wouldn't it be nice not having to have sex with an unconscious woman, Blake? Let Ali go. I'll fuck you so hard even your eyeballs will throb."

"Missy. Missy. Missy. As tempting as that sounds, you've already turned me off with your insults. Tone it down a bit. Then we'll see. Okay," he said, clapping his hands once, "who's hungry?"

He knelt before Ali. "How about you, sweets? Sandwich?"

Ali looked at him between her fallen hairs, and if Missy could patent the look, she wouldn't need any inheritance.

"Okay. That looks like a no. How about you, Missy? Can I make you a sandwich?"

"I could chew on a tube steak, as long as it's not so small it gets caught in my teeth."

Manning just smiled and walked into the kitchen.

Sturgeon

When they got back to the department, Travis went right to his desk and began going through the Manning files again. Willow knew he was trying to get anything that would lead them to the man before he killed again. She got on her phone and began by calling Palo Alto. She would touch base, one at a time, with everyone she could think of that had some connection with the man or the case.

She knew she was pacing, but she always did that. Bad habit, maybe, but it helped her think. She needed to find a way to get this guy in custody.

Willow really liked the Gaudiers. They were good people. They weren't mean or vindictive, and never hurt anyone. Except detectives, but in today's society, they might get good reviews for that.

She got nowhere with her calls, and now Travis saw her in deep thought and began following her throughout the bureau. Willow had one more phone call to make. She dialed the phone.

"Trevor, this is Willow Sturgeon. I hope it's not too early. Doing well, thank you for asking. May I ask if you have told Missy yet of her possibly being in danger? No, I can respect that. I guess I wouldn't want to know, either. We do have information, though, that Manning was headed this way. Can you keep her at home today? When? Do you know where? I would appreciate that, and I know how to be discreet. She knows about the harbor, so I'll just say I want to talk to her about Amy. Thanks, Trevor."

"What's up?" Travis asked when Willow hung up.

"I wish those girls would stay home. Especially Missy. She's out shopping already. Tomorrow is Lauren's birthday. Trevor's going to have Missy call me."

"You've gotten quite chummy with the Gaudiers. I could use a new car." Travis smirked.

"This isn't funny, Travis. I'm worried about her. They are all a rare breed. Kind, considerate and well-mannered. Not the type of people bad things should happen to."

"Um... five words. Battery on a police officer."

"I'm not totally certain she knew it was me, and I really don't care. I used poor judgement in not pulling my badge. They are good people."

Travis looked at Willow and could see in her eyes, the concern was genuine. At least in one eye. The other was still a little funny looking. He called dispatch and had them inform the patrol unit to spend as much of his time as possible close to the Gaudier home. Willow smiled at him and patted his shoulder, mouthing a thank you.

∞∞∞∞

Willow didn't like this. It had been a half hour and still no call from Missy. Trevor had said he would text his daughter and tell her to call Willow. She had gotten the impression from the captain that those kids were responsible. Willow had an uneasy feeling in the pit of her stomach. She called Trevor again.

"Willow. It's been a while."

"I know, Trevor. I'm sorry. I still haven't heard from Missy. Did she get back, yet?"

"No. She's shopping for her mom's birthday. I would be surprised to see her before dinner. I'll give her another call."

"Thanks, Trevor. I'm sorry to be such a pain."

"Not a problem. Later."

Willow looked at Travis and Mark and saw they were both looking back at her, so she guessed they were ready to hit the road.

"Let's head down to the mall," Willow said. "I want to see if I can see any sign of Manning."

"At the mall?" Travis asked. "Willow, we need to get to the coroner and see if he received anything else on the other victim, and we need to make sure the lab received the DNA results from San Pablo."

Willow knew she wasn't exactly following protocol, but she felt her first priority was Missy's safety. She and Travis continued to stare at each other. He must have seen the concern in her eyes.

"Okay. The mall it is," he said. They departed the station. On the way to the car, Willow's phone rang.

"Sturgeon."

"Willow, it's Trevor. I had to leave a message. As soon as she calls, I'll have her call you."

"Would you consider that unusual, Trevor? Not answering a call from you?"

"Not at all. If she's in line or at the register, she'll blow off any call."

"Okay. We're headed to the mall area. Where does she frequent?"

"For her mom? She'll be at Macy's."

"Okay, thanks. What does she drive?"

"Lexus 350. Tan, or to some, light brown. Hang on. I'll grab the plate number."

Willow waited while Trevor searched for Missy's plate number and when he provided it, she wrote it down and they were on their way to the mall parking lot.

When they arrived, Willow asked the guys to watch for Manning as they drove up and down the lot. She would watch for Missy's car. After five rows, her phone rang. It was Trevor. Still no call from Missy and now even he was beginning to worry. Willow got Missy's phone number, wrote it down and passed it back to Mark, asking him to find her.

After several minutes had passed, Mark said Missy was there. They continued to drive through the lot while Mark tried to narrow the location down. He eventually began giving Travis directions. Those directions led to Carl's Jr.

They drove through the lot, but there was no sign of the Lexus. "Are you sure that thing's working?" Travis asked Mark.

"Stop the car," Willow said, and when Travis complied, Willow stepped out and went into Carl's. She checked every customer, but Missy wasn't inside. She went to the restroom and found it empty. She went into the men's room, got a querulous look from the only occupant, but found no Missy. Then she walked back to the car, now parked.

"Are you sure, Mark?"

"I'm telling you. She's here." Mark looked at Willow. Willow looked at Travis and saw a disgusted look. Willow knew that look was an expression of frustration. They had just lost the case. She looked back at Mark, and he was on his phone.

"Lisa. This is Mark," he said into the phone.

Tanner

FBI Special Agent Lisa Tanner stood at the garbage can, looking in the burger bag. Not only was there a cell phone in it. There were two. She opened an evidence bag and inserted the two phones and bag and sealed it then walked over to her car and placed the bag in the trunk. She looked in the window. The two detectives still had not come out of the back room. They must be having trouble uploading the video of the drive-through.

Lisa looked up at the sky, gauging the space between the three helicopters. One FBI, one police and one civilian, all searching for the Lexus.

"Mark, call the office. Have them load google Earth, or whatever they're using these days, and search the country roads. Then call the sheriff, CHP, Park service, wildlife and whoever else you can think of. Make sure you note who you spoke to. Did you get teams to the harbor and marina?"

"They're already there, Lisa. I also have someone working on the county looking for abandoned buildings, and there are two agents digging into his family records and bank accounts. We'll know if he even uses an ATM."

"Good. Once you're done with that, start contacting storage companies."

Mark stepped away from the car and began working his phone. At the same time the two detectives came out of the restaurant. "Any luck?" Lisa asked.

Sturgeon held up a flash drive. Lisa took it, went to her car and loaded it into the computer. She watched a few minutes and then the Lexus came into view. Missy Gaudier was driving and there were two people in the back seat. Because of the angle of the camera, she was unable to see faces. She rewound it and watched it again. She rewound a third time and this time watched it in slow motion. The detectives watched with her.

"One of the people in the back seat is Blake Manning," Lisa said. "The second person is someone named Ali."

"How the hell do you even see that?" Detective Birch asked.

Lisa climbed out of the car. "Here. Sit. Watch the fingers of her left hand on the steering wheel, as she's waiting for the food. One tap is an A, two taps is a B, and so on. A swipe is a new letter. She spelled out Blake first and then Ali." Lisa walked off and dialed her phone while the detectives were watching.

"Mrs. Gaudier, this is Special Agent Tanner again. I wonder if I could ask you to invade Missy's privacy and see if you can locate a full name for a second victim. Missy has used a code in a surveillance video telling us someone named Ali was in the car. It may be Alison or any other like name. Okay. Thank you."

Lisa wasn't totally certain this Ali person was a victim, but it was more likely than not, and she was going to go on the assumption that she was. If she was in league with Manning, it would have been stupid for them to both be in the rear seat.

The only thing that had given her pause about the back-seat thing was the fact that Manning had left his DNA all over the abandoned boat. Either stupid, or uncaring. Detective Sturgeon had thought the latter. She was convinced Manning only had one more victim in mind. She felt he hadn't even given thought past that point. The Ali woman may be killed for no other reason than being a friend of Gaudier's.

When Lisa had received word that morning about the kidnapping, she had called Detective Sturgeon right away, informing her this was now an FBI matter. Sturgeon understood, but Detective Birch had been upset, saying he had just come back off medical leave and was eager to put an end to the case. Lisa felt somewhat sorry for the man, so she told them if they could get the okay from their supervisor, she would allow them to assist. They, evidently, had gotten that okay. Her phone rang.

"Tanner."

"Lisa, it's Stephanie. I'm in Macy's in the surveillance room. I have Miss Gaudier in the women's wear department with another woman about the same age. An inch or two shorter. Long blond or light brown hair. Jeans and striped blouse. One to one-ten. No visible tats or piercings. Both women are carrying bags. Gaudier from Sears and the other woman from Penney's. Exited the front door at 10:18."

"Okay. Upload it and bag it."

"Will do."

Lisa clicked over to a second call. "Tanner."

"Alvarez here, Lisa. Traffic cams have the Lexus pulling out of Carl's onto Shane, heading east and then turning left on a residential street immediately. Hard to tell which."

"Okay, Carlos. Check every intersection going north, on both Brown and Fillmore, all the way out of town."

"On it."

Lisa walked back to the car and the detectives. "The Lexus pulled out on Shane, going east, and then turned north on one of those side streets," she said, pointing. "Can you get patrol units to canvass that entire area for the Lexus?"

"I got it," Detective Birch said, as he pulled out his phone.

Detective Sturgeon handed Lisa her phone. The detective had an email opened from the lab. The DNA from the razor and from the Simmons woman's fingernails was a ninety-nine percent match.

"There's a conviction," Lisa said. "Now all we have to do is find him."

"Hopefully," Sturgeon added, "before he hurts those girls. I should have called them earlier. I knew she was in danger."

"That'll be enough of that, Willow. I need you on top of your game. We don't have time for 'If only's'."

Lisa got on the phone and called the office, having them switch the helicopter north of Shane. When she hung up, she stared at the residential area north of Shane.

"You know this area better than me, Willow. If you were going to leave town using back roads, what direction would you go?"

Detective Sturgeon looked thoughtfully at the residential area. "It would depend on my ultimate destination. I would either take Fairmont or Blanchard. Either way, I would have to get on Conner Parkway first. That tract ends at Conner."

Lisa's phone rang. "Tanner."

"Hey, Lisa. This is Anderson. I finished at Comcast. I'm at PG&E now. They're starting a search for electrical surges. This really cute blonde is asking if you have a specific area in mind."

"Tell the wife hi for me, Marshal. See if she can focus, first, north of Conner Parkway. Cabins, farms, etcetera. I'm mainly interested in places that were dormant and are suddenly using power."

"We're on it."

"Marshal?"

"Yes?"

"Don't linger too long."

"On that, too."

"How is your pull with Mr. Gaudier?" Lisa asked Willow.

"I don't know that anyone has pull with the man, actually. Why?"

"He's in the way, Willow. There's already two birds up there."

"I'll try," Willow said, as she walked away dialing her phone.

Mark returned. "Okay. I have no storage units registered to Blake Manning. I called every department I could think of. I have research calling every coastal city and bordering city to get their eyes on it. NCIC is up to date. What's next?"

"Call Stanford," Lisa instructed. "Explain the gravity. See if they'll loosen their lips a little bit. Specifically, people Manning hung with in school. Anything they can volunteer, actually. If you get any names, check to see if their family owns property north of here. Houses, shoreline, cabins or anything else you can think of.

Be as quick as you can. I have an uneasy feeling we're running out of time.

"When you get done with Stanford, run the Sanders guy. Same story—any property, storage, etc."

Detective Birch rejoined her and said he had six units in the area. Then Detective Sturgeon relayed the good news that Mr. Gaudier was moving north of town. Lisa's phone rang.

"Tanner"

"Alvarez here, Lisa. The Lexus turned left on Conner and then right on Alderman. I watched it all the way. It made no more turns and disappeared over a hill."

"Thanks, Carlos. You know what to do?"

"Yup. Calling CHP now."

Lisa hung up and called the office to have the bird start refueling and where to focus. She also told them to let SWAT and the negotiator know it was time to move. She keyed her mic. "This is Tanner. I want all units north on Alderman Highway. All units, file in formation north on Alderman." Then she spoke to the detectives, "You're welcome to tag along. The Lexus was spotted going north on Alderman. If you do, stay behind my car. The others will be breaking off as we come across roads."

Lisa jumped in her car and noticed the detectives running to theirs. She proceeded out on Shane, made the U-turn and drove to the northbound ramp of Alderman. She saw the detectives in her rear view and an increasing number of vehicles fall in line behind them.

Delany

Ali wiggled, twisted and did everything she could to loosen the cords, but she didn't feel as if she was making any progress. She knew Missy was handcuffed, and if the two of them were to get free of this asshole, she would need to be the one who broke them.

Missy was providing encouragement, constantly urging Ali to keep at it. Ali had even tried to use her nails as a saw on the cords, but that had been useless. Currently, Ali was rubbing the cords as fast as she could against the post, hoping to burn them loose, but that wasn't working either.

Ali kept apologizing to Missy for being unable to free herself, but Missy being Missy, just kept urging her to work the cords and quit apologizing. Missy had worked herself to a standing position and worked her arms enough to be able to see the cuffs, but the look of frustration Ali saw in Missy's eyes pretty much said it all. Missy just sat back down.

Manning returned from wherever he had gone this time and went behind Ali. She didn't care. She continued to struggle against her bonds. She couldn't see what he was doing but judging by the look of hatred Missy was fixing him with, Ali guessed she could.

Manning walked back and stopped beside Ali. She ignored him and kept working the cords, but she did notice he had a needle in his hand.

"I really wish I had the patience to just sit and watch if you could get those cords off, sweets," he said "Alas, as your friend Missy will attest to, patience is not my best virtue."

"You have virtues, faggot?" Ali asked as she kicked out at him. Missy laughed. Her laugh stopped as he knelt beside Ali with the needle.

"Hey!" Missy screeched. "I'm over here, shrivel-dick."

Manning looked at Missy and then back at Ali. He slapped Ali hard. Her head hit the post with force. Her face burned and her head ached from the jolt, and she was dizzy. Yet she gathered saliva and spit in his eye. He stood and wiped his face with his sleeve.

"You've been hanging around Missy too much," he said. "I'm definitely saving you for last."

He turned to walk toward Missy. Ali timed the step and kicked his foot behind his other. He stumbled forward toward Missy, hitting the floor hard. He fell perfectly, and Missy wrapped the inside of her leg under his chin and locked the leg behind the other. Ali could tell by her facial scrunching, she was squeezing for all she was worth, trying to cut off his breathing.

Manning tried to reach for the dropped needle, but Missy jerked him back. He tried to stand, pounding her leg, but she wasn't letting go. He got his leg up underneath him, but Missy used her left foot to catapult him off the floor and rammed his head hard onto the floor. He swore at her and struggled to free himself but couldn't. Minutes passed as the two swore at each other.

He reached up with his left hand to try to push Missy's head against the post. *Yes,* Ali thought, *push her face.* Ali silently directed him, as he couldn't see, having his face down and being pounded constantly into the floor. A little to the right. A little more. There.

Manning had Missy's face and Missy turned the advantage. She opened her mouth and clamped down on his thumb. Manning's screams turned manic as the cursing stopped. His attention went to his thumb, and Missy rammed his head into the floor again and again.

He was weakening, Ali could tell. She could hear his gasps for breath. With a lunge, he threw his foot toward the needle. He reached it and hooked it closer to him. Missy rammed his head into the floor again, but he reached out and grabbed the needle, then jammed it into her leg. She screamed, losing his thumb before she had severed it. Still, she lifted him as high as she could and rammed his head once again. They fought for what seemed like an hour. Ali couldn't understand how he was still breathing. This would be something she could tell her grandkids, if she survived it. Missy was winning this fight with her hands tied behind her back.

Manning was about to pass out. He could barely move. His strikes against Missy's legs were lacking force and his legs were becoming limp. Missy tightened her grip, but Ali saw tears begin to stream down her face. The drug was working.

"Stay with me, Missy. Fight it. Deep breaths. Try to calm yourself. Slow the blood flow." Ali was hurtling every word of encouragement she could think of, but she could tell, both combatants were weakening fast. Manning was nearly limp. She could hear every breath he took, and Missy was looking no better.

"You... fucker," Missy uttered as she fell to the drug's influence. Manning forced his hands between her legs and pried his head free. He rolled away and took several loud and deep breaths, and just lay where he stopped. He continued to struggle to get his breath back, slamming his fist on the floor and screaming as the thumb throbbed and bled.

Manning rolled over onto his knees and continued to suck air for several minutes. Then he looked at Ali with hatred. He pointed at her, shaking his finger, but no words were spoken. He couldn't formulate them and inhale, too.

"You're a real piece of work, aren't you, Shrek face?" she spat at him. She needed to sacrifice herself to keep him from hurting a defenseless and unconscious Missy. "You got the better of her. Wanna come over here and give me a shot, you coward? Pussy! Cupcake!" He held up a finger as if asking for a minute.

"Yeah," she continued. "Need to get your strength back, huh? You loser. Oh my God. Are you growing breasts? Are those breast humps taking the place of your balls?" Manning rolled off his knees into a sitting position, flipped her the middle finger, but was obviously still unable to talk. She continued to hurtle every insult to his manhood she could think of, some of which she knew were repeats, but she had to keep his mind off Missy.

"This is going to be the most fun I've had in years," he finally said, stuttering between breaths. "Missy gets to be first, just so you know. That's important. When I'm done with her, though, I'm going to piss all over you."

"Fuck you," Ali spat out.

Manning stood and moved on Missy. Ali screamed at him and spit at him, but he was undeterred. He unhooked Missy's legs and spread them in front of her drooping head. He ripped her shirt open and stood back, looked at her, and began rubbing himself. Ali was about to puke, but she took a deep breath and began again with the loudest scream she could muster. It had no effect on him. He knelt beside Missy and ran his injured, but unoccupied hand along the inside of her leg, all the way up, rubbing at her vagina. Then he fondled her breasts and Ali screamed and spat again.

Ali knew if the situation were reversed, Missy would do what she needed to in order to save a friend. Ali calmed herself. She knew what she had to do. She would have to play at the Stockholm Syndrome. The thought repulsed her, but she got herself under control and began working herself up. Her breathing became deeper and she let out a tiny squeak. Manning noticed and turned his gaze on her. She opened her legs so he could see.

"I... I've never been involved in this kind of excitement before," she breathed out. "Can you untie me so I can finish myself, or maybe help me finish."

Ali knew that eventually someone would be concerned she or Missy weren't answering their phones. She just needed to buy some time for the police to get here. They would find them. She had to believe someone would. Manning stood and walked toward her. She squirmed and moaned and then focused on his erection, opening her mouth and breathing heavily.

"Please," she nearly whispered, grunting. "Untie me. I need you. Help me."

He knelt beside her and slipped his hand between her legs, rubbing her gently. If she had Missy's training, she would have wrapped her legs around his throat, but she didn't. She wasn't a fighter. If they were to get out of this, she would need to do him over and over, if necessary. Please, Missy. Wake up.

He unbuttoned her jeans and unzipped them, shoving his hand down and his finger in. She groaned again and looked again at his erection. Does she call it a dick? A cock? No, he has a fetish for the innocent.

"Can't you use your penis? I know it will feel better." She wriggled herself so he could see her hands and she made caressing motions with them as she reached for his zipper. Then she began using caressing motions with her fingers. She licked her lips and looked into his eyes with the best longing look she could muster.

Without warning, he removed his finger and reached into his pocket, pulling out his phone. He stood over her but stayed far enough away that she couldn't kick him.

"Do you want me to kill Missy?" he asked her.

"No. Please. Leave her alone. Why won't you take me? I need it."

"Then keep your mouth shut while I make a phone call. If I hear so much as a whisper, I'm hanging up and right back on Missy. Do you understand?"

"Yes. I won't say a word."

Manning dialed the phone and began pacing back and forth. Each time he walked toward Missy, he glared at her exposed bra. He was talking to a woman. Ali could tell. He was talking to the woman, staring at Missy, and rubbing himself erect. Ali kept quiet, but kept her eyes peeled for anything she could use against him. She had screamed so much her throat hurt. Her head still hurt from bouncing off the post, and her face felt swollen from his slap.

She was picking up bits and pieces of his speech. Something about the harbor, a coffee comment, and then a word that sent chills through Ali. He had used the word bodies, but she didn't catch in what context. Had he made up his mind to kill them? They certainly hadn't made this endeavor easy for him. He had stood in front of Ali with the needle, but Missy had saved her by distracting him. Were Ali and Missy going to be 'the bodies'?

Sturgeon

Travis was driving and Mark had climbed into Lisa's car, so Willow pulled out the tablet and began checking her emails to see if any of the queries they had sent out had yet returned with info. The email from San Pablo that had the info about the razor also listed the pictures found in the cabinet. She scrolled the list of items found, but none of the addresses listed were in the direction they were traveling.

The address on the registration was a post-office box in San José, but there wasn't a response from them yet on the address that post-office box was registered to. They had found a lot of clothing, assorted food items and a good deal of personal items. They had not found a knife, a pick or anything else linking Manning to any of the six victims, except the DNA in Heather's fingernails, and the photos.

Willow was concerned that, when caught, Manning would off himself. They needed to find a way to take him alive. She wanted to know where the other bodies were. She wanted to give the families closure.

They had only been driving for about five minutes when Travis began to slow. She looked up from her tablet and saw Lisa pulling off to the side of the road and stopping. Travis stopped behind her, and when she turned around she saw the other FBI cars had, as well.

She and Travis shared a confused look and then turned their attention back to Lisa's SUV. Willow's phone rang. The sync was still on her phone, and she and Travis stared at the screen. It was Heather's number. That was why Lisa had pulled over. Mark must have noticed the phone had been activated. She nodded at Travis, and he thumbed the sync button.

"Sturgeon."

"Hey, sweets. Long time no talk."

"Yeah. I've really missed our conversations, handsome. How ya doin'?"

"I'm doing well. Was that you at the harbor last Friday?"

"Yup, and just so you know, I didn't break my word. I was all ready for you, but I got a little distracted by an uninvited guest." Dirt and small rocks banged against the cruiser as Lisa was tearing back onto the road, heading north, flashing lights and all. Travis was on the gas and racing after her.

"Well, I'm just calling to let you know this will soon be over, and you and I can sit down to a nice cup of coffee and a decent meal." Willow looked at the dash and saw their speed was 95 and climbing.

"I'm looking forward to that. I have a lot of questions, the girls having family and all. Maybe you can tell me if I need to look anywhere else besides our little neck of the woods. We found number three, or what was left of her, out in the Pacific Ocean. Kind of lame of you. Where's the suspense when you send them swimming?" Their speed was 110 and still climbing. Willow wondered if Travis was going to make a woman-driver comment regarding Lisa's speed.

"That would be mighty nice of me, wouldn't it? Letting you know where all the bodies are. Maybe I'll use that as a negotiation tactic, if you ever do catch me. You guys are really not all that good at what you do, are you?" The speed was beginning to decline rapidly. Mark had him.

"Well, we do have other cases, you know. It's not like our every move hinges on your dumb ass. Plus, I'm a new detective. This is my first case, and I drew you. You should be flattered." Lisa's break lights blared as she swerved onto a dirt road, Travis right on her bumper. Lisa pulled in on the dirt road about fifty yards, and then pulled over and stopped, bolting from the car and charging past Willow and Travis toward the others.

"Aw, come on, sweets. You know very well you haven't had this much excitement since you lost your cherry." A woman charged past Willow's side of the car, carrying a sniper rifle, and three others ran past Travis' side with assault rifles. Then there were agents everywhere, branching out and along the dirt road.

"I have a surprise for you. I still have that cherry. You want it?" Lisa opened her trunk and pulled out a bullhorn, unsnapped her holster, and then she and Mark walked along the road. Travis pointed and followed the two, intentionally not shutting his door.

"Of course, but it's going to be a bit. I have a decision to make, first."

"Maybe I can help. What's the dilemma?"

"Well, I was supposed to be content after I earned my seventh unit, but I don't see a way around an eighth, and eight is an unlucky number for me."

"Hmm. Yeah. I can see that being a problem. Have you considered forgetting about number eight and just focusing on number seven? Or better yet, how does this sound? Make the seventh unit your grand escape. Leave the two other numbers. Tell me where to find them, and high tail it. You'll be in the history books like your idol, Jack the Ripper. Never caught."

"Wow! You really think..." The rest of his question was interrupted. Willow heard it very clearly through the receiver... "Blake Manning," the woman's voice came over clearly and loudly, "this is the FBI. You are surrounded. Come out with your fingers interlocked on your head."

"Well fuck, sweets. Were you lying to me?"

"Here's what I want, Blake. I want to stand in front of you and look in your eyes. I don't want to be looking down at your corpse. Let them go and I will walk right through your front door. I'll put the cuffs on you myself. No FBI. No firing squads. This is me getting out of the car." Willow put her phone to her ear, slammed the door shut and began walking toward the others.

"I guess the 'never caught' thing isn't going to happen. Hang up the phone, sweets. I'll call you back in a couple of minutes. I have to think."

"Wait, Blake. The FBI is going to want to know I have proof the two women are still alive, or they're going to Waco your ass. Let me talk to one of them." She heard him mumbling, and then she heard a female voice.

"Hello?"

"This is Detective Sturgeon. Is this Missy?"

"No. My name's Ali."

"Ali, is Missy still alive, as well?"

"Yes, but..." Ali was interrupted and Blake came back on.

"Keep your phone on you, sweets. Tell those FBI assholes that they don't call the shots here. I do."

Manning hung up on her and she quickened her pace. She reached the area of Lisa, Mark and Travis after a little more than a minute, but she didn't see any of the other agents.

"He's thinking, Lisa. He said he'd call me back in a couple of minutes. Both women are still alive." Willow got no reaction at all from Lisa. The woman continued to stare at the cabin. Willow knew the special agent's mind was racing, trying to figure a way to separate the man from the women.

"I think I can talk him down. I just need some time," Willow offered.

"It's been my experience, Willow, that the longer a hostage situation lasts, the worse it is for the hostages. If he calls, keep his mind off the women if you can, but make no mistake. Stephanie is out there somewhere with her M40 and standing orders."

"Lisa. You need to call that off and give me a chance. I can get him out. I know it. I need to know where the bodies are. Maybe we should wait for the negotiator." Her words fell on deaf ears, as Lisa just shook her head and continued to stare at the cabin.

The helicopters were beginning to arrive. Willow was worried that the noise would cause Manning to up the stakes. Kill one as a warning. Occasionally, she would catch sight of an agent in the woods on either side of the cabin, but they weren't moving in, and she saw no sign of the woman sniper. She looked up. One FBI and one civilian.

She wondered what would happen if SWAT arrived. Would Willow have a say in things? Would Lisa? Willow was really worried about Missy and Ali. Manning didn't seem like a time bomb, but she didn't know him very well. She wiped the perspiration from her eyes, staying focused on the cabin. She glanced at her phone, but it was just as dormant as it had been for the last several minutes.

Willow wanted to warn Trevor away, to cut some of the noise, but she didn't want to be on her phone in case Manning called.

Without warning, one of the front windows thwacked, followed almost simultaneously by a gunshot, and the area around the cabin was chaos. Lisa was charging the cabin with her sidearm poised and Mark right beside her. Other agents were converging from everywhere. Travis was on Lisa's heels, and Willow was on his.

One of the agents threw his body at the door and it shattered inward. Lisa burst through second and went right to the prone figure, with her gun poised to fire. There was nothing to shoot. Blake Manning's head looked like it had exploded. His lifeless body was sprawled between the two women, both covered with his splatter and secured firmly to support beams.

Ali was bawling and her eyes showed her terror, but Missy looked like a lifeless lump. Her legs were spread, her blouse ripped open, and her head was hanging with the hair falling in her face. Travis was untying Ali, so Willow felt for Missy's pulse. She found one. It seemed strong. She covered up Missy's bare chest and called her name, lifting her chin.

Free of her restraints, Ali scurried across the floor and hugged Missy's head. "He drugged her with something. Then he pawed her like the pervert he was. His hands were everywhere. I just wanted to kill him. I screamed at him and spit at him, but he wouldn't stop. He came at her with the needle and she clamped his head between her legs and locked her legs together. He was choking and fighting to get free. He couldn't get loose, so he stuck the needle in her leg. I couldn't tell which one. Sorry. I thought she was going to kill him, but she finally passed out and he just ripped her shirt and began fondling her.

"I think he was going to rape her, but I got his attention for a little bit and then he suddenly walked away and called someone on the phone. He was rubbing himself all the time he was on the phone. Then the FBI girl shouted and he hung up the phone and began pacing. He went to look out the window and his head exploded."

"I'm sorry this happened to you, Ali," Willow said. "And I'm sorry it happened to Missy, but it's over now. Did he hurt you?"

"No. Missy thought he was going to rape me, but he didn't pay much attention to me at all. I lured him away from her, but only for a little bit."

"Rescue is on the way," Mark said as he walked up.

"Thanks, Mark." Willow looked over at Manning's body. "I guess we don't get to learn where the other bodies are."

"Well," Mark said, joining her stare, "not from him, for sure. Stephanie blew his brains out. Lisa did have me order cadaver dogs for here and that park, though. They might find one or two."

Lisa walked up and knelt beside Ali. "Ali, I'm sorry this happened to you. Do you feel up to a couple of questions?"

"Sure."

"What happened to the Lexus?"

"He said he was going to drive it into the drink. I'm thinking Missy's probably not going to want it back, though."

"I'm sure not, but he may have disposed of some evidence in it, so we need to find it. What happened to Miss Gaudier?"

"He drugged her. I hope it wears off soon. Is she going to be okay?"

"Rescue is on the way. We'll know more then. Did you see where he pulled the drug from?"

"Somewhere behind me. I couldn't see. Missy may have."

"We'll talk again. I'm glad you're okay." Lisa patted her shoulder and then went to the area behind the beam Ali had been bound to and began searching the kitchen cabinets.

Willow pulled out her phone and called Trevor as she walked out the front door. She looked up as it was ringing, and the only helicopter still up there was his.

"It's about time. Is she okay?"

"I'm sorry, Trevor. I was talking to her friend. She's alive, but she's been drugged and is unconscious. I think you should go home and get a car. As soon as rescue gets here, I'll call you with the hospital name."

"Did he rape her?"

"No. He molested her, though. Ali said he became distracted with a phone call."

"Is he dead, or do I get to do that?"

"He's very dead, Trevor. You need to calm down. Missy is going to need your support."

"You're right. I'm calm. Thanks, Willow. Call me. I'm going to get the family."

"I will." Willow hung up. All the cars had been brought up, and she saw several agents taping off the area, as well as an area nearly fifty yards out, which was probably where the sniper was. She heard the siren of rescue, so she went back into the cabin to find Travis.

Birch

Travis stood at the back wall, looking through the hole. An FBI agent was setting up a laser near the front window. The bullet had gone through the window, through Manning's head and through the back wall. Granted, it was a cabin, and the wall didn't seem all that thick, but still. The laser hit the wall, so he stood back and watched as it lined up with the hole. He stepped out the back door and watched the sniper agent and another agent searching for the round.

He walked back inside and saw Willow coming through the other door. She asked for the cruiser keys, so she could bring the car up. He handed them over, and she went back out. Lisa was still searching cabinets, so he went to join her.

Travis didn't know whom he agreed with more, Willow or the FBI agent. He could see Willow's point. She had wanted to give the families closure. Closure is a good thing, but it does remove all pretense of hope. Sometimes hope is all that keeps families strong. On the other hand, the FBI did see to it that no other woman would suffer at this psycho's hand. He did have two hostages that were still alive because of an FBI sniper.

There had been no attempt at negotiation, though. Lisa had given the order to the sniper prior to approaching the cabin. He wondered about that. Were the FBI so wrapped up in terrorism that they had to end these kinds of situations quickly? Lisa had approached this cabin with the intent of rendering Manning dead. Save the hostages above all else.

"Any luck?" he asked her.

"We have a large quantity of knives that we're going to have to confiscate. I don't know if any were used in the stabbing. We'll have to wait for lab results. No sign of the pick yet, but it's the drug I want to find."

"More so than the pick? Why?"

"Your case is solved, Detective. The man who murdered Heather Simmons is lying on the floor over there with half a head. Ours is just beginning. We have to find his supplier, if he bought the boat legitimately, whose cabin this is, where his permanent residence is, when this spree started, and I could go on and on."

Travis took a pair of gloves from the box and asked her where she wanted him. She directed him to the bedroom. He thought he'd seen her already go that way, but she must have been just doing a quick scan for suspects.

He headed for the bedroom and left her to her search. The bedroom door was cracked open, so he elbowed it aside and looked around. There wasn't much to write home about. A four-drawer dresser, small closet and a bed. Not even a chair. Even Travis had a chair.

He started with the closet, and his eyes went right away to the overnight bag on the floor. Very wet. Manning must have had the bag with him when he abandoned the boat. Travis opened the bag and began rifling through the damp, mildew-smelling clothes. A toothbrush, a tube of toothpaste, two disposable razors, a military-style knife, an ice pick and two bottles of some kind of pharmaceutical.

"Special Agent!" he screamed. Lisa came running in. He met her eyes and then looked down at the bag. She raced to the bag and dug out the vials.

"Apache," she said. She laid the vials face up in the bag and went to the door. She yelled toward the front, "I'm ready for my photo shoot."

An agent walked in with a camera and Lisa pointed to the bag. The agent began snapping picture after picture, and Lisa pulled Travis out of the room.

"What's Apache? Is that a date-rape drug?" Travis asked.

"Fentanyl-laced heroin. Absolutely, it is."

"Would that put her out?"

"Big time, in the right dose. Will you leave this to us and let rescue know? They need to know so they can bring her down."

"Can I have that knife and pick?"

"Nope."

Well, shit. Travis walked back out front in time to see the EMTs checking Missy's eyes and blood pressure. "Special Agent Tanner wanted me to tell you he gave her Fan... Fen... uh, Apache."

The female smiled. "China Girl, TNT, Tango and Cash, He-Man. Thanks. That helps. Any idea how much?"

"No clue," Travis offered, and the female immediately pulled out one of Travis' nightmare weapons of mass destruction. A needle. He turned to find somewhere else to be. Best go out back and call the captain.

"Carson."

"Hey, Cap. We got him. Or I should say an FBI agent with a cannon did."

"No shit, teddy tardy! I already got the word from Trevor Gaudier. You want to tell me why someone from the victim's family informed me of a case closure?"

"Sorry, Cap. We were processing the scene."

"Bullshit, Birch. FBI case. FBI processing. You know how embarrassing it is to hear this from a family member? Get your asses back here."

"On our way," Travis finished. He went in search of Willow and found her talking to Agent Maxwell, out front. As he was approaching he saw smiles and eye contact. Maxwell was asking her out. He stopped and pretended to be searching for something, giving her space for a few minutes. When the two broke apart, he delivered the news to Willow.

"The captain's pretty pissed, Willow. Your good buddy called him about the killing of Manning before we did."

"Yeah. I guess that figures. They are good friends. So, we have to go back?"

"Nah. He's already pissed so no harm in hanging out awhile. You want to flirt with the fed some more?"

"I wasn't flirting," she said with an angry look. He folded his arms across his chest and raised his eyebrows. She met his eyes, but the look of anger turned to one of being caught with her fingers in the cookie jar. Then she smiled and began poking his ribs. "Okay, maybe I was a little. So what?"

"So, I'm going to run a background check."

She punched his arm. "You are so not running a background check. I can handle myself, thank you."

"Wow. He stuck it out, even with that face, huh?"

She gasped and her one good eye flew open. "I'm going to kick your ass."

Travis saw rescue exiting toward their bus, and he and Willow quickly walked toward them. Missy was semi-conscious. She had a look of bewilderment and was obviously not feeling any pain, but she wasn't yet speaking or focusing her eyes on anything. They loaded her in the bus and Ali climbed in behind. Willow patted Travis' arm. He nodded and watched her climb in behind Ali.

Travis went back in the cabin, weaved around the body and about six agents and back to the bedroom. He saw Lisa bagging and labeling the knife, and the pick and vials already bagged beside her. The sniper agent was standing beside her, holding another evidence bag with a single round in it.

"Our captain has instructed me to beat it, Special Agent. Anything you need from me before I go?"

"Yes," Lisa said. "I already have Willow's info. Why don't you give me your phone and e-mail?" She stood and pulled out a pocket notebook and wrote down Travis' info. He bid his adieu and left the cabin, hoping Willow had left the keys in the car. She had. He cranked the engine and began his way back to town. He switched the sync to his phone and called Mrs. Simmons.

"Hello."

"Mrs. Simmons. This is detective Birch. I'm calling you to let you know the man who killed your daughter was caught this afternoon. He was fatally shot, and we will be closing the case. Those files will be available for the insurance company in two days. Once again, we are very sorry for your loss."

"Thank you, Detective, and thank you for helping us get closure. Do we get to know who?"

"It will be in the report, Mrs. Simmons. Goodbye. Godspeed."

Sturgeon

The paramedics wouldn't let her use her phone in the bus, so when it stopped at the hospital, she quickly jumped from the back and called Trevor, letting him know where Missy was. The call was short, as she didn't want to lose sight of the gurney. She ran to catch up and walked beside it, clasping Missy's one free hand, with Ali already attached to the other.

When they got to the emergency room, Willow pried Ali off Missy and led her to the waiting area.

"Why can't I be with her?" Ali asked.

"Her family is almost here, Ali. The staff is only going to allow so many people at a time in there, and they have to change her and hook up the detox."

Willow no sooner got the words out when a frantic Amy ran into the room, tears streaming down her face. She saw Willow and ran to her. "Where is she?" Trevor, Lauren and Tony were right behind her.

"She's with the doctor and nurses now. They are hooking up fluids and changing her. They said they would let us know when we could go in." Willow introduced them all to Ali, and the Gaudier family clamped on the usual hugs and blubbered their apologies that this had happened to her. Amy and Tony ushered Ali to a chair and sat beside her, thanking her for supporting Missy.

"Thank you for being here, Willow," Trevor said. "Did you take him out?"

"No. It was an FBI sniper."

"What's his name, so I can provide a reward?"

"You can't reward someone for killing a human being, Trevor, and it wouldn't be allowed, anyway."

"Human being?" Lauren screeched, and then looked around to see if she'd disturbed anyone with her tone. Then, more quietly, she continued, "He wasn't a human being. He was a rabid animal that needed to be put down." She started crying, and Trevor put his arm around her shoulder.

"You'd be surprised at what I can do, Willow," Trevor added. Willow was about to respond, but the doctor came out of Missy's room and walked toward them. She introduced herself to everyone, and then began explaining her need to do tests. She said Missy was awake, but not all that alert. They could see her for a few minutes, but the doctor wanted to get the testing started.

The four family members made a mad dash for the room, while Willow and Ali took a seat and waited. Willow wanted to check her email, but her first priority was seeing to it that Ali got some help, as well. She looked over at Ali's wrists and saw they were rope-burned and bruised. The girl also looked like she had been punched. Willow stood and walked to the nearest nurse and explained her concern. The nurse took Ali to another room.

Willow got herself started by listening to her voicemails, then she began cleaning up her emails. After about twenty minutes, the family came out of Missy's room toward her. Amy asked where Ali was and Willow told her, so the entire family was once again gone.

Willow knew she needed to get back to the station, but she also knew the captain would be showing up soon, so she would just hitch a ride with him. She texted Travis to ask him if he had notified Mrs. Simmons, and he replied that he had and that the captain was on his way. There was nothing more Willow could do now, except wait.

Fifteen minutes later, the captain arrived and sat down next to her, congratulating her and thanking her for closing the case. They talked at length about the harrowing last hours of the investigation and killing of Blake Manning. After a short period, the Gaudier family reappeared and the captain joined them leaving Willow once again alone. A nurse came up and asked Willow if she wanted her eye bled. Willow thanked her, but refused.

The captain visited with the Gaudiers for nearly a half hour before a nurse interrupted and said Missy had been transferred to a room while awaiting additional tests, so the family departed for the room. Fifteen minutes later, Willow, the captain and Ali were heading toward the station, where Ali would give her statement and be reunited with her own family.

Sturgeon

Two months later

Melissa (Missy) Gaudier had somewhat recovered from her ordeal with the help of her loving family and friends. Blake's actions against her hadn't fazed her, but his actions against others because of her were hard for her to shake. She completed her degree at Stanford last June and moved her education to Johns Hopkins University in hopes of becoming a pediatrician. She was there now, starting her first year.

Alison Delany was not as fortunate. Although she continued her courses in Oceanography in order to obtain her degree from Oregon State, she developed a fear of men. She received counseling and saw a therapist regularly, but the trauma she witnessed and suffered kept her in the company of those therapists for several weeks. Her friends and co-workers had said she worked well alone, but they had noticed when she worked with men, she was constantly 'looking over her shoulder'.

Willow Sturgeon and Mark Maxwell became an item. Their dates were all pleasant and filled with fun and laughter. Mark became a regular staple on week nights for exercise and dinner at Willow's. Their weekends were spent at Mark's place for the most part, taking in attractions in and around his home in Petaluma. Willow became good friends with the Gaudiers, as well. Despite Amy being six years her junior, the two of them spent time together often, until Amy returned to Minnesota.

Travis Birch continued his diligence with his alcoholism. He was able to see the kids every weekend, and a little more than a month after the take-down of Blake Manning, Kris brought the kids by on a Friday night and stayed the night. She never left.

Not all the good fortune Travis gained was of a personal nature. The annual Department awards that were held every October 1st found him at the podium accepting an award for his ability in POI interviews. At the same ceremony, the captain walked up to the podium and presented Travis with a new badge. He was being promoted to Detective First.

This promotion meant a new cruiser, a raise, and a choice of partners. Without hesitation, he chose Willow.

Willow suffered from the same disorder Travis seemed to. He didn't like loose ends, and she was beginning to see his point. It had been two months since the take-down of Blake Manning and Charmaine's hectic drug raids, and not only was there still a body missing, but Charles Logan was nowhere to be found. Despite all the technology brought to bear on the wife, the DMV, the social security department, the search turned up nothing.

All the victims had been known to Melissa. Heather Simmons, she knew and hung out with as a friend to Amy. The other four were all friends of hers at Stanford and it was believed the sixth, number four, would be, as well.

Numbers one and two were found buried at the cabin. Numbers five and six in the park, and number three in the Pacific Ocean. Number four was thought to be in the ocean, as well, and may never be found. They thought they had a name. Melissa had painstakingly agreed to go through the missing persons reports and identified one as a friend from Stanford. Nicole Franks.

Melissa wanted to call all the families, but the combined efforts of her father, mother, brother, sister, Willow and Travis convinced her otherwise. It wasn't her fault. She needed to stop acting like it was.

The Chulo man had developed an escape plan, and he had worked it well. He had disappeared from sight. No cell phone. No job. No bank accounts or insurance policies. Just gone. His cell phone had been found in a rest stop south of Carpel. Everyone knew he hadn't gone that way. He would have disposed of it in a direction he wasn't headed. He hadn't used his credit cards and probably didn't need them. His escape plan would have included a lot of cash.

Willow didn't know why this bothered her so much. It wasn't even their case. Logan lived in Carpel, but his criminal activities had been in Charmaine. It was their case. Maybe it was that he had been a Carpel resident that bothered her so much. Maybe that was it. In any case, the guy was sharp. All indications were, he had actually begun his flight before or during the raid on the ranch.

The manager at the ice company had said he was off that day and the next, but during subsequent interviews, the wife had said he was gone when she woke up at 4AM. She had no knowledge of him being off that day. The DEA felt it had something to do with Sanders. Sanders had somehow got the word to him of the impending raid. Willow wasn't so sure. She tended to side with Travis' view that there was a mole.

If she didn't stop thinking about this, she was going to drive herself bonkers. It was Saturday afternoon. It was supposed to be the time she didn't think about work. She was at Mark's.

Willow surfaced and treaded water in his pool, glancing his way and then admiring his form as he worked the steaks on the grill. He was the guy. She somehow could feel it. Was it love?

Saturday night was supposed to be dinner and a movie night, but this had been a very lonely week for her. Lisa was on vacation or special assignment, or something, so Mark and the others were picking up the slack and working long hours. Willow hadn't seen him all week. She had missed him horribly. So, yes. She was sure this was love.

There would be no movie tonight. She had bought a new bikini for the pool, just to let him know she wasn't interested in a movie. Slowly, she climbed the steps out of the pool and walked over to get her towel, which she had intentionally left close to the grill, and began drying herself off. She was watching out of the corner of her eye to see if he noticed. He not only noticed, he did a double-take. Yes! No movie.

"How about we skip the movie tonight and go right to dessert?" he said with a smile as he turned the steaks over.

"What kind of girl do you think I am?" she answered, continuing to dry.

"Considering how little you're wearing right now, I would say my kind."

"I think your imagination is not on your cooking. What's taking so long with those steaks?" She walked over and leaned against his back, circling her arms around and caressing his chest. She planted a kiss on the back of his neck.

"Careful, now," he said. "I may decide to forget about these steaks altogether."

Willow kissed him again and her hand slowly made its way toward his abs.

"Okay," he said as he switched the grill off. "I wasn't hungry anyway." He turned and swept her up in his arms and dashed for the house as she continued to smother him with wet kisses.

Preston

Banff was the most beautiful place he had ever seen. Pristine waters, beautiful mountains that went on forever and ever. He could see himself retiring here, easily. Of course, he would be. He had enough money that he didn't need to go back into business. If things got bad, he would, but he didn't see that happening.

This was a welcome place. He wasn't getting any of those annoying phone calls, and she'd had one of her most stressful months and needed the peace of mind. They never did seem to have a lot of alone time. There was always something, either with her work or his, that kept them from being together for extended periods.

Today, they were going to hike one of those mountains. Provided, of course, that she ever got her ass out of bed. He had gone in to wake her once already, but when he saw that naked, perfect body, he had gotten carried away, and she had fallen right back to sleep afterward.

Coffee in hand, he stood at the dinette window, staring out at the beauty. This was one of the more expensive resorts, but the view made it worthwhile.

He sat his coffee down, went to the refrigerator and pulled out the bacon and eggs. The smell of the bacon cooking would get that carnivore out of bed in a hurry. She did love her bacon.

He set the skillet on the burner, turned it on, and laid the bacon in carefully. He would use the bacon grease to fry the eggs.

He put two slices of bread in the toaster and then went and set the table. Even if she didn't get up right away, he was going to eat. He would fix hers when she got up.

As the bacon began to spit, he realized he was cooking bacon wearing nothing but his boxers. Not a good idea. He went into the bedroom and grabbed his robe, throwing it around him and making sure the door was open wide so the smell wouldn't have any obstruction.

"Get up, damnit. I want to go hiking."

"Come over here and whisper it in my ear."

He rolled his eyes and went back to the kitchenette, flipped the bacon and pushed the toaster down. He poured himself a glass of orange juice and was about to set it on the table when he heard the bathroom faucet. He sat the juice in her spot instead, and poured another for himself.

He went back to his bacon, done to her liking, so he forked it out and broke two eggs into the skillet, turning the heat down. He threw the bacon on paper towels and began patting it down. Her arms were around him and inching toward his cock.

"Knock it off," he said. "We're going hiking, and that's final."

She released him, walked to the table and downed the juice in two swallows. Then she put the glass in the sink, poured herself a cup of coffee, and walked it to the table.

He put the bacon and eggs on her plate and began to butter her toast. Her hands were again around him, but this time right to his cock, and she began a vigorous stroking. He swirled around in one fluid motion and pushed her to the floor. He was inside her and thrusting fast before she'd even settled.

"How do you like your new name?" she asked. "I couldn't decide between Wilson Preston and Preston Wilson." She laughed between gasps.

"Well, I have an advantage now," he said, increasing his speed. "I can go by either. You, on the other hand, can't exactly go by Tanner Lisa."